Forever Carly

MICHELE SIMS

About the Book

Secrets, deceptions, and lies.

Carly Rivers, a small town girl with big dreams to become a renowned expert on historical African American communities unexpectantly encounters her college sweetheart, Mason Moore, after ten years apart in Charleston, South Carolina.

Mason has transformed his family's business into an international conglomerate. Both are rising from the ashes of a failed marriage. Can Carly survive in Mason's world of secrets and feelings that have yet to be acknowledged? Can they rediscover the love they once shared, peeling back the layers one at a time? Or will the untold truth cost them the second chance at love they both deserve?

Acknowledgements

I would like to thank my husband, Tony for your love and endless patience in completing this project. A special thanks to Ms. J. Melvin and Ms. D. Hunter for your support. To Ms. S. Lewis, thank you for your invaluable insights on this project. Thank you, The Book Khaleesi for guiding this project to completion.

My thanks also goes out to you, my dear readers. Thank you for reading and sharing my stories. I hope you all enjoy the book, Forever Carly, the first in the Come to the Carolinas series.

I dedicate this book to God, the source of all good things, and to my forever firstborn son, Jonathan McNeil, a storyteller, a fellow lover of words and to those who believe that true love never dies.

Chapter

1

Watch your step. Hold on," a loud voice called out, piercing the silence of an inky December evening. The unexpected sound of the heavy door as it was forced open, the rush of wind, and the flashlight shining in her face overwhelmed her senses. Dr. Caroline "Carly" Rivers stumbled as she tried to maintain her balance. Her heartbeat quickened and she panicked while reaching for the cold wrought-iron railing.

"You scared me," she yelled while walking up the concrete steps of the old courthouse. The building was covered with white snow and patches of ice. Stopping to catch her breath, she wrapped her fashionable heavy woolen coat around her. "What the devil were you thinking? You almost made me fall." She knitted her brow, looking up at her lawyer, a tall young man wearing owl-eye glasses and holding a flashlight in his hand.

"That's what I was trying to prevent. It's dark out here. I

didn't want you to hurt yourself." He lowered the flashlight, so the bright light illuminated the slippery spots covered with ice instead of blinding her and placed a hand on her arm. Slowly, he helped her up the stairs to the warmth of the large entryway of the courthouse with its worn honey-colored hardwood floors.

"We're in the room to the left." He led the way down the wide corridor lined with large portraits of former judges in their black robes and opened the door to a room with a long conference table surrounded by leather-covered chairs. Large windows provided a view of the gusty winds blowing through the trees outside.

"I hope you're right this time." She pulled out a chair. "The weather is too bad to be out chasing false hopes." She took her time unwrapping the scarf around her neck and climbing out of her coat, but still shuddered from the chill in the room. Dressed in a black, long-sleeved sheath dress accessorized with pearls and matching boots, the ones that made her feel confident, she smoothed back her hair and wiped her tired eyes.

"I've got a feeling about it, Carly. I think the jury is going to come back with a verdict tonight. They've been in deliberations longer than expected."

"Is that good or bad, Counselor?" She folded her arms across her chest and looked at the baby-faced man she had hired months ago. Attorney Jason Aaronson worked for a firm that was highly regarded and recommended by her friends, but she didn't have the college's deep pockets.

Her former employer, a small college, was paying for the legal representation of the dean of the history department after she sued him for sexual harassment. The firm she had hired was supportive, but couldn't offer representation by one of their senior, more-experienced members with the money she was able to pay.

Sighing, she paced while he sat looking over notes on several of the yellow legal pads on the table in front of him.

In two years, she had gone from being one of the history department's most sought-after professors and favorite of the students to being an outcast among her colleagues. Her chances for the tenure she knew she deserved were slim.

"It's neither good nor bad." He shrugged and peered over his glasses, resting low on the bridge of his nose.

"What did you say?" She returned her attention to their conversation.

"I answered your question. I don't think the time the jury is taking is a good or bad thing. What I think is that you should have a seat and wait. The fact that one of the dean's former students came forward and testified that he harassed her too sure didn't hurt your case. It didn't prove it, but it didn't hurt. She was credible and did better than I thought under cross examination."

Carly bit her lip and slowly slumped into her chair. Casting her gaze out the window, she looked at the snow as it fell on the small Maryland town. It was Christmastime and she couldn't deny the beauty of nature as the snow outlined the landscape. The holiday season was once her favorite time of the year, but the crushing weight of debt, a blistering divorce, little hope of having children of her own, and a career on life support had taken its toll. Tough times. That was an understatement, and she had receipts to prove it.

She placed a hand to her forehead and turned her head as tears formed in her eyes.

"Are you all right?" Jason pulled a clean tissue from a box on the table and handed it to her.

Before she could answer, there was a knock at the door. A grim-faced representative of the courts dressed in a dark suit, a white shirt, and matching tie opened the door and stepped inside the room. Carly studied his appearance. If she didn't know better, she could easily have mistaken him for a man dressed for a funeral. *Her* funeral.

Jason pushed his chair away from the table and stood at attention.

"The jury has returned with a verdict," he advised them. "The judge is in the courtroom waiting for you."

Despite her attempts to calm her anxiety, her palms moistened. She made tight fists and dug her nails into her palms to stop the fleeting tremors as she hid her hands below the table.

"It's time." Jason reached out and touched her shoulder.

She briefly wondered if she stood, could her legs bear her weight? She didn't worry long, since comforting thoughts of her Aunt Nora came to mind, calming her fears. *"We'll handle whatever happens together,"* her aunt had told her during a recent phone call. *"You needed to speak your truth."*

Taking a deep breath, she said a quick prayer before rising from her seat. A heavy pit formed in her stomach as she followed the men to face the jury who held her fate in their hands.

Chapter

2

Bernie. Tell me again how this screwup occurred." Mason Moore, CEO of Moore Investment Group, drummed his fingers on the mahogany-wood armrest, barking at his friend, Bernard Morgan, who was also the VP of Finance and Acquisitions for his growing company. Mason took a sip of his drink then sat back in his cushioned seat aboard his jet. He touched the video button on his cellphone. Bernie's face appeared on the screen.

"Listen, I've said the same thing twice already. The house on Hagood Avenue was included in the deal with all the other houses in the area. They made us a deal we couldn't refuse. It made sense to sell. Besides, aren't you the one who always says good business maneuvers don't involve misplaced sentimentality? Are you getting soft in your old age?" Bernie joked.

"The only one who's getting soft is you from eating too much of your wife's cooking."

"Ouch, bruh." Bernie visibly winced. "You know I'm

sensitive about my weight."

"You know I'm protective of my reputation in the community." Mace leaned in closer to the screen. "I still have family and good friends in Charleston. People who don't really know me think that since I inherited my grandfather's wealth, I've become a man without a heart. It's not true and I don't like the possibility of bad press that could follow this deal."

"Listen, we have Autumn Jackson, our own Olivia Pope, here in New York, working for the company to avoid scandals. She's one of the best PR folks around. She can spin anything. I'll tell her to get on the next plane to handle the matter," he assured him, then paused. "We sent Fletcher Daniels, one of our contract investigators, ahead of Autumn's arrival. He gathered information on the prior owner of the house. Her aunt is a leader in the community. We're hoping she can calm her niece's fears and the concerns of others who sold their homes thinking we were going to rehab the neighborhood. I found that uncovering hidden facts can help in the... *negotiations*. Have you had a chance to look over the information?"

"No, Bernie." He took another swallow of his drink. "Been busy running an international conglomerate, remember?"

"Check your bag. I spoke to your assistant this morning. He said he placed the information in there for you to review while on the plane."

Mason hit the intercom button on the side of his chair. "Andrew, bring me the info from Fletch."

Andrew came from the rear of the plane carrying Mason's Italian leather bag. "Here it is, boss." He opened the bag and handed him a folder marked "Confidential" in bold red letters. The plane hit a patch of turbulence causing Andrew's body to sway and he dropped the folder in the aisle of the plane. A dark and grainy eight-by-ten picture of a younger woman in the arms of an older man fell out of the folder. Mason looked on as Andrew dropped to his knees and gathered the contents.

"What's that?" Mason extended his hand and took the picture with the date stamped three years earlier. He noticed the young woman had a butterfly tattoo on her right shoulder.

Andrew finished gathering the papers before quickly returning to his desk in the rear of the plane.

"Let me give you a quick background on what he sent. Fletch also sent me a copy." Bernie swallowed hard. "I know it's not your style but Fletch discovered some potentially embarrassing information about the prior owner of the home, Professor Caroline Rivers Matherson."

Mace's jaw tightened as Bernie said the name Matherson.

"She's one of the country's leading experts on preserving historically black neighborhoods," Bernie continued.

"I know who previously owned the home. Tell me about the people in the picture." Mason looked again at the photo, which appeared to have a dark filter covering it. "This can't be her. The date stamp shows it was taken three years ago. She looks like a younger version of the woman I once knew as Caroline Rivers. Maybe she's a relative."

"I believe Fletch said it was a picture of her, Professor Matherson."

"Who's the guy?" Mace leaned in for a closer look.

"That's Dean Thompson, head of the history department at Middleton State College in Maryland, but I'll need to check again with Fletch to be sure." He picked up his pen and made a note to himself before continuing. "Professor Matherson worked under him. She's brilliant. We've hired her before to do research on property before we acquired it. Her life has recently taken a hard turn for the worse. She was the plaintiff in a sexual harassment suit against the dean. Fletch sat through most of the trial. There should be transcripts of the proceedings in the folder, containing allegations that she slept her way to the top. It was believed she was involved in a consensual relationship with him. When he refused to help her gain tenure, she filed a suit against him in retaliation. She's also in significant debt. Maybe we can offer her a financial incentive to lend support to our deal, one she won't refuse."

Mason's eyes narrowed as he listened before tossing the file into the adjacent seat. "You're right. Gathering opposition research on folks isn't my style." He cleared his throat. "The professor isn't my enemy. Whatever happened in Maryland is her business, not mine. If Fletch has her under surveillance, tell him to end the investigation."

"Fine. When are you due to arrive at the office? We have a late-night meeting, don't we?"

"I won't be able to make the meeting. Let's reschedule." Mason frowned.

"But—"

Mace cut off his response. "The flight plan has already been changed. I'm handling this myself. I should be landing in Charleston in the next few minutes. Goodbye, Bernie."

He pressed the end-call button.

"Buckle your seatbelt and prepare for landing." The voice of the captain filled the cabin. "There's a little more turbulence. We may have a bumpy ride."

Mace threw back his head and finished the last of his drink. "A hard landing is the least of my worries."

* * *

"Yeah. This is Fletch." He placed the call on speaker. "What do you need, *Ms. Moore*?"

"Save the sarcasm." Her response was quick and as usual, her tone had a bite. "Take me off speaker. Did you send Mason the information like I told you?"

"Of course. You know I did." He paused. "That's why you're paying me the big bucks."

"Including the picture?"

"Yes, Jamillah. Including the picture." Fletcher Daniels placed his fingers to his forehead. "Don't you think it would be better if you just settle your differences with Mason?"

"Stay in your lane, Fletcher, and stick to the plan. Talk to you later."

"Yeah, not as late as I would like." He pressed the end-call button.

Chapter

3

How could he?" Carly gripped the edge of the breakfast table, unable to believe what she was seeing and hearing from the small television on the kitchen counter.

Her jaw muscles tightened as she sat straight in her chair, listening intently.

"Most of the homes on Hagood Avenue near Spring Street will be torn down to make way for a new, upscale development," the newscaster announced with an air of authority that it was already a done deal.

"I don't believe it." Carly tightened her lips, then blew out a breath. "How could Mason allow this? His group bought up most of the homes in that area. If what we just heard is true, the plans will mean that the neighborhood around my parents' home will be destroyed."

A tight pain gripped her chest as the camera floated past her childhood home. It was already painful being back in Charleston. She hadn't visited since her mother's death three years prior. Now her parents' home was slated for destruction.

Her Aunt Nora sat down at the breakfast table across from her and placed her hand on top of Carly's. Carly knew the gesture was supposed to be comforting, but seeing the wrinkles and the age spots on her skin that traveled from that hand up the arm to the smiling face that looked so much like her mother's only caused more pain.

Aunt Nora's kitchen was small and quaint but filled with loads of memories. The dark wood cabinets provided a nice contrast against the cream-colored walls. The matching cotton curtains were starched to perfection. Tea towels that Carly had given to her mother and Aunt Nora years ago still hung on the oven door with a crown and the saying, "*The cook is a goddess*," embroidered on them. Beautiful cookbooks, some for display, and others with Aunt Nora's handwriting in the margins of the pages, worn with age, were on the counters. These were the memories that filled her soul, especially during difficult times.

She knew Aunt Nora's health wasn't good, but she was trying to hide it with plenty of her delicious food and Southern hospitality. Her aunt was a proud woman who never wanted to admit she needed help. Carly squeezed her aunt's hand, offering her a smile. Aunt Nora was like a second mother to her. She was able to go to her doctor's visit with her the day before. Her diabetes and high blood pressure were out of control. Poor control of the same diseases had eventually led to her mother's heart attack. The thought of losing Aunt Nora caused Carly to place her other hand to her chest to massage the weighted feeling away.

She was glad she had decided to leave Maryland right after the verdict was rendered in her sexual harassment case.

"Verdict for the plaintiff," the jury foreman had read to the quiet courtroom.

It was two weeks ago when she sat beside her lawyer in an uncomfortable wooden chair holding her breath. It took a few moments before she would allow herself to believe what she had heard.

"Carly, they ruled in your favor." Jason's big smile brightened the otherwise drab room. It was then that she allowed herself to breathe.

She had called her best friends that night, after returning home, screaming with a mixture of joy and relief. She knew she needed to check on Aunt Nora, but afterward, they all agreed to leave from Charleston's port to go on a cruise to the Bahamas the week before Christmas to celebrate her victory.

Her eyes trailed back to the television. The reporter was talking excitedly about the new development and the new jobs it would bring, but all Carly could think about was how this was something that's going on all over the country. Destroying historical black neighborhoods for the sake of progress and development.

As an associate professor of history, Carly had done extensive research to establish the provenance of many dwellings in Southern cities, especially those on the west side of Charleston, South Carolina. Concerned that tearing down large portions of African American communities in many Southern cities robbed history of the richness of the culture and the contributions of the inhabitants of those neighborhoods, Carly had become one of the country's leading experts on preserving historical communities. It was not only her vocation – it was her passion.

"Has Mason completely lost his heart?" She looked at Aunt Nora, and then back at the television. "Our family and

Mason's have been friends for years. He has to know that my parents would never have agreed to the sale if they were still here and knew of his plans for the property. How many times did he sit at their table or play basketball with the guys from the neighborhood in our backyard? Does that mean nothing to him now?"

But did anything have meaning for Mason Moore? The way he had dumped her all those years ago when she thought they would have forever… If her heart hadn't mattered to him, what could a house possibly mean?

Carly paused before pushing the carved oak chair away from the table.

Aunt Nora placed a hand to her ear to dampen the sound of the chair scraping across the floor. "Let's not jump to conclusions, Carly. We don't know the whole story."

"We know a lot about Mason Moore. He's arrogant, self-centered, and blind to his own ambitions. His whole life, he's been groomed to take his place in the family's business. I'm sure he's a heartless shark by now. And you know he's never been comfortable with the word no, especially if it stood in the way of him getting what he wanted." She took her half-full teacup and placed it in the sink. She couldn't drink or eat anything now.

"Yes, that's the impression I had about Mason before I spoke to him earlier this year. I agree he's a driven young man, but he's willing to listen to reason. I've placed a call to Mason to talk to him about it. I'm sure there's a good explanation. Please, don't worry about it."

"Has he returned your call?" Carly looked at the older woman straightening her glasses as if they were askew, but they weren't.

"Not yet, but he's a busy man." Aunt Nora got up and

turned off the television.

"Sure. He's busy and so is everyone else in that neighborhood. They're *busy* trying to make ends meet and raise their families."

Carly took a deep breath to calm herself. She looked over at her aunt, who had turned away and cast her eyes on the view outside the window.

"Come sit with me." She urged her aunt to return to their chairs at the table, sensing that there was something that needed to be said. After they reclaimed their seats, Carly placed a hand on her aunt's hand. The same hand that had soothed her fears, braided her hair, and with just a touch reminded her that every problem in her life had a solution. Rubbing her thumb across her aunt's knuckles, she hoped to soothe her concerns.

"You're telling me not to worry, but I can tell something is concerning you." Carly pulled her chair closer.

Aunt Nora turned to look into Carly's eyes. "You know I've always loved you and your brother. You were my sister's kids, but I loved you as if you were my own. I've always tried to do right by the two of you."

"I know that, Aunt Nora." Carly's eyes moistened with emotion. She wondered why her aunt needed to say what she knew to be true and had never doubted.

"I hope I didn't make a mistake acting as your representative in the sale of your parents' home."

"Aunt Nora, please…" Carly rose out of her chair, hoping to allay her fears. "I never meant to make you feel like I was blaming you for—"

Aunt Nora raised her arm and waved Carly away before she could place an arm around her shoulder. "Have a seat. This needs to be said."

Carly sat back in her seat. Leaning forward, she placed her hands on the table.

"You were so overwhelmed with everything going on with you." Aunt Nora lowered her head. Her aunt had walked with her through all the painful battles of the last year and knew it had been the fight of her life.

"I just thought that after you gave me the power of attorney, I could lessen your burdens by arranging the sale. I reviewed the paperwork with recommendations from my lawyers before I sent them to you. I thought the deal was a good one."

"To be honest, I didn't review them as closely as I could have." Carly raised her aunt's hand off the table and kissed the top of it. In the absence of her parents, Aunt Nora had stepped in to ease her burdens. Swallowing the hard lump in her throat, Carly reflected on how difficult the last few years had been.

"Believe me when I tell you with all sincerity that I don't blame you." Carly bit her lower lip to fight back the tears.

"Well, if we're being perfectly honest, you shouldn't blame Mason for what has happened, either."

"What are you saying?" Carly tilted her head, looking into the eyes of the woman who had never lied to her in her life. Not once.

"My meetings were never directly with him. He was out of the country when the deal was finalized. One of his vice presidents – of acquisitions, I think – acted as his representative. He said he had the authority to make real estate decisions for Mr. Moore."

"So you're telling me that you never spoke to Mason?" The frown on Carly's face softened for a few seconds.

"I spoke to him after the deal was agreed upon, but he

wasn't involved in the negotiations. Remember, those real estate agents approached me about the house." Aunt Nora rubbed her forehead. "Big, fancy, prestigious firm with all sorts of money. With everything you've been through and what it's done to your finances, I felt like they could get the best deal and help you get out of trouble."

Up until a few months ago, Carly couldn't bring herself to sell her parents' house, despite the avid interest in it. But since she had remained in Maryland after graduating college and her older brother, John, now lived on the West Coast, they both decided it was time to let the home go. He signed over his interest in the home to her before the sale to help ease her financial problems.

"Wow, he sure has a lot of people insulating him from whatever fallout may happen. The realtors point a finger at the Moore Investment Group and Mason has his people protecting his interests. Just great."

"Carly, I never thought anything *nefarious* was afoot."

She burst out laughing. "You're being funny, Aunt Nora."

The older woman's eyes twinkled.

"N-e-f-a-r-i-o-u-s, typically something wicked or criminal." Carly had won her elementary school's spelling bee in the third grade correctly spelling the word. Aunt Nora was there standing proudly as one of her greatest cheerleaders.

After a few moments, a solemn hush enveloped the room. Aunt Nora straightened her glasses. "I never asked them what they planned to do with the house after the sale."

"That doesn't mean they didn't take advantage of your trust that they would do the right thing." Carly folded her arms across her chest. "You've always been good at handling business. I know you made the best decision at the time. I've always trusted your judgement."

Carly took in a breath before continuing. "None of this is your fault."

"I see I'm not cooling off your anger. Like I said, I've placed a call to Mason. Let me talk to him."

Carly rubbed her chin. "Tell me, how did you get a call through to him? He's such a busy man."

"His mother and I have remained friends for decades. We're on the planning committee for the Clarkson Symposium. She gave me his direct number." She paused and smiled. "You know his firm is sponsoring the symposium this year?"

Aunt Nora had served on the *Selma Poinsette Clarkson Symposium* planning committee every year for the past ten years. They provided scholarships for first-generation college students, and also protected historical sites in Charleston.

Carly began to wonder why her aunt was defending Mason with everything she was saying. The sly smile on her face almost made her roll her eyes. Her entire family loved Mason.

Her aunt's next statement confirmed the gnawing suspicion. "If I can't clear up the misunderstanding, maybe you can contact him after you return from the islands. That's something great to look forward to, don't you think?" Aunt Nora flashed one of her broad, sunny smiles. Time had done nothing to diminish her beauty, nor her desire to look on the bright side of life.

"No, I don't think so. I have absolutely no desire to talk to Mason Moore ever again, in this life or the next."

Her aunt pursed her lips. Carly didn't bother to ask what words she was biting back. She tilted her head to the side, something Carly knew she did when she was about to change the subject.

"You said you were going to do some research while you're in the Bahamas. Are you still planning to make it a pleasure trip with a little bit of business?"

"Yes, ma'am. This entire trip will be a tax write-off. I need it." She also needed the fun in the sun with her friends that had helped her make it through this hell of a year. Carly sighed and closed her eyes as she imagined enjoying a cool, refreshing drink and the pleasures of calm island breezes.

She opened her eyes and looked at her watch. "Well, with all this happening, all the more important that I get the rest of the stuff out of the house."

"I'm sorry I didn't check to see if all the furniture had been removed from the house before the sale, but... Well, you know I haven't been feeling that well lately." Aunt Nora's eyes dropped to the table.

Carly knew she hated admitting she wasn't feeling well. "Don't worry about it, Aunt Nora, I'm glad the doctor was able to adjust the doses of your medicines. You'll be feeling better in no time." Carly hoped her voice sounded more confident than she felt inside.

"I'm better. I can go to the house to help you finish packing. There shouldn't be much left at this point." Aunt Nora extended her hand and placed it on top of Carly's, giving it a quick, supportive squeeze.

"Let me get ready for this meeting with the real estate agent." The agent had graciously agreed to meet Carly at her parents' home for a final, sentimental walkthrough. "I can make plans to have the furniture placed in storage until I come back."

"If you wait, I can go with you."

"No, I don't want to be late. I would feel better if you get a little more rest. I won't be gone long." She kissed her aunt on the cheek before heading to her bedroom to get her purse.

Chapter

4

Carly took in the sights as she made the short drive from her aunt's house on Henrietta Street to her childhood neighborhood. Charleston, South Carolina was one of the beautiful crown jewels of the New South. She looked forward to seeing more of the city. It was always gorgeous at Christmas and steeped in history, it rang in the holidays with its unique charm inviting all to come and stay awhile. Decorated with sparkling white lights and shiny bows, Charleston donned all its finery. Storefronts, homes, antebellum mansions, churches, boats, parks, and its majestic bridge over the Cooper River arching over the city's background were fashioned with lights, garlands, and holly, showing their yuletide cheer.

So many emotions coursed through her on the short route. Much like the history of Charleston, Carly hadn't fully reckoned with the truth of her complex past and all its contradictions.

Carly parked her car in front of her parents' home. She

got out and looked around the old neighborhood. She was struck by the reality that the things and people who lived in the neighborhood during her childhood, those who provided her with a sense of belonging, were no longer there. Mrs. Mary – a guardian angel of children – who wandered into the streets to retrieve their rubber balls, no longer sat on her porch. She had gone to glory many years ago. Gone were the views of the shallow salt marshes across the street from her home. She didn't hear the cacophony of seagulls that once gathered for their daily chats with each other along the Ashley River. The sweetgrasses no longer waved hello in the wind.

As she walked along the brick path leading to the front door, she smelled fish frying on someone's stove as a recording of Charles Brown's hit, "Please Come Home for Christmas," sounded through an open window near her. The agent from Reilly Realty had assured her the locks wouldn't be changed until after their meeting. She took her keys out of her purse and opened the door.

Most of her parents' furniture was gone from the living room, but her heart was still full of the memories of a happy childhood and loving parents. Her father died before her thirteenth birthday. Despite the grief after her father's death, her mother continued the tradition of filling the home with delicious treats and fresh poinsettias at Christmastime.

Carly stopped in her tracks as she looked at the two poinsettia plants with vibrant red leaves in the same corner where her mother had always placed them, next to the fireplace. She blinked away the tears threatening to fall as she focused on the pots wrapped in bright green foil with large red ribbons tied around them.

"Leave it to Aunt Nora to do something kind when I need it the most."

Coughing, Carly cleared her throat and waved the dust from in front of her face. She managed a smile as she walked toward the plants and noticed there was no card.

"Curious..." she said to herself, uncertain the plants *were* from Aunt Nora.

Before turning on the lights, she rubbed one of the satiny leaves between her fingers, then flipped the switch as she continued on the way to her bedroom. She'd paid the utilities every month prior to the sale, even though she knew she would never return to inhabit the house. She rubbed her chest, which was unable to fully expand as it tightened with grief. Three years had passed since her mother's heart attack.

Opening a few windows in her room and her brother's room before going to her parents' bedroom, Carly made her way at a slow pace. It was almost as if she heard the television her mother watched most nights before going to bed. She envisioned the smell of honeysuckle, the familiar scent of the perfume her mother wore, as she looked at the top of the dresser covered with old Avon bottles.

Her aunt told her she had packed up most of her mother's things except for the chair and vanity dresser. Her brother's trophy of his last victory on the football field and a picture of Carly smiling at her graduation remained on top of the dresser. Aunt Nora thought Carly should take the vanity since she had spent hours in front of the mirror playing dress-up as a little girl.

Carly looked at her reflection in the mirror and twisted her ringlets of curls, frizzy from the humidity. She moved closer to the mirror as she looked at the circles forming under her eyes from fatigue.

Better pack a light foundation and concealer for the cruise, she thought to herself.

"Hello."

Carly turned at the sound of someone entering the home, suspecting it was the real estate agent who had agreed to meet with her.

She noticed an old dress box in the corner, discolored and wrinkled with time. Bending to touch the top of the box, she rubbed her fingers across the cracks in the cardboard, worn with age. She wanted to see what was inside, but she ran out the door to meet the agent before opening it.

"Hello. I'm Carly Rivers, and you must be Janice Blake?" Carly was sure it was Janice, since the name tag on her blazer identified her as an employee of Reilly Realty.

"Yes, I'm Janice, and I'm pleased we meet at last. I'm sorry I'm a little late, but we have a bit of a problem."

"It's fine, Janice. I haven't been here long, but what's the problem?" Carly knitted her brow.

"Well, this is quite unusual, and I know I promised you one last walkthrough, but—" Janice's phone rang before she could finish her thought. She frowned as she looked at it. "Pardon me, Carly. I really have to take this." She walked away as she spoke to the caller.

Carly returned to the bedroom to get the box on the floor. She didn't intend to eavesdrop, but she couldn't help overhearing Janice's conversation, which was more important to her than whatever was in the box.

"So, Mr. Moore wants to come here to look over the property? Dan, I assure you I sent him all the pictures and specifications he requested before he sold it to the new buyer." The sound of Janice's deep, audible sigh filled the room. "Well, I have another appointment and I can't meet with him."

Carly inclined her ear to listen to the conversation. There was a long pause.

"If the deal is contingent on his final request, I can make it happen. Ms. Rivers is still here. Yes, you heard me. She's here and…" She paused again.

Carly wished she could hear what was being said on the other end of the call.

"Yes, I understand he wants to view the property by himself before it's torn down. He won't be here before the next hour? Okay."

Carly's head snapped to attention. So her parents' house was on the list of properties to be destroyed. Her heart sank into her stomach. Another reality hit her. If Mason wanted to see it before it was torn down, then he knew! He knew they were going to destroy her family home.

She paced the floor, wringing her hands. She had to do something, even if it meant pleading for her home. Well, it no longer belonged to her, since she had already sold it, despite her original misgivings. What could she do? Did she really have the strength or inclination to engage in yet another bruising legal battle?

"Carly, I'm so glad we met each other. Now that you've seen the property one last time, we can lock up and walk to our cars. I have the information you requested on local movers who can assist you in removing the rest of your mother's belongings in my car."

"Janice, I know you have other appointments. I appreciate that you squeezed in time for me on such short notice, but I left a box in the bedroom. I'll be right behind you. You can send the information to me by email since I'll be heading out of town for the holiday. I won't be able to make arrangements with the movers for another week."

"All right." She checked the time on her phone and bit her lip. "I really have to go or I'll be late again. It's been one of those days. Take care."

"Thanks, Janice. Don't worry. I'm right behind you. I'll lock up before I leave." Carly smiled and waved as Janice rushed out the door.

She turned and headed back to the bedroom. She heard the sound of the keys as Janice tossed them into the metal mailbox on the side of the door, followed by the sound of her heels clicking against the brick as she scurried down the steps to her car.

Carly knew she needed to come up with a convincing argument if she wanted to save her old home. She didn't want to live in the house anymore, but she'd never imagined that someone would tear it down. What she didn't know was how she could save it.

A gust of wind blew through the house and rain began to patter on the tin roof. Carly went to the window and stared out at the vacant lot where homes filled with love once stood. She pondered their history as time slowly ticked by while she waited in her mother's bedroom for her showdown with Mason.

Her mother had always liked Mason – no, she'd *loved* Mason.

"I don't know why you can't see that his cockiness is only a cover to protect his tender heart. That boy feels too deeply about too many things. He's got a good heart. Remember my words. He's going to make some woman very happy one day," her mother once told her.

She had hoped her mother was right about him.

Carly heard the keys clanging as they were removed from the metal mailbox and placed in the lock to open the door. Her muscles tensed at the sound of footsteps across the wooden floor, stopping and proceeding in the direction of the kitchen before returning to the front of the house.

Summoning her courage, she willed herself to face Mason, the person who held the fate of this home in his hands. She walked down the hall, carrying the old box.

There he was, dressed in a black suit, tailored to fit his broad shoulders and muscular body. He initially stood in front of the poinsettias, looking away from her, then he turned, pivoting to face her as she entered the room. Self-assured, with an ego that filled the length and breadth of his tall, powerful frame, he could charm any woman with his inviting smile and smooth baritone voice.

"Caroline?" He tilted his head. His jaw dropped as he awaited her answer.

"Yes, it's me, Mason."

Chapter

5

Hello. How have you been?" Carly placed the box on the floor and wiped the dust off her hands as she tried to gather her thoughts.

"Hi. I've been fine." Mason shook his head and stared at her as if he was trying to figure out if she was really standing in front of him. "I didn't expect to see you here today. I thought you were living in..." He searched his brain for a moment. "...Maryland?" He clasped his hands at his waist and didn't move closer to her.

Just being in his presence was too much. She became flustered and stumbled over her words. "I'm here for the holidays. I...I thought you had settled in New York." Her mouth felt like she had stuffed it with cotton balls. She rubbed the back of her neck as she pondered if she should get right to the point or fill the time with cordial niceties between old acquaintances. She didn't have time for niceties. This was all about saving her home.

She took a deep breath. "Anyway, why are you here? At

this house? You wanted to see it before tearing it down?" She shook her head, narrowed her eyes at him, and spoke through gritted teeth. "You...you knew...you knew the plans. I overheard the real estate agent. Aunt Nora trusted you, but I didn't. You betrayed me in the past and you're doing the same thing now."

"Wait a minute. Let me explain."

She looked at him, raising his hands in a defensive posture while her heart raced. She erupted in volcanic anger, blurting out feelings she had carried for so many years. "What can you possibly explain? Haven't you done enough to hurt me and my family? Now you want to level our home?"

Mason winced. She knew they were both thinking of the last time he had hurt her family. He stared at her as she wiped away the tears that fell down her cheeks but didn't cool her anger.

Her phone buzzed and she reached for it in her crossbody purse.

She stared at the text from her aunt, then mumbled as she read it aloud, "Don't forget to bring the box in your mother's bedroom. Your mother saved the contents for you."

She texted her aunt back.

Do you want me to bring the poinsettia plants too?

Aunt Nora: What plants?

Carly frowned. So the plants weren't from her aunt. She sent one last text.

Never mind. I'll be back soon.

She placed the phone back in her purse.

"What are you staring at?" she snapped at Mason as he gazed at her in her form-fitting black jersey dress that clung to her curvy figure. The last time they saw one another, they were in college and the woman she would become hadn't revealed herself yet, at least not to him.

"It's *who* and not *what* I'm staring at."

His eyes travelling the length of her body in seconds didn't escape her attention.

"I didn't expect to run into you." His eyes didn't lie as they looked directly into hers. "I surely don't mean to upset you."

The heat of her anger gradually cooled hearing more of his smooth voice. He still had an effect on her, despite the passage of time. She felt a familiar tingling sensation throughout her body – the same feeling she'd had when they were in college, and he kissed her for the first time.

"I'm upset that I had to hear the plans to tear down this house on television. You've been in touch with my aunt. A simple phone call would have been a great gesture." Her body betrayed the hostility she wanted to maintain towards him, and his direct eye contact with her was more uncomfortable than she cared to admit. She looked away as she repositioned the strap of her pocketbook on her shoulder.

"I'm sorry about that. I know it's upsetting, but I wasn't directly involved in the acquisition of this property. I have a team of portfolio managers who buy and sell properties for me for investment purposes. I run a large company with shareholders who expect a return on their investments."

He looked at his hands and intertwined his fingers. "I came down here when I learned this house was one of the holdings that was bought and sold. This home was not a part of the original deal. When I learned of your decision to sell the house, I envisioned renovating it and making it a part of a future development. But I learned after the fact that one of my VPs included it in a quick sale for demolition. The property is more valuable than the home and we were given a very lucrative deal to sell."

"So, it's just business? There's nothing you can do about the plans for this home?"

"I'm afraid I can't promise to change what has already happened." His tone softened. "Now you have another reason to hate me."

Again, they weren't just talking about a house. They were talking about years of lost love. Missed opportunity. Regret…

"I don't hate you. It's just…ironic seeing you here, but yet so detached from this place. I never imagined I would have to plead for it, since you spent so much time here when we were younger."

She turned toward the fireplace. "My mother used to take pictures of us standing right there at Christmastime. I think she took one of you, but…"

Carly held up her hands and squeezed her eyes tight, shutting out the pictures from the past that were flooding her head and all the feelings that went with them. "You know what? I can't do this with you right now. Too many bittersweet memories. I think I'd better leave and allow you the private walkthrough you requested."

He held out his hand to slow her progress toward the door after she leaned down to pick up the box to carry it to Aunt Nora's house.

"Please don't leave. I have memories of this home too, mostly good ones. For instance, your mother always placed two live poinsettia plants right there. That's why I had them delivered here one last time." He pointed to the marble slab at the base of the fireplace.

She halted and turned to look at him. Her eyes softened for the first time as she blinked, caught off guard by his remorse.

"And I'm surprised you kept the box I had delivered to you so many years ago. The first kiss we shared meant a lot to me. *You* meant… You still mean a lot to me." He touched the lid of the box. "I bought that present many years ago because I wanted to show you how much I desired for us to be together."

"What are you talking about? I've never seen this box before. I think it belonged to my mother."

"Well, open it and see what's inside."

Chapter

6

C arly took the lid off the box. Inside was a varsity cheerleader jacket with the block number twelve sewn on the front. She looked up at his smiling face and took the jacket out of the box.

Damn, he's still good-looking. She didn't want to admit it, but it was the truth.

"I purchased this jacket as a gift for you. Your mother sewed my team number on it. I asked her what she thought about me asking you to be my girl and she said, 'Go for it.' I intended to ask you on that night of the game, but you know how that ended."

They both sat for a moment in complete silence, remembering the outcome of that night. That last night...when things fell completely apart.

"I don't understand why you thought it had to end that way between us." Her jaw slackened.

The more she thought about that night, the more her anger and regret started to simmer. "Why did you do it?

Why? You wanted to get all the glory, so you ruined John's chances of making it to the pros. Your decision on the field ended up causing my brother to suffer a career-ending injury. He had no chance of making it to the pros after that game. He was your friend, yet because of you, my brother lost his scholarship. What were you thinking?"

She paused for a few moments. "I'll tell you what you were thinking. 'I'm Mason Moore. I'll do whatever I want. I'll throw a dangerous pass, and I'll jilt his younger sister on the same night. And—'"

"No, stop it, Caroline. I didn't mean to stand you up. I suffered a concussion and had trouble remembering my own name that night. All I remembered was my parents taking me to the ER to get me checked out. I forgot we had a date until days later. It's the truth. I'm many things, but I'm not a liar."

She paced before him, surprised she was allowing her feelings about the deal with the house to quickly morph into something much deeper.

"All right, I can accept that, but one week later, I still didn't hear from you. Then you leave town and transfer to another school months later without an explanation. Did I mean nothing to you?" She crossed her arms and turned away, unable to look him in the eyes.

"So, we're going there now? I didn't know you still held so much anger against me after all these years."

She frowned while watching him clear his throat and briefly shift his attention to look at his feet.

He raised his head and stood still as he observed her. "Are you willing to listen to me now, or do you want me to listen to you make accusations against me? I can do this either way, Caroline. I didn't come here to fight with you."

Carly took a deep breath. Got her emotions back under

control.

She hadn't come here to argue either.

Mason paced the floor for a few seconds then stopped, measuring his words. "I looked up at you on the sideline. Your hands were covering your mouth, but I could still hear you screaming. From the look on your face, I thought you'd never forgive me when John didn't get up after taking that nasty hit. I was so sorry. I carried the guilt for years."

Carly bit her lip. Somehow, hearing that he actually felt guilty about it, and for years, calmed her ire. She paced slowly, back and forth, the length of the living room a couple of times.

He was completely silent, waiting for her response.

She decided to hold out an olive branch. Her anger and bitterness over all those years were no longer a weight she wanted to carry. "I'm sorry too. You took a nasty hit as well. I wasn't screaming just for my brother, I was concerned about you. The trainers had to come take you off the field."

"You were worried about me? My memories of that night are spotty, but I thought I saw contempt, not concern."

"Was I rolling my eyes, sneering, or crossing my arms?"

"No, not like you were doing a few minutes ago when I feared for my life."

She laughed, despite her attempts to suppress it. They stood looking at each other for a few moments. Looking at their past from a different perspective.

Mason finally spoke. "Let's see if the jacket will fit you." He took it out of her hand and held it up as she placed her hands in the sleeves. "It's perfect." He tilted his head as his boyish grin spread across his face.

"Thank you, Mace. As I think back on it, my mother did place a white satin-covered box with a red ribbon tied around it on my bed, but when she told me it was from you, I refused to open it. I told her to return it. You didn't deserve all of my anger back then, and I didn't plan to unload on you today, but..."

But what? She paced back and forth in front of him, unable to believe everything she'd said. She pulled the jacket tighter around her.

Anyway, this wasn't about their past. It was about their present.

She decided to refocus the conversation. "I'm shocked you're willing to let this house be torn down without a fight. I remember a man who once stood by his convictions."

He winced and placed his hands behind his back. "It's not my decision anymore. Please say you understand that."

"I don't understand it, but I have to accept it." She looked away toward the ray of light shining through the window. "It's not like I was misled. When my aunt told me Moore Investment Group had purchased the property, I just thought you would take a personal interest, as the owner of the company, and restore it. So much for assumptions."

"We can't relive the past." He looked at her as he pleaded with puppy-dog eyes filled with remorse.

"Sure, it's not personal. So I'll ask, why are you here? Do you ask all those involved in your business acquisitions to wear a jacket you purchased?" She placed her hands on her hips and waited for his response.

"No, I don't, but I wanted to see this house one last time, I guess. I'm not exactly sure why, but I know I would have regretted it if I didn't see it again. The house I grew up in on Henrietta Street was torn down." He sighed. "This house is one link to the past, but I don't feel the need to dwell on the past."

"Like I'm doing?" She peered into his eyes, then backed away to increase the space between them. "This house, this *neighborhood*, is special to me, even though I don't live here anymore."

"I haven't forgotten the good times I had here with your family. I just carry them inside me. I remember all the great meals your mother prepared for us – the red rice, seafood dishes, and the best macaroni and cheese in the world. Don't tell my mother she isn't as good a cook." He smiled, having gotten another laugh out of her.

He moved to the center of the room and stood before her, his eyes downcast. "Caroline—"

"Call me Carly. I've gone by the name Carly for years."

"*Carly*, I should have come to you and explained myself all those years ago. I tried, but you were with Tyson before I got the nerve to talk to you. He told me you hated me, and I should man up and leave you alone." He rolled his eyes. "I thought he was right after you never reached out to me."

"At that time, I thought it was on you to reach out to me first." She looked down at her feet. "The intimate moment we shared was special to me, then one week later, I heard nothing from you. I thought I was just another woman you grew tired of and cast to the side."

"It wasn't like that. I left campus quickly after my injury because I didn't bear up well under the harsh scrutiny of others. Some told me to my face that I deserved what happened to me. I admit, I was arrogant, but I never meant to be callous." He closed his eyes and rubbed the side of his face. "You're important to me even though a lot of time has passed since we last talked. And your brother was and still is my friend. It hurt me to see him lying in that hospital bed. It hurt even more thinking you would never forgive me."

She reached out and grabbed his hands. "You visited him? I never saw you at the hospital."

"Yes. I came to the hospital one day while you were being comforted by Tyson. He snarled at me when he looked up and saw me. I didn't want to cause a scene, so I left. After that day, I only came after I checked with John to make sure you weren't there."

She wrung her hands. Mason had said her ex-husband's name one too many times. "He was there when I needed a shoulder to cry on in college, but after we married, he wasn't there for me. It got so bad, it was best we separated and divorced."

"I regretted my decision not to talk to you for years, but now I know I could have handled things differently." Mason looked at her and raised an eyebrow. "Wait. Did you say you were divorced?"

"Yes, it was finally legal a few months ago."

"It must have been difficult for you, going through a divorce not long after losing your mother." He squeezed her hands.

Her heart quickened as if threatening to beat out of her chest.

She took in a deep breath and savored the masculine smell of his cologne. His luscious lips beckoned her to him. She wished she could taste them as he looked at her face. She wiped the sweat off her brow and pursed her lips as she exhaled.

"Let me help you out of this jacket. You look flushed."

His hand brushed her chest while helping her out of the garment.

"Thank you. It's getting warm in here."

He smiled as he helped her out of her jacket before taking

off his own. "I agree. It is warm and inviting in here, just like I remembered."

Her phone rang in her bag. "It's probably Aunt Nora wondering if I'm all right. She knew it would be hard for me coming back here."

The door opened. A man wearing a dark suit and crisp white shirt entered the room. "Pardon the interruption, Mr. Moore." He stopped near the door and clasped his hands in front of him. "There's a business call in the car that requires your attention, from the firm in New York. VP Morgan instructed me to inform you that it was urgent. Can I tell him you will take the call? Your pilot also sent a text to get the estimated time we will arrive at the airport to leave."

"Well, I guess we need to say goodbye." Carly backed away from him and looked at her pocketbook. Her phone was still ringing.

"Wait a minute." Mason held up one hand in Carly's direction and the other at the driver. "Let me take this call." He looked at the driver, who was turning and headed toward the door. "Carly, I'll be right back. Promise me you'll be here when I get back."

"I promise." She crossed her heart.

He turned and hurried out the door.

"Yes, Aunt Nora." She picked up the phone and absently answered the call, without looking at the caller ID on the screen.

"This isn't Nora." A familiar male voice filled her ear. "It's Tyson."

She closed her eyes. Inhaling a slow, deep breath, she focused on calming her heart, which was thumping in her chest. She'd had at least a hundred missed calls from him over the past few months. He kept calling and she kept ignoring his calls. She would have done the same with this one if she had bothered to look at it before answering the phone.

Storms of emotions swirled within as his voice registered in her mind, conjuring up ghosts of memories. When things were good between them, they were very good. The bad experiences, however, outnumbered the good. Over time, the pain of their failed marriage stuck with her like shards of glass, piercing her body where it could do the most damage.

"What do you want?" Her response was sharper than she wanted it to be. He still had an effect on her. She wasn't neutral when it came to him.

"Glad to hear your voice too, Carly." His laugh was lighthearted in contrast to the harsh tone of her voice. "I've been thinking a lot about you, about us."

"Why?" She frowned, looking at his name on the screen. She considered hanging up, but maybe if she went ahead and talked to him, she could put to rest whatever had him calling the past few months. Her divorce was final. She had no reason to ever talk to Tyson again.

"The holidays were always a special time for us. I just thought it would be good for us to talk about old times. You know, the good times. Admit it, Carl, we had some good times."

"I don't have time to revisit the past, Tyson."

"Fine. Let's talk about the present. I know you're in Charleston and planning to go on a cruise. I remember how much I used to beg you to take time off to visit relatives. I also wanted *us* to go on a cruise." He hesitated. "You were too busy chasing the chance at tenure to work on our marriage. I wasn't the only one at fault."

"Wait. Tyson, are you stalking me? I don't need this. Good—"

39

"Carly, wait." His voice was urgent. "I spoke to your...*cousin*."

"My cousin shared information about me?" She paused. "Is *that* what you want me to believe?"

"It's true. He told me when you were leaving. I did a little research and found out that there was only one seven-day cruise leaving out of Charleston. I booked a suite on the top deck so we can watch the sunset together. What do you say? You, me, and a beautiful sunset."

She rolled her eyes. "Don't do this, Tyson." She rubbed her temple. "I'll be busy spending my time with my girlfriends. We're over."

"I disagree. I don't think it's over yet." His smugness had returned. "What I think is that I want to go to the Bahamas too. Did you buy the cruise ship and I'm not welcome to board?"

She began to feel the heat of anger again. Her heart rate accelerated, and her stomach began to churn. "Go to hell, Tyson," she blurted out.

"Wait. I'm... I'm sorry," he choked. "Please don't be angry with me. I guess the holidays are playing with my head. The truth is..." He paused. "I still love you. I think if we're both willing to work at it, we can regain what we lost. We had good times too. Don't tell me you've forgotten."

"I can't do this with you. Goodbye." She clicked off the phone. Digging her nails into her palm, she tried holding back the tears. "Maybe I needed this reminder." She let out a sound deep in her throat. How could she forget how caring, funny Tyson could turn into a raging monster in a matter of minutes? Placing a hand on her stomach, she diminished the rising waves of nausea.

"I promised myself I would never let Tyson hurt me the

way he did ever again. I'll never let him take me back to that dark place that I prayed my way out of."

She turned and went to the bathroom to regain her composure.

"I'll say goodbye to Mason and then I'm out of here."

Chapter

7

Mason hurried to the limo. He opened the door to the back seat and slammed it behind him. The privacy partition was raised between him and the driver.

"Speak, Morgan," he demanded in a harsh tone.

"Mace, I thought you would be in the air by now. Where in the hell are you?" Bernie raised his voice, returning the hostility in equal measure. The two of them had been best friends since grad school. "The markets are imploding. I don't know how many times I tapped your cell and nothing. *Hellooo.* You're the CEO of a major conglomerate. I don't get why you're still handling business in Charleston when the holdings we have down there are such a small part of your portfolio. You promised we would make some decisions about the subsidiaries, including the lifestyle company, *Moore for You*, that Jamillah wants you to sell to her."

"She can't afford to buy me out." He pressed his fist to his forehead. "And no, I don't plan to give it to her."

"Well, one way or another, we need some direction from you," Bernie persisted. "Sell your shares of that company to someone else? Expand more into mass media? What do you want to do? I'll call an emergency meeting for a face-to-face discussion with the board in the next two hours. You should be back in New York by then, right?"

Mason leaned his head back against the plush headrest and looked up. He had spent most of his adult life growing the business he had inherited from his maternal grandparents. While his grandfather had significant holdings in South Carolina, Mace had elevated the business to the international stage. He paid a high price for it. He had no personal life. His business *was* his life.

"Mason, what is going on with you, man?"

He responded with a deep groan.

"It's not like you to be indecisive."

Mason remained motionless, unaffected by the anxiety in Bernie's voice.

"Is everything all right down there? I mean, is your mother okay?" Bernie's voice went high.

"She's fine," Mason responded in a monotone.

"Your brothers?"

"Everybody is fine." He turned and looked out the window at the house where Carly was still waiting for him. "An unresolved past is never the past." He murmured under his breath the old saying her mother had often said to the both of them. "Meet your challenges head on."

"What did you say? I didn't understand you." Bernie briefly awaited his response.

Mace straightened his posture, holding his head high.

"I may not be making myself clear as your VP of finance. More importantly, as your friend, you need to understand what's at stake. You have a lot of money tied up in the overseas market. If you don't respond with something definitive, you stand to lose millions," he screeched. "It could also threaten our domestic holdings, Mace."

Mason cleared his throat. "I need you to handle this for me. Something important has come up. You know my long-term business plans. I trust you."

"What could be more important than a business emergency that could cripple your company?"

Mace laughed and placed his hand on the door handle.

"You're not caught up in a *Christmas Carol* experience down there, are you?" Bernie chuckled. "Have you seen the ghost of Christmas past?"

Mason's posture loosened. Turning his head, he looked through the glass with an unfocused stare. Hesitating while weighing his words, he finally spoke. "I've been singularly focused on growing my business. I've made sacrifices and hard decisions, but I've never been an Ebenezer Scrooge. I've never taken advantage of people, even when it was profitable to do so."

"I'm sorry, Mace. You know that wasn't what I meant. I wasn't implying anything negative about your integrity." He stumbled over his words. "Things are just crazy up here. It was a stupid thing to say."

As an adult, Mace had viewed the time he spent in Charleston with family as an obligation, not something he looked forward to. For the past few months, he had felt gnawing regrets about past failed relationships. It was a feeling he couldn't shake. Maybe he wanted something different than growing his fortune.

"I need you to handle things for the next few hours." He lowered the partition screen. "Don't sell. I'll call you as soon as I can."

"Before you hang up, I wanted to let you know that I followed up with Fletcher about the picture he sent last week. He admitted that he made a mistake identifying the female standing with the older man as the owner of the home in Charleston. The woman in the picture wasn't Carly Matherson. She was one of the dean's former teaching assistants. Her social media handle was Tam P. Sorry, I don't do the social media thing. I had one of my younger associates do some research to identify her."

"Thanks. Goodbye, Bernie."

"Goodbye."

He looked at the driver in the front seat. "Stay here until I return."

"You got it, boss."

Mason opened the door and climbed out of the vehicle. He turned and made his way back to the house. He needed to discuss some important matters with Carly. The two of them had an unresolved past that needed to be settled.

Chapter

8

After a quick tap on the door, Mason entered and looked around the room. Carly was coming down the hall.

"Bathroom break." She gazed at him.

"Sorry for the interruption. It took a little longer than I had hoped." He crossed the room, narrowing the distance between them.

"No problem." He noted her faint smile. "I returned a few phone calls."

Focus, Mason, he thought to himself as he stood in front of her. Concentrating his efforts on slowing his heart rate, he made sure his gaze didn't settle on Carly's breasts or her sensuous hips. He knew he wanted to spend more time with her. He needed to reconnect after being apart from her for years. Business matters could wait.

"Can I invite you to dinner so we can share a meal and talk? I'm grateful we've cleared up our misunderstanding. Or at least have started to." He stopped in front of her and grabbed her hands. "I'd like to catch up on all the things you're doing. We could also use the time to talk about the plans for the new development. You're not looking at the future jobs the project will create, the increased tax base, and the increased funding for schools. We've got to be more forward looking. I have my eyes on the future."

She frowned and released his hands.

"Did I say something wrong?" He tilted his head and placed a hand on her shoulder.

"No, nothing wrong." She raised the corners of her lips. "I have to meet with my Aunt Nora this evening. Tomorrow night, I'm scheduled to give a talk at the Notable Women of Charleston Poinsettia Symposium at the Gaillard Center to honor the works of Mrs. Selma Clarkson."

"My company has given funds to support their programs. So, you're on the panel of speakers tomorrow?"

"Yes, the featured speaker had to cancel at the last minute and I'm filling in."

"Oh, I thought I heard on the news this morning that they had another speaker – a college history professor with a specialty in African American history in Charleston and the Sea Islands, Professor Carly Morrison."

"Carly Matherson, not Morrison. I haven't had time to update my speaker's bio since my divorce. I'll be using my maiden name and marketing myself as Carly Rivers after I return from my vacation."

"His last name wasn't once Morrison and he changed it to Matherson?" He smiled, recalling the memory of taunting Tyson while they were in college by intentionally calling him by the wrong name.

"No, it was always Matherson. You and Tyson didn't like each other much, did you?"

Petty. I get it. He shrugged. "Tyson wasn't someone I wanted to get to know, so it wouldn't be accurate to say I didn't like him. But enough about him, unless you want to talk about him."

Please say no. I don't want to waste my time talking about your ex, but I don't want to mess things up between us either.

"No, I don't." She shook her head.

"Good. So, what about tomorrow after the event? Can we get together then?" He smiled and grasped her hands, rubbing her smooth skin with his thumb. "Please say yes. There's so much I want to catch up on."

"I'm afraid that won't work either. I'll be heading for the cruise terminal for a getaway to the Bahamas before the holidays roll in."

Mason looked around the stark room. He reflected on the comfy La-Z-Boy chairs and couch that once occupied the room. "You're going to the islands for Christmas instead of staying here with family? I remember when your mother had this room decorated with lots of poinsettias. This room always felt like love to me, filled with the smells of her cooking and the plants which made it look so festive."

"Yes, but as you said, we can't dwell in the past." She took small steps toward the door.

"Maybe I was wrong, Carly. It wouldn't be the first time."

"Goodbye, Mason." She walked to the door and crossed the threshold without looking back.

"Goodbye, Carly." Mace ran his hand through his hair. *I can't let it end like this, but I'm not sure what to do.*

He was pacing the floor when his phone began buzzing with notifications. Pulling it out of his pocket, he looked at the messages popping up on the screen.

FOREVER *Carly*

Volatility in the foreign markets triggers a day of massive selling.
The Dow plunges in the midst of high-volume trading.
NASDAQ drops to its lowest level this year.

His heart was thumping out of his chest. He wiped the sweat from his brow with the back of his hand. While struggling with the urge to flee to New York, he became overwhelmed and flooded with fear. Placing his hand on the mantel, he braced himself.

He didn't want to be a disappointment to his family. A failure.

Unexpectantly, a warm wave of calm flowed from his head to his feet.

"You can't take it with you." The reassuring voice of his supportive maternal grandmother, Ella, filled his mind.

"Don't pay attention to that old woman," he recalled hearing his grandfather, Pops, responding to her advice. *"Everybody can't be leaders,"* Pops once told him. *"But you, Mason, you were born for this. Leaders have to make hard decisions."*

He looked at the space in front of him, imagining he was seeing his grandfather, a man of imposing stature.

"You may not like it, but regardless of what you decide, you'll have to live with the consequences of your actions."

"Maybe she was right, Pops," he said out loud as if speaking to his grandfather. It was painful accepting that Pops and Grandma Ella were gone. The money they left was firmly in his hands. He placed the phone, still buzzing, in his pocket and walked out the door.

"I'll figure something out. First, handle business in New York and then I can focus on winning Carly back." He opened the door to the limo. "Take me to the airport."

Chapter

9

I think the meeting with leadership went well." Bernie fidgeted with his gold cufflinks as he sat in a plush leather chair across from Mace in his spacious corporate office. Everything about the decor spoke to the power of its owner. From the sleek, modern design of the silver light fixtures, to the black executive desk with its highly polished black oak finish, and the built-in, floor-to-ceiling shelving which provided a stark contrast against the white walls and the high architectural ceiling.

Mace focused his attention on the large monitors mounted on the wall in front of his desk, keeping up with his holdings in real time. "I agree." He stroked his chin with his hand. "We need to divest ourselves of assets that no longer fit in with our core business of real estate, financial investments, and mass media. Social media and promoting fashion and lifestyle products were Jamillah's thing. She won't like it, but it's time to sell my shares in the companies she founded with my money. I'll announce it after the new year."

He sat quietly for a moment, lost in thought. He finally said, "Yeah, let's announce it after the new year." He uncrossed his legs and rose from his seat.

"Today, we celebrate." Bernie pulled out his phone and looked at the screen. "The department heads are meeting downstairs for cocktails with this year's Young Heroes in Business Ethics and Integrity recipients. Are you coming?"

"I've got too many loose ends to tie up. Besides, I met and congratulated all of the recipients except for one during their tour of the building. She had a prior engagement. I'm expecting Andrew to bring her to my office for a quick meet-and-greet."

Andrew stuck his head in the door. "Are you ready for us?"

Mace rose from his seat. "Come in."

Andrew stood to the side, allowing the young woman to come into the room. Mace's jaw dropped as he saw that the woman looked like a younger version of Carly. Her brown hair – lighter and longer than Carly's – cascaded down, with thick curls framing her face. The bright twinkle in her eyes felt familiar to Mason. He observed her as she walked across the room with poise and an air of self-assurance. He was so taken by her appearance, he failed to verbally acknowledge her presence.

An awkward silence filled the room until Andrew cleared his throat and began the introductions. "You've met Mr. Morgan."

She nodded.

"Now, I'm pleased to introduce you to our CEO, Mr. Mason Moore." He directed her attention to Mason.

"Tamara Phillips." She extended her hand and smiled.

"Pleased to meet you." Mason shook her hand, holding it

a little longer than usual for a first-time introduction.

"I'd better get downstairs." Bernie cocked his brow, giving Mace a questioning look. "Miss Phillips, I'll make sure you meet the department head who will be your assigned mentor."

She turned to face Bernie, revealing a small tattoo of a butterfly on her right shoulder, peeking above the fabric of her black A-line dress with an off-the-shoulder design. "Thanks."

"No problem." He offered a smile before exiting.

"I'll return in about ten minutes to escort you downstairs." Andrew walked across the room and closed the door behind him.

"Have a seat." Mason directed her to the chair that Bernie had previously occupied.

"Thank you." She smiled and smoothed out the fabric of her dress before sitting down. "I appreciate that you took the time out of your schedule to meet with me. I'm sure you had more pressing business to attend to."

"You're welcome," he replied, still focusing on her soulful eyes. There was an aura behind them that called out to him, something that spoke to him. "I meet with all of the recipients of our Hero Awards every year. I have a special connection to them." He paused and swallowed hard, uncomfortable with the sentimental feelings rising up within him. "They were named in honor of my grandmother, Ella Jefferson. She was one of my personal heroes."

"Now I understand why family is so important to you." She leaned forward in her chair. "I was honest with Andrew and told him the real reason I wasn't able to make the meetings this morning. I've been waiting for months for the final fitting of my wedding dress. My mother and two sisters flew to New York to be with me. It was too difficult to change the schedule for the fitting." She buried her lower lip between her teeth. "Andrew assured me that it wouldn't be a problem if I came later in the day. The first mentor I ever had always told me to set my intentions and establish my priorities. My career is important to me, but I couldn't imagine not having my future husband by my side to share in my success. He's been very supportive of me even in the tough times."

"Congratulations on your upcoming wedding. Support from those who love us is important." Mason interlaced his fingers, resting his hands on his lap. "It also sounds like you had a very inspiring mentor."

"I did." She looked away with sad, downcast eyes. "Her advice and example of integrity are what contributed to my winning the award."

"I sense that it wasn't all good times." He sat back, hoping she would share more information. He had read her bio – and those of all the other winning candidates – but was still interested in hearing how she'd turned her challenge into triumph.

"I wrote about my experiences as a teaching assistant at a small college in the essay I submitted to win the award. My mentor at that time was Professor Matherson."

Mace's head tilted, inclining his ear to hear more after the mention of the professor's name. "Interesting."

"Yes. After winning the Heroes award, I found out that she was also a consultant for your company. She was a great role model for me." She paused while Mason nodded in agreement. "When I worked with her, she tried to advise me about the complications... No, call it the possibility of a disaster with workplace relationships. She actually warned me against it, but I had to find out the hard way." Tamara joined her hands and pressed them against her lips. She sat silently, briefly lost in her thoughts.

Mason broke the silence using a supportive voice. "Please continue."

"I left the college and came to New York to work in my uncle's marketing firm when it became clear that the man, the dean of the history department, wanted more than I was ready to give, if you know what I mean."

"I'm getting the impression." He nodded.

"Well, I blame myself for what happened to Professor Matherson." Tears welled up that didn't fall.

"How so?" He knitted his brow.

"Everyone told me how much we looked alike. We have similar facial features." She pushed the strands of her curly hair behind her ear. "After I left, some of the other assistants told me that he started going harder on her. As I look back on it, his attraction to her may have been what led him to start coming on to me. I had heard rumors that he had a thing for her before I got there, but she rebuffed him."

She made fists with her hands at her sides. "I blame myself that I didn't have the courage to turn him in years ago when it was happening to me. Instead, I ran. I kept in touch with some of the teaching assistants on social media under the name Tam P. When I saw how her so-called colleagues were trashing her online, I realized I had to do something. She had the strength to file a harassment suit against the dean. I prayed on it, talked to my fiancé about it, and agreed to testify for her. I have also used my experience to advocate for others in the workplace." She let out a deep breath. "It's still difficult talking about it."

"I'm sure it is but, your courage and willingness to help others is what we're looking for at Moore Investment Group.

Ethics and integrity are some of the core values we have here. I'm glad you accepted the mentorship." Mace looked over his shoulder at Andrew entering the room. "There's a meet-and-greet downstairs with members of the leadership board." He stood, signaling the end of their time together.

"Right this way, Tamara." Andrew stopped beside her and extended his hand, pointing in the direction of the door.

Mace waited until they left before returning to his seat behind his desk. A fleeting thought ran through his mind. *Was the mistaken identity of the woman in the grainy photo Fletcher sent me a week ago really a mistake or intentional? And why?*

He picked up his cell phone and pressed a number on speed dial.

"Have the jet ready in the next two hours. I need to fly back to Charleston." He smiled and ended the call.

Chapter

10

C arly was the last speaker at the podium. As a child, she'd never imagined herself as the guest speaker at the Gaillard Center, an institution in the heart of downtown Charleston known for its stunning architecture and commitment to providing a venue for the city's diverse voices. She looked over the room, filled to capacity, noticing the decorative touches of European-style Christmas baubles in bright red and gold accenting the sweetgrass baskets and wreaths of African origin.

"I've been told that the future holds the promise of progress. Higher wages. Answers to the affordable housing crisis. A better life for our children. Who wouldn't desire that?"

The audience participated in a call-and-response manner, similar to that of a gathering at a revival meeting.

Carly raised her hands like a prophetess inviting her followers to engage and interact with her. "What if the future is a bright star, far off in the sky, shining brightly on all of us, but unattainable to most of those shooting for the stars? What if the belief in a bright future is a fantasy?"

The audience moaned but maintained their focus on her.

"Let's take a moment to look at the present. Our beloved Charleston. The Holy City. A city of manners, gentility, contradictions, and tradition is changing in front of us. Neighborhoods built and sustained by minority groups have become less diverse, homes more expensive to own. Yes, some folks are more affluent, but at what cost? Are we watching the city's identity and culture being diluted? The effects of gentrification are felt all around us. The downtown has become the 'hip place' to live." She held her hand up, making air quotes.

"Charleston has become a much sought-after destination, attracting newcomers while long-time residents are eventually displaced or priced out. We need to strike a better balance. But how?"

Carly paused for emphasis, turning her body to different sections of the room. She spoke for several more minutes. "I was born and reared in Charleston. The memories I have of this city are like salt in my blood. They sustain me, energize me. Some of you may say, she's not one of us. She doesn't live here anymore, but as a historian, I understand the intended and unintended effects of tearing down landmarks and whole neighborhoods. If there are no historically black-owned homes and businesses, it would be like we didn't once exist and thrive here. Visitors would think we were not an integral part of this community." She placed her hands on the podium.

"It's as if I turned my pencil upside down and used the rubber tip to wipe over a line of text that once meant a lot to me, but the line no longer fits. Poof. Just like that, it's erased – gone from history. Can a plaque or marker in front of a factory say anything about the fears and strength it took for workers to strike for higher wages and a better life? What does a highway coursing through a formerly thriving neighborhood that was destroyed in the name of progress say to future generations? It's up to all of us to find the answers, to strike a balance."

Carly ended her talk with a question-and-answer period. Afterwards, the audience gave her a standing ovation. She bowed to them, smiling as she looked around the room filled with vibrant red poinsettias.

After the event, Aunt Nora came up on stage and hugged her while a group of well-wishers surrounded them. "I knew I could depend on you, my beautiful and talented niece. I got emotional listening to you break it down for the audience."

"Nora, Nora. We have a few reporters who want to get a statement from you about the event." Her co-chairwoman tried ushering Aunt Nora and Carly off the stage.

Although surrounded by a crowd, Carly felt a pull drawing her eyes to the corner of the room. The vibration was strong and undeniable. She turned, noticing Mason standing before them and applauding. He stepped out of the shadows and locked his gaze upon her.

He came back to Charleston. She had begun following Moore Investment Group on social media. With all the bad financial news reports, she was surprised he hadn't stayed in New York. She felt the heat of his stare pulsing throughout her body. Grabbing the papers on the podium, she fanned herself to cool the flames stirred up within her.

There was a time when she loved everything about Mason Moore. His confidence. His sexy swagger and the way his quarterback uniform hugged his rippling, hard muscles. There she was, standing before the upstanding women of

Charleston, entertaining scandalous thoughts of him. He was dressed in a well-fitting suit...one that could easily have been worn by a model on the cover of *GQ* magazine. She imagined what it would be like to see him naked.

Closing her eyes, she willed herself to banish the thoughts. In a few hours, she would be sipping her drink at the *bon voyage* party. *Stay focused, Carly.*

Mason headed straight for her. His gaze never faltered as he drew near to where she was standing.

"The program was wonderful, Mrs. Robinson." Mason lavished praise on Aunt Nora with a smile.

Carly's eyes widened as her auntie, a woman she knew could not be swayed by praise or criticism, smiled back at him.

"I have to thank you and your employees for all these poinsettias gracing this hall tonight. Your crew of volunteers swooped in, decorated the halls, and set up the book fair earlier today."

"Nora, we need to speak to the reporters. Come on." Her co-chairwoman tried again to get her off the stage.

"I'm coming, Edith. Please let them know I'm on my way." Aunt Nora sighed. "Carly, I thought we could enjoy a cup of chai tea together backstage before you go to the cruise terminal, but I guess we're running short on time." She looked at her watch.

"I don't think I'll have the time to sit with you, but I would love a chai tea latte to go." Carly stroked the top of her aunt's hand.

Mason interjected, "If I may, Mrs. Robinson... Carly, I would love to escort you to the terminal since time is ticking away. We can use the opportunity to talk and share a cup of tea in the car on the way there."

Nora tightened her grasp on Carly's hand. "Carly, what do you think?"

"What I think is, I don't want to miss my sailing to the Bahamas. I'll let Mace take me to the terminal and I'll call you when I get there."

"I love you, sweetheart. Don't forget to call me."

"I love you too, Auntie Nora." They hugged and kissed each other goodbye before the committee members whisked Aunt Nora off the stage.

Chapter

11

C arly gathered her things. "We'd better get going. I didn't expect the question-and-answer period to last as long as it did. The audience asked great questions."

"I agree. Your points were well taken and received. The audience asked questions because it was clear you knew your stuff." Mason looked around them to make sure she wasn't leaving anything.

"We'd better get the tea now. I don't want to miss the ship's sailing."

Mason placed his right hand on Carly's shoulder. The same surge of energy as when he'd touched her the day before ignited his nerves. He felt exhilarated. "I wish we had more time to spend together." He tilted his head and rested his hand on the small of her back before walking toward the exit. This time, he saw her arch her back and offer him a satisfying look as if she felt the same thing too.

A frisson of excitement spread throughout his body as he looked down at her and smiled. She was once his cherished

Caroline. The desire to get to know her now as Carly had invaded his every thought all night. He'd barely gotten two hours of sleep, counting the time until he saw her again.

Maybe I can convince her to stay. The idea crossed his mind. He opened his mouth, about to speak, but decided against it. The smile spreading across her face as she looked at the boarding pass peeking out of her purse told him the time to say goodbye was drawing nearer.

Her phone buzzed. He noticed the mild tremor of her hands as she looked for it. To him, the look in her eyes made it appear that alarms were going off under her skin.

"Is something wrong?" He turned to face her.

"No," she answered while looking down at her phone.

His phone buzzed moments later. He looked at the screen. It was full of notifications about headlines from leading financial journals, and he briefly perused them.

CEO Mason Moore, once touted the Boy Wonder of Wall Street, scores again with his unconventional management style.

The Dow rebounds to record highs.

Mason watched as Carly quickly typed a text.

"Are you sure everything is all right?"

That time, she looked up and met his concerned expression with a smile. "It's just one of my girlfriends telling me she's at the terminal. We'd better go."

Mace pointed to the black limo with the driver standing in front of the vehicle. He opened the door for Carly upon their arrival at the car and waited for her to enter before sliding in the back seat beside her. The driver hurried to his seat, and they pulled onto the street.

Ahead of them loomed Mother Emanuel AME Church, dressed in white, with its impressive Gothic Revival architecture and large steeple that appeared to reach high into the sky, piercing the heavens.

Carly looked out the window at the quiet, tree-lined street that during recent years had been transformed from the sleepy northern edge of the city's tourist experience to a district with a vibrant mix of hotels, offices, and residential areas. Lush, landscaped areas dotted their route along the Calhoun Street corridor leading to the Cooper River waterfront.

"I love what is happening on this side of town." She touched Mace's arm. "Your company has had a lot to do with revitalizing this area."

"Yes, we're proud of the role we've played in the city's expansion." He leaned closer and looked out the window over her shoulder. People dressed in jackets and comfortable shoes walked along the sidewalks of the area, heading toward the popular King and Meeting Streets. "The International African American Museum is open. Maybe we can tour it together when you get back." Mace grabbed her hand and looked down at their joined hands resting on the black leather seat.

"That will be nice." She looked up at him.

He pointed out several other landmarks along the route on their short ride to Union Pier, seventy acres of downtown waterfront real estate.

"You'll be happy to know that the plans for redeveloping this property will include honoring the past. The Bennett Rice Mill façade will be retained," Mace shared as the driver brought the car to a reserved place near the ship.

"Now that is good news." She loosened his grip to unlock her seatbelt.

He frowned, missing the warmth of her hand in his. He got out of the car first, looking down at her sexy legs stepping out of the vehicle. They walked hand in hand, as close to the large white ship as allowed by security for visitors. He wanted to enjoy as much time as he had left with her.

* * *

Standing on the pier, Carly held Mace's hand, oblivious to others as they whooped and yelled while walking the gangplank on their way to the cruise ship floating on the Cooper River with the Ravenel Bridge rising behind them. She was looking forward to a week of fun with her besties.

The sun was setting and there was a chill in the air, making her shiver. She placed her carry-on bag at her feet.

In the distance, a man with Tyson's build, wearing a dark trench coat that looked familiar, caught her attention. He was pulling his suitcase and walking toward the pier where she was standing with Mace.

"Oh, no," she murmured under her breath.

Mason took off his jacket and placed it around her. "You said you're cold?"

"Yes, a little cold." The temperature was chilling. Her hands had become icy with fear that Tyson was making good on his threat to join her on the cruise. She twisted her neck as if it was sore to draw out the mounting tension. He was getting closer, but she couldn't make out his facial features in the dim light of dusk.

"Carly."

It took her a few seconds to register that Mace was calling her name. She turned her head to give him her attention.

"It's been a long time since we've been together, but I remember how you would freeze up when you were scared. Are you hiding your fear of being on the water for a whole week? Is that it?" He placed a hand under her chin. "I thought this was your idea, but you look like a doe in the headlights."

"No, I'm not frightened. I love cruising." She managed a smile with her whole face. "What you're reading is excitement mixed with a little fatigue." She placed a hand behind her neck and stretched. "It's been a busy week."

Raising her head, she peered in the direction of the ship's deck, but kept the figure of the man approaching in her peripheral vision.

"I guess I'd better go." Her heart skipped a beat as it pounded against her chest. The man drew nearer. A whiff of wind blew a recognizable scent of strong cologne her way, invading her nostrils.

"Oh no." She placed a hand on her chest. "This can't be happening to me."

"Carly, you either tell me what's going on or I'm going on that ship with you to make sure you're all right." Mason placed his hands on her arms and drew her close to him.

She turned her head, looking the man straight in the eye as he passed by them. She let out a breath. It wasn't him. Her heart calmed, grateful that it wasn't Tyson ruining another minute of her life. Her eyes moistened with relief that it was going to be okay.

Turning her attention back to Mason, she placed a hand on his arm. "Don't worry about me. I was just having a moment." She raised her hand and placed it on the side of his face. "I remember how you used to give me that look of genuine concern. It touched me." She reached for her bag at her feet. "Well, this is goodbye."

He pulled her to his chest for a final hug. "Yes. We'd better say goodbye."

"Before I leave, I need to tell you I spoke to my brother last night. Why didn't you tell me your family loaned him the money to set up his business?" She turned his chin so he couldn't avoid looking into her eyes.

"It wasn't my story to tell. I'm curious why he told you now since a nondisclosure was a part of our deal."

"We rarely keep secrets from each other. He said it was time I knew the truth. He didn't think we needed to keep things from each other, especially if it had something to do with him."

"Carly, I want to get to know you again. Since my divorce three years ago, I've plunged my energies and attention into my business. I feel like it's time for a change. I agree, we can't move forward without an honest friendship." He placed a hand to his mouth and cleared his throat.

Carly leaned in and brushed her lips against his. "I'm all for getting to know you again," she responded as a slow, sweet smile spread across her lips. "But did I hear you correctly? You said you were divorced?"

"Yes, I'm divorced with no children."

"And you're an international jetsetter with a company projected to make the *Fortune* 500 list in the next five years. You have holdings around the world, and you spend most of your time out of the country."

"You've done your research, Dr. Rivers. Did you discover that I've found a reason to stay in the country, especially since I can look forward to spending Christmas Day with a woman who loves a hall decked with poinsettias?"

She repositioned her carry-on bag in her hand. "I'd better get going before I miss my sailing."

"Carly…" He grabbed her forearms again and pulled her closer.

"Yes, Mace?"

"I'm asking if you would like to spend Christmas Day

together. Will you join me for Christmas dinner when you get back to Charleston?"

She took her time answering while looking at the boat with all the cruisers walking on the deck. "Yes, I would love to spend the day with you."

Mace gave her his megawatt smile, the one that arose from a place of genuine happiness.

"I hope we talk about more than just property and research." She smiled back.

"I think I can accomplish that." He took his time grabbing the lapels of his jacket and wrapped her up in the warmth of his arms as he leaned in to kiss her.

She closed her eyes, taking in his lust-worthy fragrance. Warm, woodsy undertones mixed with the creamy smell of the tea they'd drunk, with ginger, allspice, and cinnamon wafting in the space between their lips like an aphrodisiac, demanding they make an intimate connection.

The sight of his full lips and chiseled jaw coming closer made her heart thump. At first, the pressure of his soft lips against hers was light as she surrendered to the urgings of his tongue entering her mouth.

Her breath quickened while his tongue explored the soft sweetness of her lips.

He placed his strong hands on her cheeks and applied soft pressure to her bottom lip, caught between his. The darting of his tongue, in and out, *deep* and sensuous, left her breathless.

He continued the mating dance with his tongue colliding with hers.

Drawing her breath as if it would be the last one, she took before her pleasurable death, she delighted in the passion they shared. Despite her hurt from the past, she desired more of him. Her heart beat wildly as the heat within rose from a slow burn to a roaring flame, from her belly down to her toes.

Carly tried in vain to pull away, shocked that her heart would give up its secrets, held inside for a decade. The fires within her roared, fueled by lust kept hidden for far too long, but now she refused to deny it.

I want you, Mace.

She tried to step away as she shuddered at the thought, and recoiled from the wave of fear that maybe she was the only one caught up in the experience of the moment, but she looked up and searched his eyes, finding the answer – *No. You're not the only one.*

"Carly, I'm sorry I was so forward with you, but—"

"There's no need to apologize, Mace. I enjoyed our kiss goodbye." She lowered her eyes.

He lifted her chin. "So did I." He brushed his lips against hers one last time. "I've waited a long time to kiss you again. It was worth the wait."

The ship's whistle blew and the seagulls walking along the pier scattered into the air.

"Hey, lovebirds. You coming, Carly?" one of her girlfriends yelled down from the deck of the ship.

"I'm coming," she yelled, waving back at her.

"In one week?" He released her from his embrace, and she returned his coat.

"Yes, Mace. In one week. I can't wait." She grabbed her bag and waved goodbye to him before walking toward the gangplank.

Her phone buzzed and she looked back at him as she waited her turn to board the ship.

Mace: Miss you already.

Carly: Miss you too. See you when I get back.

Chapter

12

C ome on, Carly. It's Christmas Eve. Let's enjoy this last night together. This has been the best cruise ever." Yara Shephard shimmied her shoulders and swayed her curvaceous hips, wrapped tight in a black silk dress fit for turning heads. "I think I'm going to get lucky tonight." She smiled at Carly, who looked up from her screen and stopped typing a text.

"Don't let me hold you back. I'll join you later." Carly looked around the suite at clothes thrown on chairs and on the couch. "My things won't pack themselves."

"Bags out in the hall before midnight," their cabin steward reminded them in a loud voice after knocking on the door.

Carly turned away, looking at the blue waters of the Caribbean. "I knew I needed a break. I just didn't know how much I needed it." A smile spread across her face, reaching her eyes.

"That's what I'm saying, girl. You need this last-minute fling to get your freak on." Yara looked over at the table where the contents of Carly's bag had spilled over. "How do I look?" she asked, walking over to the table.

"Like you own the club, queen." Carly lowered her head and continued typing.

"No, you're the queen bee." Yara picked up Carly's eau de parfum vial and uncapped it. "You're the one who has been turning heads. Men have been sending you drinks all week long. They've been drawn to you like a bee to honey." She turned and placed a finger on the nozzle, spraying a mist in the air.

"Yara, don't," Carly yelled, trying to stop her. Too late. A foul odor with undertones of hot pepper filled the room.

"What are you trying to do to me?" Yara dropped the bottle and covered her nose and mouth with her hands. In between coughs, she managed to speak. "Are you trying to kill me?" She leaned over and placed her hands on her thighs. "You know I normally wear your perfume." Her eyes were watering and becoming red from the lingering fumes.

Carly opened the sliding glass doors to allow fresh air to enter the room, then rushed to the bar to grab a bottle of water. "Here, take a few sips of this."

Yara snatched the plastic container and squeezed it, gulping down a mouthful of the cool liquid and setting off a second round of spasmic coughs.

"Easy, easy." Carly patted her on the back then went back to the bar to place a few ice cubes in a cloth. "Pat your face with this." She cocked her head and examined Yara's eyes, which had begun to swell.

"That container was labelled perfume." Yara's voice went up an octave as she pointed to the vial on the floor. "Why did you bring pepper spray on the ship?"

The door opened before Carly could answer. Ariel

Dennison, their other bestie and suite mate, pranced into the room with a bottle of wine in her hand. Her jaw dropped. She covered her mouth with her hand. "Yara, what happened to you?" Her friend's face, which was normally attractive, with large brown eyes, looked like a mini-gargoyle capable of scaring any child on Halloween.

"Carly tried to kill me," Yara remarked. Her words were garbled as she spoke through swollen lips. She rubbed her eyes.

"I didn't tell you to uncap the pepper spray." Carly came toward Yara with a small first-aid kit containing anti-allergy meds in liquid form. "Take this." She tore open the foil. "You're not having problems breathing, are you?"

Yara shook her head.

"Stop rubbing your eyes. You're only making it worse."

"I'll stop rubbing my eyes when you answer my question. Why the pepper spray?"

Carly took in a deep breath. "Do you think they would have let me on board with a knife or a gun?" She looked between Yara and Ariel.

"Let me be clearer, Carly." Yara rolled her eyes. "Why did you feel you needed a weapon?" She looked around the well-appointed, luxurious suite, an upgrade courtesy of the captain of the ship. She swallowed the liquid.

Falling back in the chair, Carly folded her legs under her and pulled at the hem of her oversized t-shirt. "Tyson threatened to come on the cruise." She rubbed her forehead. "I've had that pepper spray to protect myself since our last argument a year ago. He said he was just trying to get my attention, but no man will ever grab me again."

"He must have lost his mind." Ariel's eyes widened. "Tyson did that?"

Carly nodded.

"Oh no." Yara stood up, gasping for air, and placed a hand at her throat. "He doesn't want any of this smoke."

Ariel and Carly passed a knowing look between them.

"I saw that." Yara turned in the direction of the bathroom. "I know I sound bad, but I still have my strength. I remember there was a time when I respected Tyson...until we found out why he wanted to be the father to your baby, our angel who's in heaven."

Carly's eyes moistened. She buried her lip between her teeth and quickly looked away.

"Sorry, talking too much. Forget I said that." Yara quickly covered her mouth and widened her eyes.

Ariel and Carly remained quiet, refusing to acknowledge her words or respond.

"I should see how I look." Yara got up, attempting to leave the room, but not before Ariel sprang into action.

"Let me get my jar of cucumber facial mask. It's in my room. I'll apply it for you." She left Yara and Carly to gather her supplies.

"Put this on." Carly gave Yara one of her robes to cover her dress. She knew Yara had a habit of failing to filter her thoughts, but she had a heart of gold.

Ariel returned before Yara could find a mirror. "Don't worry about it," she reassured them. "You know I'm a wiz with makeup. If need be, I'll cover up the red blemishes. This mask should ease the swelling."

She opened the container and covered Yara's face with the green paste. "There." She stood back, then applied a little more paste. "Let it dry. It should feel cool on your face. Time for some wine."

"I agree." Carly retrieved three glasses while Ariel opened

the wine.

Yara touched her face lightly. Some of the swelling had started to disappear.

"We're missing a great party." Ariel poured the wine, ensuring that each of them had a generous amount. She gave her friends their glasses and then lifted her own to take in the aroma. "One of the ship's officers came to my table, where I was enjoying a little cuddle time with Sam, the sax player, who was on break. He said it was courtesy of the captain. Sam doesn't drink on duty, but he suggested that I come get the two of you. But under the circumstances…" She cleared her throat. "Maybe we should have our party here in the suite."

The sound of the band playing jazz music on the deck could be heard through the open door. "They're having a DJ for a midnight party after the band finishes their set. We're going to party 'til we're broke." Ariel laughed.

"After all the shopping we did this week, we're already broke," Yara added. Her speech was less garbled.

Carly took a sip from her glass. "Oh, this is so good." She closed her eyes, savoring the flavor.

"I was told this wine was from the captain's private stock." Ariel licked her lips after tasting it. They all held their glasses up in a toast. "The captain wanted to make sure we had a good time. He and your boyfriend, Mason Moore, are good friends."

"He's not my boyfriend," Carly said quickly, placing strands of her curly hair behind her ear. "I don't have time for such things. Besides, I'm in my thirties. What am I supposed to do with a *boy-friend*?"

"That's right." Yara looked at both of them. "You've already married and divorced a mama's boy. Since he was stalking you, all you had to do was call his mama and let her know about what her mess of a son was up to now. She would have set him straight."

"Right, right. He's a mess." Ariel waved away the comments about Tyson. "Let's talk about Mason. He's rich, generous, and far more interesting." She wiggled her eyebrows. "Did I mention that he's rich and has friends in powerful places? The man doesn't know me or Yara, but because we're your friends, he arranged for us to get one of the most lavish suites on the ship." She began counting the benefits on her fingers. "He gave us each thousands of dollars of shipboard credit, and he got us seats at the captain's table on formal night. Now, that's clout." She leaned forward. "Do you think he can get us VIP tickets to a Bruno Mars concert?"

Carly placed a hand to her mouth and closed her eyes. "Ariel, if I didn't know better, I'd think you were turning into a gold digger."

Ariel made her counterpoint. "I've dated more than my share of broke men. It's time for something different."

Carly's phone buzzed on the table next to her. She picked it up and looked at the message, typing a quick reply.

"Your phone has been going off a lot today," Yara told her. The green paste on her face had almost dried.

Carly glanced at Yara and giggled.

"What's so funny?" Yara cocked a brow.

"Your green mask is starting to flake, Miss Hulk." Carly hit the send button. Her voice then took on a more serious tone. "My cousin Daniel has been texting me. He came from Chicago to get Aunt Nora and take her back to his home. Her water pipes broke and several rooms in her house were flooded."

"I'm sorry to hear that," Yara and Ariel said in unison.

"Thanks." Carly tightened her lips. "The house was

damaged, but she's okay. Literally, when it rains, it pours. I was planning on staying with her for the week of Christmas. After that, I planned to get my career back on track in Maryland."

Yara touched Carly's thigh in a show of support before getting more wine from the bar. "It's been a tough year, but together we're going to get through it." Yara got a glimpse of herself in a glass vase on the bar. "Yikes. Thanks to Miss Queen Bee, I'm too scary-looking to go to the party."

"Not my fault." Carly held up her hands.

"Carly has attracted lots of *friends* this week, but not as a queen bee. More like a praying mantis who's looking for some sex before she lures men to their deaths by chopping off their heads." Ariel side-eyed Carly. "Sam told me how you blew off his friend who just wanted to have some fun."

"I drank a little wine with him, listened to his corny stories, and danced with him. That didn't mean I wanted to have sex with him or see him after this week is over."

"Why not have a little fun? After all, you and Mason are just *friends*, even though you get all giggly every time he calls," Yara reminded her. "I thought it was the men you attracted, like Mason, who you've said had commitment issues, but I'm beginning to think it's you, Carly."

"You're one to talk, Yara. How many times have I heard you say you don't need a man? I actually agree with you. After this year, I need to focus my full energies on saving historical African American communities. My career is very important to me."

In spite of the green mask covering her face, the sadness could be seen in Yara's eyes. Their sparkle was momentarily dimmed as she spoke. "I admit that I've said that I didn't need a man, but I never said I didn't *want* a man. I've been alone for years, but it's hard pulling in these streets by yourself, even with a high-income job." She swallowed hard and pointed a finger at Carly. "What about you? Weren't you the one who planned to have it all? A career and at least two kids running around the house by now?"

"So much for best-laid plans." Carly looked away. "At least we have each other."

"You know we'll always ride or die for each other," Yara said. "It's not too late to have it all if you allow yourself a chance to rekindle a relationship with Mason."

Carly got up and took her glass of wine to the large window. "I...I just can't open myself up to that kind of pain anymore. I admit that something in me was reawakened by our kiss on the dock, but it's been ten years since we dated." Her voice was low and full of remorse. "It may not work out." She rubbed her chest. "I'm afraid to take that leap into love again."

Ariel treaded lightly, taking her time addressing Carly's concerns. "I've tried to stay in my lane this whole week. I wanted us to focus on having fun and keeping it light, but as your friend, I've got to say this. You can't let your past dictate your present circumstances. The two are different."

Yara raised her eyebrows and nodded.

"Yes, and presently, I plan to enjoy Christmas dinner with Mason, then he'll go his way and I'll go mine. I've tried to tell him I didn't want to impose upon him, but he refused to let me cancel. He said a deal was a deal."

"So, let me know if I've got this right. Until last week, you hadn't seen Mason in ten years?" Ariel tilted her head, awaiting the answer.

"That's right." Carly furrowed her brow.

"He owns a large company that you found out acquired

and sold your parents' home and the homes of your former neighbors in a big real estate deal."

"All true." Carly took a sip of her wine.

"And after the sale, you discovered that they planned to tear the homes down to make room for a new development." Ariel cocked her brow.

"Yes. Get to the point, Ariel." Carly pursed her lips.

"I will." She began pacing as if she was in a courtroom, skillfully presenting her case. "I can only imagine that the confrontation between the two of you was not...pleasant, wouldn't you say?"

"I admit I unloaded on him, but he took it." She placed a finger to her lips, recalling their initial meeting the week before.

"I see," Yara added, observing the exchange between Carly and Ariel.

"We were able to clear the air after he explained what happened. I guess my anger cooled when he agreed to look into the matter. I hope he's able to use his influence to prevent the home from being demolished."

"So you agreed to spend Christmas Day with Mason to discuss business? All the phone calls you received from him this week sounded personal."

"Yes, Attorney Ariel." Carly rolled her eyes. "It's business."

Ariel looked at Yara. "I would like to go on record that I have a hostile witness."

"Overruled. Continue, counselor, with your questioning of the witness."

"Now that your aunt is in Chicago and her home is damaged, you don't have a place to stay." Ariel leaned in.

"All of the hotels are booked. Mace offered to let me stay

at his place. His house manager, Marlena Johnson, was one of my mother's friends. He said she was happy to prepare one of the guest rooms for me and ensure I was comfortable." Carly sat back in her chair.

"How convenient." Ariel placed her index finger to her cheek. "I don't think this is about business at all. Again, I will state my case. What happened between the two of you is in the past. Let it rest. If I base my assumption on how often he called, I will say he wants to get to know you better. This is personal."

Carly paused, taking it all in. "To address your concerns, Mason has a condo in downtown Charleston. We'll be discussing business. His family owns a large home on one of the islands outside of the city. I plan to spend a few days in Charleston while I consider going to Chicago with Aunt Nora. Maybe Mace and I will stop by and see his family before I leave. You know, for a friendly visit. End of story."

Yara and Ariel looked at each other.

Carly turned away. Placing a finger on the pulse at the angle of her jaw, she felt her heart rate slow. The view of the moon shining over the dark water calmed her while Yara and Ariel allowed her a little silent time to reflect on her thoughts. Did she need to be cautious with Mace?

The sound of sultry music from the deck filled the suite. The DJ was playing a sensual song, one of Muni Long's hits.

Betraying her words about being satisfied with a mere friendship with Mace, she hugged herself and began swaying to the music. Her mind drifted as she began fantasizing about what she could enjoy with him if only she could let go of the pain of the past. Her body heated with longing and desire. It had been a long time since she'd allowed herself to think about enjoying being with a man.

She couldn't help thinking about the next day. She had agreed to spend Christmas with Mace. Hours and hours alone with him.

Shaking the thoughts out of her head, she turned to face her friends, unaware that her nipples had hardened and could be seen beneath her shirt.

Yara laughed, breaking the silence. "Do you think Carly is thinking about her love for saving old neighborhoods? You know, *business*?" She directed her attention to Ariel.

"Nope." Ariel smirked. "I think she won't admit that she still has feelings for a particular neighbor."

One of the cabin stewards walking through the hall announced again, "A friendly reminder – bags in the hallway. We'll be docking in Charleston, South Carolina by ten o'clock tomorrow."

"I don't have time for the two of you." Carly placed her hands on her hips. With an exaggerated sway, she walked in the direction of her bedroom. "I have to pack."

Chapter

13

Mason couldn't believe his good fortune. For too long, he had been unlucky in love and now his life had changed for the better. He got up early and walked across the hardwood floors in his bedroom, with its contemporary, soft-gray walls, on his way to the bathroom.

How could he sleep knowing that Carly, the most gorgeous, sexy woman in the world, was on her way back to him?

Looking at his reflection in the mirror, he ran his hand along his cheek, touching the coarse stubble on his brown skin.

"I'd better shave." Normally, when on vacation, he preferred the rugged-man look. However, knowing the burning desire he had to kiss Carly's soft lips and rub his smooth cheeks against her silky body in intimate places that he could only explore with a close, clean-shaven face, he searched for his razor. He took in a deep breath to slow his racing heart as it skipped a beat at the thought of reuniting with her. Not wanting to nick himself and draw blood, he knew he had to calm down.

After he finished shaving, he pumped his fist, elated that he was being given a second chance to win Carly's heart. Before taking a phone call he was expecting that morning, he jumped into the shower.

"That felt good." He turned off the water and dried himself before heading back to the bedroom to get dressed. It was Christmas morning. He had a feeling he was on the cusp of happiness. Surely, misfortune couldn't happen again, and he'd lose Carly. Not this time. Not ever again.

Just two weeks earlier, he'd been dreading the thought of another holiday season spent at a large family gathering – or, worse yet, *alone*, without someone special. Then Carly reentered his life. He would have been happy spending a day alone with her, but since he'd found out her aunt Nora's home had flooded, he had to watch himself. He shouldn't seem glad for the mishap, but he *was*. It meant Carly could be spending the entire week with him if he played his cards right.

He pulled back the custom shutters covering the abundance of windows, flooding the room with morning sunlight. Looking out at the unparalleled views of the picturesque Charleston harbor, he still marveled at the beauty of the city. At the time of purchase, he had insisted on central views of the city from his condo, which included the well-known landmarks of the St. Michael's and St. Phillip's churches' steeples from above, and lush landscapes bordering the marina below.

It was a new day, and he would begin it with a new resolve to think pleasant thoughts. In a few hours, he would be waiting at the cruise terminal for the ship returning Carly from her weeklong vacation.

He turned his head toward the phone ringing on the desk, interrupting his thoughts.

"Good morning, Mace." Bernie's voice was cheerful and upbeat, despite the fact that it was Christmas morning, and he was working.

"Good morning, Bernie. Give me the details quickly. I have someplace to go and there's no doubt that your wife won't be happy with you if you spend the entire morning working."

"You've got a point, so I'll get right to it. The emergency meeting that was initially scheduled for last night was cancelled. The rumors that the board of directors and a group of vocal shareholders were going to call for a vote of no confidence against you have calmed down. Nothing takes the oxygen out of conflicts at a company like all the positive press you've been getting. Mace, I've got to tell you that you ruffled some feathers when you initially told them that you weren't coming back to New York for a sham meeting. It was a good thing that you came back for a few days."

"What were they going to do if I didn't come back? Replace me? I'm the largest shareholder in the company." Mace looked at his face in the mirror. "I wasn't worried, but you're right. I'm the leader. People need to see that the leader is with them and firmly in charge."

"That's the point, man. Seeing is believing. You were cool as a cucumber, even when the company's stock plummeted last week."

Mace took a seat behind his desk. "We can't lose focus on our goals. We need to stay the course."

"Do you have ice water running through your veins?" Bernie's comment sounded more like a statement of fact than a question. "You've got to know that the captain of the ship needs to be on board, even if it's about to go down."

"Spare me the melodrama." Mace retorted. "As I told you, I had matters down here that I had to take care of first."

"Well, that's the second reason for the uproar at the company. Yes, it's the week of Christmas, but no one here has ever thought of you as the devoted family man who needed to spend time with his loved ones." Bernie's exasperation was audible. "What we were hearing was that the matter involved an old flame that you were pursuing. Folks thought you were thinking with the wrong head, man. You know better than I do that in this small business circle of high finance, pursuing matters of the heart is never a good look for the man in charge."

Mace stiffened his back and sat upright. "As the CEO, I'll tell you that my moves were calculated and well thought-out."

"I didn't mean to question your authority, but you're going to give us all heart attacks with your unorthodox decisions. We weren't born with trust funds. We depend on the price of the stock to finance our futures."

"Come on, Bernie." Mace bit his lip to hold back mounting frustration, tinged with disappointment. "Not you too. How many times do I have to hear, 'Your grandfather, who toiled to build this company, would never make those types of decisions'? Well, I've sacrificed a lot to build this company into a conglomerate. Do I need to pull out spreadsheets showing how much it has grown under my leadership?"

"I know that, Mason," he conceded. "I've been here with you the entire time. I know all you've done."

Mason pressed the point. "So, you don't think I'm entitled to a personal life?" He looked at the phone screen.

"You know that's not what I'm saying," Bernie quickly

responded. "How many times have I said all work and no play makes you a boring guy?"

"Plenty." Mason stopped speaking, giving himself a moment to calm down. "I don't mean to unload on you. It's just irritating knowing that it never matters how much I give. For some on the board, it's all about profits and more profits."

The silence lasted for seconds before Bernie spoke. He took his time asking the question. "So, are you planning on coming back to New York tomorrow after your dinner date with Carly?"

Mason stood up. "You're really trying to tick me off, aren't you? Don't press me. I want to spend time reconnecting with Carly. I haven't decided what day I'll return."

"No offense intended. I didn't mean to over-step." Bernie lowered his voice. "I heard the two of you dated back in the day. Are you saying this could develop into something serious?"

"Listen..." Mason contemplated his answer. "Don't expect me back until the end of the week."

"What?" Bernie screeched. "We have meetings the day after Christmas."

"Tell my assistant to cancel them."

Bernie began stumbling over his words. "What...what about the press conference? The *Times* is calling you the new wonder boy of business."

"Cancel." Mason went to one of his two closets in the master suite to start getting dressed.

"We cancelled the meeting with our international investors last week when you went to Charleston earlier than expected. We can't cancel again."

"Tentatively keep it on the books." Mace took out a pair of slacks. "I'll call you back about it."

"What about the New Year's Eve party?" The party was a tradition started by Mason's grandfather. The only one he'd missed was the year he died.

Mason held up his shirt on the hanger. "I'll be back in time for the party. I'm thinking about asking Carly to be my date. After this year's party, let's talk about discontinuing it. It's an old tradition. I believe it's time for a change. I want to modernize the company's culture by taking it in another direction."

"Some will be unhappy if you end it," Bernie countered. "But people like me will be glad to save the company some money. That party is costing more each year. Will your ex, Jamillah, be there?"

"Probably, but don't worry about her. Give me an update on the Hagood Avenue house in Charleston." Mace lowered his head and placed three fingers between his brows. "It's important to me."

"I know, it's personal." Bernie tightened his lips. "There's a clause that would allow us to modify the contract. We should be able to finalize the new deal soon."

"Thanks." Mason smiled. "I've never forgotten something my grandfather told me. The statement, 'It's not personal, it's business,' is false. All business is personal."

"Yeah, Mason. I got it. I think we can buy our way to a happy solution to this problem. Assume it's taken care of."

"Good. Merry Christmas, Bernie."

"Merry Christmas, Mason. Goodbye."

Chapter

14

Mason arrived early to get a parking space close to the terminal where the ship would be docking.

Who was he kidding? His decision to get there early had more to do with his excitement about seeing Carly again and less to do with parking. He looked at his Rolex watch while tapping his feet, anxiously anticipating her arrival with a bouquet of red roses in hand.

Mason stood a head above most of those waiting inside the building for the arrival of their loved ones. He didn't have to stand on his toes as he looked out the large glass windows to see the cruisers disembarking with smiles on their faces as they walked down the gangplank.

He had a bottle of wine chilling in the ice bucket on the table near his couch. The lights had been left on a low, warm glow and with a touch of the remote he could turn on soft music to play in the background, welcoming her to his home.

He had spent most of the previous day preparing for their date. The oysters on the half shell had been delivered from his favorite seafood restaurant in Charleston. He had made many lists for his housekeeper in preparation for an evening of romance.

"If you change your mind one more time…!" she'd yelled at him, out of character, after he called to tell her he wanted to edit the list. Twice.

The countdown to this moment had started early. As if he was a kid waiting for Christmas morning, he was wide-eyed and smiling.

Shifting his weight from one foot to the other, Mason looked around before his gaze landed on Carly walking arm in arm with two other women. His breath caught as he looked at her confidently striding down the long corridor dressed in a red dress that billowed in the breeze. One of the porters in the crowd rushed toward her, pushing a cart. She spoke to him, appearing to decline his offer of assistance. The scene was repeated. One male porter after another approached them, slowing the ladies' arrival to where Mason was standing.

"They don't need your help. I've taken care of those things already." His tone was harsh and drew the attention of those standing nearby. He frowned, thinking about the intrusion the other men were causing by slowing down his plans. Sure, they were doing their jobs, but he looked around and saw other cruisers weren't getting their attention but could have used some assistance.

Raising his hand and waving, he caught Carly's eye. She rewarded his efforts by immediately flashing the most gorgeous smile he had ever seen.

If she had dressed to impress, she'd have scored a major victory. He looked at her dress, covered with a matching cropped jacket. She wore gold jewelry and red sandals that complimented her outfit, adding an exclamation point. *Yeah, baby!* He looked down at her legs and manicured feet in stylish shoes.

Note to self. Buy Carly more of those sexy shoes.

He closed his eyes to break the mental hold that stimulating thoughts were having on him as he thickened with excitement. He needed to pause the vision of her in those shoes and nothing else but underwear for later.

Her beautiful face with her warm brown eyes and flawless cocoa skin was framed by thick, curly hair. She wore it down around her shoulders, and it was bouncing with each step she took. At one point, she threw her head back while walking with her friends, appearing to enjoy a laugh at a private joke. All of them looked like they were in a great mood from a week of fun and sun. He had never met her friends, but she'd spoken of them during their phone calls.

He recalled her saying Yara was the most outspoken one of the three of them. The more reserved member of the trio was Ariel. They were both pretty women, but neither of them was as gorgeous as his Carly. He shrugged, knowing his bias.

Her hips swayed sensually as she got closer to him, making his pelvis throb, a reminder of how much the sight of Carly turned him on. She was within yards of him, and to his surprise, with a bright glow on her face, she broke into a run and flung herself into his arms.

He'd always had good reflexes and caught her before she landed on one of the roses' thorns. He had the bouquet in his left hand, leaving his dominant hand free to return her warm and tight embrace around his neck. Lifting her off her feet, he gave her an impromptu but sensuous kiss. Closing his eyes, he moaned and opened his lips to welcome her tongue, covered with a hint of sweet caramel. His lips lingered on hers, signaling his hunger for more. She pulled away slowly as he lowered her to the ground and inhaled her scent.

"Damn, you smell good."

"Thank you, Mace. I'm so happy to see you." She giggled.

He couldn't resist giving her another kiss. He wanted to keep her close, savoring the delicious taste of her mouth and the pleasing scent on her smooth, bronzed skin. *Intoxicating*. He looked at her, absently holding on to the flowers he had prepared to give to her.

"You don't know how happy I am to see you." He gave her a boyish grin after he saw her cheeks flush like a schoolgirl kissed for the first time.

"Are those for me?" She pointed to the flowers.

"Yes." He nodded, flustered that he hadn't realized he was still holding the bouquet. While he was leaning in to give them to her, she planted a brief kiss on his cheek.

Yara and Ariel remained behind Carly, observing their reunion.

"Didn't the two of them just see each other a week ago?" Yara spoke loudly enough to get their attention. "I'm sure she talked to him every night while we were gone." She turned to Ariel, who nodded, confirming her observations.

Carly rolled her eyes and laughed. "Mace, these are my two best friends in the world. This is Yara Shephard and Ariel Dennison. We were college roommates." She pointed to the women. "And Yara, you're mistaken. I didn't talk to Mason *every* night."

"If you didn't talk to him, you were talking *about* him every night." Yara nudged Ariel while they inspected Mason as if he was the latest man-candy waiting to be devoured.

Carly turned to Mason, directing her comments to him. "They became my college roommates after you transferred to another school."

She was smiling, but he winced, unprepared for her to refer to anything that had happened ten years earlier. The corners of his lips were downturned and trembled slightly before he calmed the fears that talk of the past would derail his plans for a delightful night.

He turned to the other women with a pleasant smile, welcoming their distraction.

"Nice to meet you." He extended a hand, first to Yara and then to Ariel, who stood slightly behind her. "I'm glad you all are back safe from your trip. I've made arrangements for both of you. I wanted to make sure you got to the airport on time and wouldn't miss your connecting flights."

"Thank you. That was so nice of you," they all responded, with a chorus of Southern accents.

Mason was ready to get the party started with Carly, just the two of them. As he had planned, two well-built, attractive men dressed in casual attire, each holding a single rose, came toward them.

"I have a reservation for Yara Shephard," the first man spoke up.

Yara raised her hand as he presented her with the rose and took her small carry-on bag from her.

"And I have a reservation for Ariel Dennison." The second man handed her the rose as Mace gave the remaining instructions.

"I have reserved individual town cars for both of you since you'll be going to different airlines at different times. Your bags are being picked up and loaded into the cars as we speak. If you would like, your attendants can give you the scenic route around Charleston and then take you to the airport."

Carly bit her lower lip. "Mason, I know I told you that Yara was flying out today and Ariel wanted to be home for Christmas, but we couldn't get her a return flight until tomorrow morning."

"No worries, ladies. I was able to secure first-class seats for both of you. I owed it to you all for the times I interrupted your girls' trip with my phone calls to Carly. Please accept my apologies."

"First-class accommodations home?" Yara looked at Ariel before they both turned to face him.

"Apologies accepted." Yara paused. "Carly…"

"Yes?" She looked at her friend.

"This one is a keeper." Yara burst out in loud laughter.

"I'll keep that in mind, girlfriend." She shook her head.

Mace chuckled. Carly had told him to expect anything to come out of Yara's mouth.

Carly opened her arms wide for Yara and Ariel to come together for their group hug. "Merry Christmas… Well, I guess we'd better say our goodbyes for now."

Mason moved behind them as Carly, with moisture glistening in her eyes, hugged her girls. He rubbed her shoulder, lending unspoken support. He knew it was hard saying goodbye to her sister-friends.

He stood with her, giving her time to watch and wave as they disappeared out the door. "Shall we go?"

"Yes, I'm ready." She took in a breath and grabbed his hand for the walk to the exit.

Chapter

15

Relaxed from a week of pampering and spending time with her sister-friends, Carly patted her full belly.

"So, how was it?" Mace refilled her glass with dark-red merlot and took her back into his arms. They sat on the couch together at his penthouse overlooking the Cooper River, finishing their second glasses. His home was decorated with a fragrant spruce tree filled with expensive ornaments, fancy baubles, and twinkling, colorful lights. Bright-red poinsettias lined the foyer and both sides of the fireplace.

"The dinner was fantastic." She smiled up at him as he planted a kiss on her lips.

"I had your aunt Nora send your mother's recipes to my cook. That's why the meal was so good, but I was talking about the trip. Were you ready to come back?"

"That was so sweet of you." She smacked her lips and gave him an air kiss. "To answer your question, I had a great time, but I was ready to come back. I needed and enjoyed my time with my girls. I don't know how I would have gotten through the past year without them. But this time with you is perfect."

"I'm glad they were there for you." He gazed into her eyes. "I need to apologize for taking you away from them while you were cruising. Honestly, I tried not to call you, but seven o'clock in the evening became my time with Carly. After the first two nights of keeping you on the phone for about a half an hour, I thought I could distract myself by arranging things to do to occupy my time. I even scheduled a conference call, but what can I say? We had tech problems and had to reschedule." He shrugged.

"Darn that technology." She gave him a playful side-eye and giggled.

"Yes, and as fate would have it, it was seven o'clock and there I was on the phone with you again. I tried, Carly. I really did, but I couldn't help myself." He laughed.

"Well, it wasn't *all* you. Midweek on the cruise, I was missing you and I called you, remember? My girlfriends said if I didn't call, they would. They were tired of my PMS."

"I remember you calling me, but what did I have to do with your PMS?"

"My girls said my PMS was my Pining for Mace Syndrome. They insisted that I didn't smile as much on the days I didn't talk to you. They got used to my constant giggling every time they mentioned your name. I looked sad one night when the DJ in the nightclub played a song by Prince."

"You remembered Prince was my favorite artist?" He gave her that boyish grin she was so fond of. "If I didn't know better, Carly, I would say we're crushing on each other again. I know I'm, at the very least, wanting you. Does it surprise you how easy it's been to reconnect with each other?" he asked as he rubbed her arms.

"No, not really. We've always had a *charged* relationship. I'm happy it's positive again instead of negative. I've always known I was attracted to you, even though you pulled my ponytail more often than I care to remember."

He stopped rubbing her arms and looked up, reflecting on his thoughts. "I was a jealous thing back then. I remember pulling on your ponytail a few times when other boys tried to get your attention, but forgive me, I think I was eight years old at the time." He smiled. "I remember calling you my play-sister, but I wanted to belong to you as your boyfriend, even back then. You were my girl, despite making me beg for the sugar cookies your mom placed in your lunchbox for me."

"Speaking of mothers, is everything all right with you and your mother? No one has called you today, and if I remember anything about you Moores, it's that you get together at Christmas and you all know how to party together."

"Things are fine with me and my family. I told my mother I was spending the day with you and I swear she leaped out of her chair, jumping for joy. She said her prayers have been answered. My brothers told me she gave strict orders, under the threat of death, to leave us alone. She wants us to have time to get to know each other again. She had the audacity to say that there were only two women in the world capable of managing me, and she was *one* of them."

Carly turned, allowing them to look at each other, eye to eye. "Who is the only other woman who has the skills to manage you, Mace? Tell me."

"First of all, I'm not sure I'm comfortable with the term 'manage,' because that would imply I'm difficult. But the other woman she named was you."

"Is that right?" She hesitated at first, then placed a kiss on his lips while he wrapped her in his arms, drawing her closer to him.

"I love my mother and I know she loves me. She'd give her life for any of her kids, but I realize she doesn't understand me and that's why she thinks I'm difficult."

"Maybe you don't realize how good you are at hiding your tender heart because it bruises very easily under layers of a cocky and contrary attitude."

He looked at her, then turned his head. A red flush crept across his cheeks as he tried swallowing his emotions.

Carly wrapped her arms around his neck and rested her head on his shoulder.

"You understand me, but do me a favor?"

"What is it?" She looked into his glistening eyes.

"Keep it to yourself, okay? People thinking I have a tender heart may not be good for my reputation."

"It will stay between the two of us. Your heart is safe with me."

"My family knows my heart has always belonged to you. It's no secret they want us to be together, but they respect it's up to us to figure out how to make that happen. My mother wanted me to tell you, you're the daughter she and my father never had. Before my father died, he told me how much he wished we could have gotten back together."

"I didn't know your father had passed." Carly raised her head, revealing her pained expression.

"He died of cancer five years ago." He tilted his head, relishing the warmth of her hand against his cheek.

"My condolences to you. I'm sorry I'm just hearing about it." She placed her forehead to his. "I've always cared about your family. They didn't need to stay away from us at Christmas. This day is about spending time with those we love, curling up in front of a fire, and having the blessing of a belly full of great food."

"Well, I can provide everything except those you love. Your brother couldn't change his plans and Aunt Nora is in Chicago, so you're stuck with me."

She pressed her hand against his chest and rested it above his heart. "I wouldn't say I'm stuck. I'm where I want to be. Thank you so much for the invitation." She looked up and slowly blinked her eyes.

He embraced her and rested his chin on her head.

"I'm the one who should be thanking you." He paused. "I don't want you to think I've only gotten caught up in Christmas cheer. I need to share something with you."

She turned and looked at him. "What is it, Mace?"

"I need to tell you the truth. I never stopped loving you." He played with her fingers interlaced with his. "I realized a few years ago that you were the ghost in all relationships I had after we broke up. For me, it has always been you." His look of remorse bore into the marrow of her being. "Sadly, it didn't take long to realize I made a mistake marrying someone else."

She locked eyes with him and placed a hand over her mouth as she ingested his words. "My truth is, I know I was also rebounding after we split up. I don't want to be the ghost in your life anymore if you're ready to be present in mine."

"I know trust is something we'll need to build with each other. I could tell when you said goodbye a week ago at the docks that you hesitated in committing to spending this day with me."

"Yes, it's true, I was hesitant because I didn't want to be disappointed again." She chewed on her lips lightly and remained silent as he rubbed her back.

"I get it. We need to take our time getting to know each other again."

They sat silently, taking in all the words that had been spoken between them.

After a few moments, Mace sat up suddenly. "I can't hold back the surprise any longer. Guess what?"

"What, Mace?"

"Your parents' home has been removed from the development deal."

"Oh my gosh!" A bright smile covered Carly's face. She first kissed him on the cheek before kissing him on the lips. "Now, that's the best Christmas gift ever."

"I'm glad I could tell you the good news today, but that's not your Christmas gift."

The song "I'll Be Home for Christmas" began to play softly in the background. Mace opened the drawer of the table next to the couch and pulled out a small, satin-covered box with a red ribbon around it.

Before he could give it to her, Carly spotted a photo placed in a silver frame. "Is that us?" She grabbed it and looked at the picture of the two of them smiling at each other.

"Yes, that's us as teenagers after we returned from the Christmas parade downtown. I kept that picture because it's how I wanted to remember us – enjoying one of the happiest Christmases I've ever had." He gave her the box and she placed the picture on the top of the table.

"Yes, it was a happy Christmas for me too, but not as happy as the time I'm sharing with you tonight."

"Open the box."

She untied the ribbon and pulled the cover off the box, revealing an eighteen-carat gold bracelet with a heart-shaped solid gold charm. Her eyes widened at the sight of the gift.

"No, I can't, Mace. This is too much. What you've done to save my family's home from demolition is enough."

"Nothing is too much for you and you need to know I'll make sure you have the funds to renovate it as you see fit. We can make plans for the house together." He grabbed her hands and rubbed the top of them with his thumbs.

She weighed her words – how transparent she should be with him.

"It's been a long time since we've spent every day together, but at your core, I think I still know you, Mace." She repositioned herself to face him directly. "This isn't just about the house anymore – it's about you and me." She raised her hand and placed it on his chest. "You've showed me how much my feelings matter to you. I don't know how you did it, but I do know if you didn't want the house to be saved, it wouldn't have happened."

She paused and struggled to swallow the lump in her throat. "The truth is, I'm scared. I don't want to get hurt, but I promise to keep my heart open. Merry Christmas. You've made this day very special."

"Merry Christmas, Carly. You don't know what it means to me to have this time again with you." He kissed her with all the tenderness and passion within him. "I'm glad you were willing to give us a second chance."

They continued their casual bantering while drinking more and more wine. She looked up and slowly blinked, trying to clear her head.

No more wine for me.

Chapter

16

Mace pressed his lips to Carly's with the fervor of unmet needs bursting inside him. His tongue glided across her lower lip. Once inside, he claimed her. Searching her mouth, he voraciously released the fiery desires smoldering for her for years. Taking in a deep breath and excited by her moaning, he nibbled with sensuous tiny bites along her neck and down to the mounds of her breasts while pulling her onto his lap.

"Oh, Mace." She panted his name as her chest heaved.

He slowed as she struggled to catch her breath.

Things are moving fast. I can't afford to mess this up. Throbbing with lust, he pressed against her. He wanted things between them to develop organically, but were they ready to take it further this soon?

I need to stop this, but I want her so badly. He warred with himself but released her from his embrace as she pulled away, blinking and shaking her head.

"I'm feeling a little dizzy. I think the wine has snuck up

on me." She rubbed her forehead and then lowered a hand to her chest.

He placed his hand over hers and felt her heart racing, so fast he became concerned. "Let's take a break." He extended his head against the back of the couch and exhaled. His body was tight and hard as a drum. He needed to release some tension.

"Oh." She looked down and raised her butt above his lap as he repositioned her alongside his boner, hard as steel.

He chuckled, entertained by thoughts that it could pierce their clothing and find its way to the soft space it had yearned to be in for the past ten years. She rested beside him as they calmed their breathing. He thought he had his impulses under control until…

Seconds later, she fumbled with the buttons on his shirt. "Do you want me, Mace?" Her words began to slur as she placed kisses along his chest. She rested her warm lips longingly above his heart.

"Were you all drinking on the ship too?" He smiled, amused at her attempts to be amorous, despite the gradual effects of the alcohol on her behavior.

"Yes, we had a few glasses of wine and champagne, and something else with cute umbrellas on the side of the glass. We celebrated having such a good trip." She placed a hand to her mouth and widened her eyes to stay awake.

He pressed her head against his chest, and she closed her eyes. As he hugged her, she began drifting off to sleep.

"Yes, I want you, but as my wife, my partner for life, and not as just someone to share my bed for only one night. When I'm inside you again, loving you like no other man ever could, I want you to know for sure that you want to spend the rest of your life with me."

He admired her beauty as she slept in his arms. Lifting her off the couch, he prepared to take her to one of his guest rooms. She stirred as he gathered her in his arms and kissed her on the forehead.

"I love you, Mace." Her eyes remained closed. Snuggling her head against his chest, she yawned.

"What did you say?" he placed his mouth near her ear and asked softly.

She took a deep slumbering breath but didn't answer as he took her to bed.

* * *

Dressed in casual couture, Mason finished his breakfast and wiped his mouth with his starched white napkin. He placed it on the table before taking a sip of water from his crystal glass. Carly sat across from him in an oversized hoodie with *Charleston* stitched across the front and skinny jeans.

She ate the last of her omelet before taking a bite of her toast, covered with strawberry jam.

In silence, Mason looked at the expanse of the river along the calm harbor, oblivious to the seconds Carly spent staring at him.

"All right, spill it, Mace. You're not talking to me and it's uncomfortable." She peered at him over her glass as she took a sip of water from it.

"I have a lot I want to say to you, Carly. I just don't know in what order and how to say it."

"Try not to waste time filtering it. Like I said, just say it." She swallowed hard and sat up straight in her chair, braced for whatever he had to tell her.

"All right, let's start with Christmas. Was it just the wine and champagne flowing, or were you telling me how you really feel when you said you loved me?"

She took a breath, then the truth of his statement hit her. *What*? *When*?

"Carly, are you listening to me?"

"Yes, I'm listening. Did you say I told you I loved you?"

"Admittedly, you were drunk at the time." He cocked an eyebrow.

She buried her lower lip between her teeth. "It wasn't just the alcohol. I do love you and I've always loved you, since we were kids. I don't deny that. I just don't want us to get into something neither one of us is prepared to handle."

He laughed. "We're already there, baby, and I'm not talking about puppy love. Christmas Day was wonderful for me – the best I've had in a long time – because of you. There has always been a spark between us. After our heavy petting last night, I was ready to go all the way, but I don't want to rush things. I want it to be right for both of us. I want it to happen only after you tell me you're sure you want me."

"I'm not accustomed to having this kind of discussion so early in the morning, but I've been celibate, by choice and circumstance. You didn't know about it, but my divorce was nasty. It's also hard to desire sex when you're having to fend off unwanted advances on the job." She turned her gaze away from him.

"I'm sorry about all you had to endure. I wish we were at a point where you felt you could have reached out to me, but I'm here for you now." He squeezed her hand.

"Thank you." She moved her hand from underneath his and looked at her phone, buzzing on the table. "It's Aunt Nora saying good morning and sending wishes that we enjoy a great day. Let me send her a quick text back."

"Tell her I said hello." His phone rang and he looked at the screen before picking it up. "Hello... Don't worry about the time. Tell me what's going on."

Carly remained quiet as Mace listened to the caller.

Mace's cook, Marlena, returned and, with adept speed and minimal noise, began clearing the table.

"Excuse me, Carly. I have to take this."

"Sure. Not a problem," she answered before he disappeared in the direction of his home office, leaving her with Marlena.

"Marlena."

"Yes." She stopped her task. "Is there something I can get for you?"

"No. I wanted to thank you for preparing the delicious Christmas meal. You probably had the day off before my plans changed and I agreed to spend this week with Mason."

"You're welcome. It wasn't a problem. When Mr. Moore is in town, he knows I'm available, no matter the day or time. That's our agreement. He's a great boss and a friend to my family. Anything I can do to make his life a little easier, I'm willing to do."

"I remember he had a problem tooting his own horn. Sometimes that can lead to people not knowing who he really is."

Marlena smiled. "Yes. There are times I think it's how he wants it. He likes being misunderstood, or maybe letting people think whatever they want to think of him." She finished clearing the table and left the room before Mason returned.

Carly turned her attention back to the river and watched the sailboats leaving trails in the water as the boaters who rose early that morning sped along the coast on the sunny

December day.

"Sorry. I had to take that call. There's trouble in the foreign markets. It means, unfortunately, that I'll have to change our afternoon plans, but I'll be free this evening."

"That's fine. I have work to do, then we can go out to dinner and walk along King Street to look at the decorations before we go to visit your family."

"We have plenty of food here, but I'm sure my mother will want us to have dinner with them. Prepare to be stuck over there for hours."

"If we eat before we go, we can stick to the plan to avoid spending hours over there. As I told you, I agreed to a visit, not to dinner. She won't insist we eat twice."

"Sounds like a good plan, but why do we have to go out?" He looked at her.

"If I agree to stay here for dinner, you and Marlena will make it nice, but very formal. I don't want to dress for dinner like we did for Christmas. My sweet booty doesn't need another eight-course meal." She turned and patted her butt. "Can we enjoy a casual night out, including a walk along a few of the downtown streets? I haven't been here for Christmas in a while. Please?" She batted her lashes at him.

"Who's being coy and manipulative now? All right, but—"

"I'm leaving, Mr. Moore," Marlena called out before entering the room. "I have to take my grandson Jalen to holiday camp this morning, but I'll be back shortly."

"Take your time. We'll be fine until you return. Oh, and another thing." He held a finger in the air. "Stop calling me Mr. Moore. Carly needs to know I'm just Mason to you."

"Fine, Mason." She tightened her grip on her apron strings. "I wanted to make sure Carly knew how much I respect you. Calling you Mr. Moore, not Mason, while she was here would convey that."

"Thank you, Marlena, for the fantastic meals you prepared." He rose from the table, looking flushed and uncomfortable with the praise.

"You're welcome." She waved goodbye and turned to leave.

Carly moved closer to him. "You'd better go handle your business."

Mason listened as the heavy front door closed behind Marlena before taking Carly into his arms. "First, pleasure." He swept her off her feet and planted a kiss on her lips. "Then I can get back to business. I promise it won't take too long." The phone in his pocket began buzzing again. "Make yourself at home." He hurried out of the room, talking to the person on the phone intruding on their time. "Good work, Bernie."

Carly listened. She couldn't hear the conversation on the other end, but smiled, hearing the elation in Mace's voice.

"Fantastic, man. I knew you could do it." His voice trailed off as he walked to his study.

This isn't how I intended to spend my week. She sighed. *What should I have expected? It's Christmastime and he's working.*

She shook her head. *The man is obviously married to his work.* She turned and headed to the guest room for a midmorning nap.

Chapter

17

It's been a long time since I dined at the Peninsula Grill, Mace. The food is still excellent and the coconut cake... Mmm, so good." Carly closed her eyes briefly, savoring the memory of each pleasurable bite. She placed her hand in his as they left the restaurant and strolled through the Market area before heading down King Street, looking at the windows decorated with Christmas themes.

"It *was* good, but I don't understand why we couldn't go straight to my parents' home. You know, get the obligatory 'you will have fun' dinner party over with earlier. We're running late. Now Mom will expect us to stay for a couple hours to make amends." Mason buttoned his coat and Carly drew her scarf around her, a protection from the cool evening breeze.

"I get the impression that your trips home are about business – a quick check-in with the family and poof, you're out." She raised a closed fist in the air, then quickly spread her fingers before placing her hand in her pocket. "I want to see the town and I want to see it with you, tonight. I haven't decided if I'm going to return to Maryland to look for another position or look at other options. One of Aunt Nora's friends called while you were working to tell me about a visiting professor position here at the College of Charleston."

He shrugged. "As long as your plans include the two of us spending time together, it's your choice."

She stopped and hugged him. "I want to make this work." She gazed into his eyes, assuring him, "I won't make a decision without input from you."

Brightly decorated storefronts and vignettes with lush greenery, poinsettias, traditional red ornaments, and twinkling lights illuminated their path with holiday cheer. They passed Horlbeck Alley, between King and Meeting Streets, one of the Holy City's nine hidden pathways of a bygone era.

Quick movements in the shadows caught their eyes.

"Please don't hurt me. Don't hurt me." As they passed by, the distressed screams of a woman caught their attention.

Mason loosened his grip on Carly's hand and leaned forward to see if he could get a glimpse of what was happening. "Carly, stay here while I check out what's going on."

A loud popping sound, as if flesh was connecting violently with flesh, could be heard, followed by another scream coming from the alleyway.

"Mace, don't go. Let me call the police." She fumbled for her phone.

"Stay here, Carly. I'll be right back." He ran into the alley and was gone before she could call the authorities. Her heart raced and her breath became shallow as he disappeared into the darkened space. She heard him demanding someone to stop, then an argument ensued between him and another male.

"What's your emergency?" the 911 dispatcher asked.

"Please come right away," she yelled into the phone's speaker. "There's a disturbance in Horlbeck Alley downtown. Send a car. I'll be here waiting to flag them down," Carly told the dispatcher, frantic to get help to the scene.

"We're on our way, ma'am."

Carly heard a scuffle coming from the alley. She ran toward the sound, uncertain of what she could do to stop it. When she came upon the scene, a man held a shaking woman in his arms at gunpoint while Mason kept his hands in the air.

"Stop right there," the man screamed.

Carly raised her hands and froze in her tracks.

"Carly!" Mason yelled, startling the man.

He pushed the woman to the ground and struck Mason hard in the head with the butt of his gun while he was distracted by Carly's appearance.

"Mason!" Shrieking, she fell to her knees alongside Mason's motionless body, crumpled on the cold brick pathway.

The man took off running.

"Thank you, God." She uttered a quick prayer of thanksgiving that no one had been killed, then added, "Please let Mason be okay."

* * *

"Marlena, I didn't know who else to call. Mason woke up and when I told him I was going to call his mother, he tried bolting out of the bed until I promised I wouldn't call her. I told him we owed her an explanation for why we didn't show up."

Carly sat on the stool in the kitchen while Marlena stirred the soup bubbling on the stove. "He told me we would call her later."

Marlena checked the bread in the oven that was filling the house with a warm, pleasing aroma. "I called her. She's accustomed to getting phone calls from me when Mason has to change his plans because of business, but she wasn't happy about it. She asked if you could come alone. I told her you weren't home. I wasn't lying by telling her you were out with a friend."

"Thanks, I appreciate it. I had my hands full taking care of Mason." After his head CT scan came back negative, they released Mason from the emergency room and told Carly to monitor him.

"Why don't you get some rest? I know you've been up throughout the night checking on him. You look exhausted. I'll take over and maybe I can get him to eat a little something."

"Caroline!" Mace yelled for her from the bedroom.

Carly jumped and stumbled off her stool as she and Marlena ran to check on him. She arrived at the door and found him sitting upright in bed, panting, his chest heaving, with beads of sweat dripping down the side of his face.

"I'm here, Mace. It's me, Carly... Caroline." She rushed to his bedside and placed her hands on his temples. When she turned his head so they could look into each other's eyes, he calmed.

His breath slowed while he covered her hands with his. "You're here. I had a nightmare that you were shot, and you died in my arms." His chest heaved again. He closed his eyes, tightening his jaw to hold back the tears, but he couldn't prevent them from falling.

She held him in her arms and pressed his head to her breast until he regained his composure.

Marlena backed out of the room and slowly closed the door.

"I'm all right, Mace. You took blows to the head. It's you I'm worried about."

He lifted his head and pressed his forehead to hers. "I thought I had lost you for good. The grief I felt was so heavy, it was unbearable," he told her, barely above a whisper. "I was supposed to protect you and fate turned on me. It was you who protected me. I was supposed to be the one who made sure no harm ever came to you. Whoever was crazy enough to try and hurt you was supposed to understand that they had to come through me to get to you, not the other way around."

"Who says that, Mace?" She placed her hands on the sides of his face and searched his eyes. "Or is it you placing an unrealistic expectation on yourself?"

"It's me telling the world I love you and you're mine. You're my woman."

"Well, then, let me put you and the world on notice. You're my man and to get to you, they're going to have to come through *me*. So, now that we understand each other, I need to get some fluids in you. I can bring a tray to you in here or help you to the table to get some soup."

He smiled and sniffed the aroma in the room. "That bread does smell good. I'll eat a little soup if I can have some bread along with it. Help me to the table. I need to get out of this bed. What time is it?"

Carly looked at the clock on his bedside table. "It's about noon the next day." She placed his arm around her shoulder and helped him to his feet.

"I can do it if you don't need me to sprint to the table."

"All right. I'll walk alongside you. We can take our time."

Marlena was bringing the soup to the table by the time they made it to the dining area. She waited until he spoke to her, but her eyes showed concern for his condition as she ladled soup from the tureen into his bowl.

"I'll be okay, Marlena. Don't worry about me," he told her in a low voice. "Thank you for the soup and being there for me. I know you called my mother, or she would have been here fussing over me by now." He blew on the spoon, containing a small amount of soup, before swallowing it, then took a bite of his bread while Marlena served some of the soup to Carly.

"Hmm, this is good." He closed his eyes, savoring the soup, and took his time raising his head.

"I'm sorry I frightened you both earlier, but I was having a nightmare that Carly was shot dead because she didn't listen to me."

Carly dropped her spoon next to her saucer, causing it to clang against the porcelain.

"That was loud." He held his head and closed his eyes.

"Who wasn't listening to whom, Mace? I begged you not to go and you went anyway."

"The two of you can call me if you need me. I need to take care of things in the kitchen." Marlena hurried out of the room.

"You never listen to me, Carly. That guy was my grandfather's former employee. I was handling it until you showed up. I wasn't worried about me. I was scared to death for *you*."

She hesitated to respond and picked up her spoon. "Eat your soup, please, Mace. You need to regain your strength." She examined the slice of bread and bit off another piece.

"This bread tastes a lot like the bread my mom used to bake."

"I loved your mom's bread. It took Marlena some time to get the recipe right, but I think she's done a good job." He took in another spoonful of soup and tore off another portion of bread. "I'm not that impulsive maverick I once was." His tone was adamant. "You don't need to protect me from myself."

She looked up from her bowl. "Get used to it, Mace. The secret is out. We know you're not a superman. You're human. If that man had fired the gun, the bullet wouldn't have bounced off you."

He didn't respond.

Moments of silence passed while she swallowed another spoonful of soup, not saying another word until she finished her meal. She looked up and saw he had emptied his bowl.

"I'm tired and I need some rest." He got up slowly and she went to his side.

"I'd sleep better if you came to bed with me. I don't want to be separated from you, at least not now."

"It would be good to take a nap." She took his hand and walked with him to the bedroom.

Chapter

18

I t's not like Mason to take a nap this early in the evening," Lucille Moore, Mason's mother, told Carly.

"The meal was wonderful and maybe he ate a little too much," Carly responded, looking down and fidgeting with her hands. "A full belly can make anyone sleepy."

Lucille placed her cup of tea on the table as she looked over at Mason in the next room on the couch in the solarium. She and Carly were enjoying after-dinner tea and petite desserts in the family room while Mason napped. "There's something else going on, so tell me, what really happened last night? I don't think Marlena told me the entire story."

"Mace was assaulted last night while we were downtown, walking back to the car near Horlbeck Alley. He didn't want you to worry, so he made me promise not to tell you, but there's no way to hide his bruises without telling more lies." Carly placed her cup on the table as well and looked at Lucille.

"So he wasn't involved in a car accident on his way home from a business meeting?"

"No." Carly shook her head. The bruises on Mason's face were fading, but there was no way Lucille wouldn't ask about them.

"Thank you for telling me the truth. I could always depend on you to be candid with me."

Carly had known Mace's family since they were children. She knew there was no need to try to keep anything from Lucille Jefferson Moore. She was like a super-sleuth who couldn't rest until she discovered the truth.

"So you were with him when it happened?" Her concern showed in her warm brown eyes.

"Yes. He asked me to stay out of it before he went into an alleyway to see if he could help a woman who was being assaulted, but I couldn't stay away. I couldn't let him go into a dangerous situation by himself."

Lucille smiled and nodded. "It doesn't surprise me. There was a time when no one would have doubted that you'd surrender your safety and maybe even your life for him. Your brother and Mason were older than you, but you were fiercely protective of both of them." She fiddled with a small tart on her plate. "It's good to see you and Mason together again. You deserve a good man in your life." She moistened her lips with her tongue. "Every woman deserves a good man, one loving to his wife and children."

She dropped the tart and wiped her hands on a napkin, her lips tightly pressed together.

Carly knew she was thinking of her own deceased husband, Cameron Moore. He had not been a good man to her. When Carly was a child, she'd overheard her mother talking to Aunt Nora about rumors that he'd had an affair.

"*Go to your room, Caroline,*" she remembered her mother telling her. "*Grown people are talking.*"

Lucille had never told Mason about it, but somehow Carly, even at that young age, got caught up in the family secret.

"The two of you are back together," she repeated, leaning over and patting Carly's hand. "I plan to do all I can do to ensure the two of you have the happy ending you both deserve. I owe it to Mason."

The comment hit Carly in a way she found confusing. She sat back in her chair and rubbed her chin as she pondered how to respond. "What do you mean, you owe it to Mason?"

"I owe my boy a piece of happiness. From the time he took his first breath, I offered my child as a sacrifice for my own happiness."

Carly shuddered. "A sacrifice? I don't think I could ever sacrifice my child for any reason."

"Don't judge me, dear, if you've never been in the situation. My father wanted a son, and I gave him mine. Mason was named for my father, Mason Jefferson, and Cameron insisted we add the name Edmund. I had to fight with him in my hospital bed to give him *my* father's name. We had Cameron the second – Deuce – and Cameron also named our second son, Evan, after his father. He only agreed to let Mason be named for my father after I told him he could give him the name of his best friend, Edmund Hollison, who died saving his life in the first Gulf War, as a middle name. Mason was an unexpected gift to us. We already had two sons and I never thought we would have a third child. Mason came into this world burdened with the names, hopes, triumphs, and failures of other men."

"All of us bear names not of our choosing," Carly responded. "Sometimes we're fortunate enough to have names that reflect who we are."

MICHELE SIMS

Lucille nodded. "My boy bore that burden and I insisted that he, more than the other boys, spend time on the farm with my parents. He knew they loved him, but I'm sure he would have preferred spending time with his friends instead of with older people. Mason had a special relationship with my parents and that's why they left him the lion's share of their fortune, more than they left me or my sisters."

"Lucille, why are you telling me these things now?"

"You're both older and I want to let you know what things have shaped the man Mason has become. He may not have had the chance to shape his own identity under the weight of my father's history in this town, but the one thing I know for sure is what he has clung to. He knew from the time he was a little boy he loved you, and he held on to that belief, even when I thought it was puppy love and the two of you would move on. You've been his anchor – the one thing he claimed for himself is his lifelong love for you."

"You don't owe me anything and I don't think Mace believes you owe him anything," Carly reassured her. "He knows you love him and would give your life for him."

Lucille sighed. "I guess we can add it to the list of things we share. It took me a while to realize it, but we know love is about sacrifice. He's not perfect when it comes to communicating his feelings, but he would give anything for you." She looked over at Mason before continuing. "You need to know more about the concussion he suffered ten years ago that ended his football career, but—"

Carly held up her hand. "Ended his football career *and* our relationship."

"I know there was a rift between the two of you afterward." Lucille spoke in hushed tones, casting constant looks over at Mason.

"More than a rift, Lucille." Carly tried to contain the bile rising within her. "He stopped communicating with me. Despite our history, our relationship was over because he felt it was over." She tightened her fists.

Lucille leaned in closer to Carly and faced her with an unwavering gaze. "Listen to me. My boy's behavior and his decisions may have seemed indifferent, but he *never* stopped loving you. I just hope this current concussion doesn't make it worse."

Carly sat back and laughed. The loud and bitter sound of it caused Mace to stir from his sleep. "Indifferent, you say?"

"There's more to it than you know. I hoped over time Mason would explain it to you, but you know he doesn't like to appear weak."

Before they could continue, the door opened and three boys spilled into the room, laughing and running toward Lucille. They were followed by their mother, lumbering into the room with her hand on her pregnant belly.

"Mom, I couldn't keep them away. The boys heard you telling me on the phone that Mason was over here. You know how they feel about their Uncle Mason."

"Yes, I do." She extended her arms to embrace the boys one at a time.

"Katelyn and boys, this is Caroline Rivers."

They smiled at her and waved.

"Call me Carly." She got up and took Katelyn's extended hand.

"I'm Kate – Evan's wife – and these are our sons, Evan the third, or Trey, and our middle child, Eric." She pointed to the young boy then turned to her third son. "The one with all the curls is our youngest, Ian."

"We know you're Carly." Ian came closer and gave her a

hug.

"How do you know me, Ian? I don't think we've had the pleasure of meeting before now." She smiled at him.

"Your pictures are in Uncle Mason's private office." He cupped his hand around his mouth and lowered the volume of his voice. "I saw them in his drawer. You're pretty like your pictures."

"Yeah," Eric added. "You smile more than Millie did."

Carly looked at Lucille, who rubbed her neck and turned her head away.

Kate pasted on a smile before quickly placing her hand on Eric's shoulder.

They all shifted their attention to Mason, yawning as he walked into the room.

"Hey. What did I say about you boys talking about your uncle and sharing secrets?"

"Uncle Mason," they yelled and ran to greet him.

He hugged the boys and made his way to the couch beside Carly.

"Hey, sleepyhead." She leaned in and placed a kiss on his cheek.

"I was more tired than I thought. Hey, Kate."

She waved at him.

"Mom, that meal was fantastic. I ate more than I should have." He yawned and patted his stomach. "Is there something wrong?" He looked between his mother and Carly. "I'm not sure what, but something seems off."

"No, it's nothing," his mother assured him. "I'm glad you enjoyed the meal. I made the bread pudding you like if you want to take some with you."

"I couldn't eat another bite now, but I'll take you up on the offer to take some with me."

"Is Carly your girlfriend again, Uncle Mason?" Ian sat on the couch between him and Carly.

"You know she is. Everyone knows he loves her." Eric covered his mouth as he giggled.

"Boys! You're embarrassing your uncle," Kate said.

Carly looked at her, uncertain she wasn't glad the boys were spilling the poorly kept secret.

"All right, guys. What about some red velvet cake in the kitchen with Grandma?" Lucille rose and helped Ian and then Eric to their feet. "Come with us, Trey."

"Will you join us, Uncle Mason? We want to show you the bikes Grandma gave us for Christmas. We didn't get to show them to you because you weren't here for Christmas." A slight frown appeared as Trey spoke.

"Sure, buddy, and I'm sorry I missed Christmas, but I brought my gifts for all of you."

"Where are they?" The smiles and merriment returned.

"Carly, are you going to be all right while I show the boys their gifts?"

"Sure, I'll be fine. You go and enjoy your time with them."

"I'll go cut the cake for the boys while you and Carly get to know each other." Lucille nodded at Kate and walked out of the room with the boys and Mason in tow.

"What happened to your face, Uncle Mason? Were you in a fight?" Ian asked as he reached for Mason's hand.

"I'll tell you all about it." Mason looked at his nephew and led the way to the kitchen.

Kate waited until the boys were out of earshot before she spoke. "So good to finally meet you in person, Carly."

"Good to meet you too."

"I apologize if Eric's comment was uncomfortable." Kate rubbed her stomach.

Carly tilted her head. "Eric said something about someone named Millie? I don't know her."

Kate rubbed her forehead. "Millie is Mason's ex, Jamillah."

"Oh." Carly interlaced her fingers and rested her hands on her lap. "Don't worry about it. He was just sharing his thoughts."

Kate bit her lip. "I hope you're alright. Evan told me about the attack. That must have been so scary for you." Her face went from worry and concern to a knowing smile. "Evan also told me you two are back together. Things are going okay?"

Carly tried to keep an even smile on her face. She and Kate hadn't been together for five minutes and she was all up in her business. "It may be premature to say we're back together, but we're trying to get to know each other again."

"Nothing would make all of us happier. Other than this little one coming into the world soon." She looked down at her swollen belly. "The two of you getting back together would be another Christmas miracle." Kate paused for a second. "I hope I'm not being too forward. Mason is more like my brother than a brother-in-law. I just want him to be happy."

Carly again tried to keep her smile even. Mason hadn't spoken much about the members of his family, so she wasn't sure who he was close to and who she could trust.

"Mason has always been the maverick of the family and possibly the smartest of all the Moore sons. I heard many times about his epic tale of trying to win you back, his true love."

Carly threw her head back and let out a hearty laugh. "I don't know how epic the tale is. Let's not forget, he married another woman."

"Have you met Jamillah before?" Kate asked.

"No, I haven't." Carly took one of the petite cakes off the tray, placed it in her mouth, and squirmed uncomfortably in her chair. She didn't know what to say. Stuffing her mouth with the delicious sweets calmed her anxiety.

She chewed the cake and swallowed it slowly. She could do it. She could handle Kate's need to spill the tea.

"Jamillah was a supermodel. She's gorgeous." Kate rolled her neck and pursed her lips. "I don't mean to gush, Carly, but the woman can command attention in any room. She's tall, and stately, but a bit vapid. I'm sure you could hold your own in any conversation with her. Google her. You need to be prepared."

Carly leaned forward with an elbow on her thigh and opened her mouth to speak. "For what?"

Kate leaned forward and whispered, "I'm sure she still says negative things about the family. She blames everyone except herself for the failure of their marriage. She told me that I supported Mason's decision to not have children because I wanted my children, whom he adores, to inherit his money. Can you imagine?" She frowned. "The nerve of that woman."

Initially speechless, Carly's jaw dropped for a moment. "I don't know what to say."

Mason returned, rubbing his head and squinting. "Carly, I called for a ride home. I can't seem to shake this headache and I think I've given Kate enough time to give you the scoop on the family."

"What makes you think I was saying anything about the family?" She had difficulty getting out of the chair with a swollen belly.

He moved forward and helped her to her feet. "It's because I know you, sis." He gave her a kiss on the cheek.

"Ready to go, Carly?"

She quickly gathered her things. "Sure."

"The boys are in the kitchen eating cake with Mom. My prayers for you and Evan trying to calm them down after she fills them with chocolate and sugar. Tell them we had to leave and I'll see them again this week before the new year rolls in. I don't want them to see me when I'm not well." He placed a hand on his belly. "I'm feeling a little nauseous."

"Sorry you're not feeling well, Mason, but the boys have seen an adult who's nauseated." She pointed to herself, and they smiled at each other.

"I almost forgot about the first few months of all your pregnancies." He kissed her one last time then went to Carly to urge her to the door.

"It was good to meet you, Kate." Carly wasn't entirely sure that was true, but it was the right thing to say.

Mason looked at his watch, which was connected to his smartphone. "That's our notification that the driver is here. Bye, Kate."

"Bye, Mason. Carly, let's get together soon." Kate waved as they left.

The driver had arrived and was waiting in the driveway. Mace opened the door for Carly. She slid in while the driver bobbed his head to an old-school rap song playing on satellite radio.

"You don't mind if I listen to music, do you, Mr. Moore?" the driver asked before he drove off.

"Turn it down a little," Mace responded, holding his head.

Carly was quiet as she reflected on her conversations with Lucille and Kate. Mason slid closer and laid his head against the back of the seat to rest on their way home while music flowed through the limo.

"*Get back. Get back.*" Carly listened to the chorus of the song playing in the background that had once been her anthem of defiance when she was going through hard times.

She bobbed her head to the beat as the car rolled away from the house.

Chapter

19

Aunt Nora, you should be having fun with Daniel and his family instead of worrying about me." Carly took the phone off speaker and placed it to her ear as she entered the condo and closed the door. The place was quiet, and a couple of lamps had been left on to illuminate the room.

"How was Christmas?" She looked around and there was no sign of Mace or Marlena, so she placed the phone back on speaker and threw her gym bag on the floor after returning from her late-evening workout.

"I'm having a wonderful time enjoying the holidays with Daniel and his family, but you know your cousin, that hard-headed son of mine. I told him I didn't need anything for Christmas, so he paid for a room addition to my home. He said it was a thank-you gift for all the sacrifices I've made for him and his family. It will be more work than I planned for the new year, but I'm warming up to the idea of a renovation. I thought while I was getting the repairs from the water damage done, I might as well let the contractor build a home office. I've always dreamed of having one. Are you back at the condo yet?"

Carly sank down on the plush couch. She knew this would just be the beginning of a talk about Mace. "Yes, I'm back. Mace hasn't returned yet, but he should be home soon."

"You don't need to stay there long, my dear. The repairs from the water damage should be completed soon and you can return to my house."

"I don't have enough time to discuss this right now." She looked around the room. "Nor can I tell you that I know what we're doing or where our relationship is headed, but it feels right between me and Mace. I want to see where things go. I'm getting tired of being afraid of what the future holds for me. Trust me, I'm not ready to throw caution to the wind either, but I'm staying here because I want to be here for now, not because I have to stay."

"I'm just saying I know things are tight for you financially, but you don't have to stay there and feel obligated to do whatever he wants you to do. You've worked too hard to regain your freedom only to get back into a relationship for the wrong reason."

Carly grabbed her belly and let out a hearty laugh. "Don't worry. I'm not giving up the booty in exchange for a place to stay."

"Sweetheart, I didn't mean to imply that." Aunt Nora cleared her throat.

"But it is what you meant."

"Who's giving up booty?"

Carly fumbled to get the phone, startled as Mace entered the room. "I thought you weren't at home." She attempted to smile as her lips quivered.

"Is that Mace asking about booty?"

"Mace is home and I've got to go, Aunt Nora." Before she could take the phone off speaker, Aunt Nora greeted him.

"Hello, Mace. Happy holidays."

"Happy holidays, Nora." Mace plopped on the couch beside Carly. He was wearing a short-sleeved t-shirt and lounge pants, while she was dressed in tight spandex exercise clothing with the black crop top and leggings she'd put on after showering at the gym.

"I was telling Carly that she didn't need to worry about overstaying her welcome. My place should be ready by the time I return in a few days."

"Nonsense, Nora. She doesn't need to worry about anything. I'm enjoying her company and I have plenty of room. We've been catching up on old times." He licked his lips while viewing Carly in her attire.

Carly chewed her lip, concerned the two of them were about to enter into a tug-of-war. Nora hesitated, but Carly knew she was preparing a counter-response.

"I see, and that's what I'm worrying about. I don't know how to be anything but honest, especially when it comes to my niece's happiness. She's been through a lot."

"Aunt Nora, I'm a big girl and all those difficult days are behind me now. We shouldn't bother Mace with unpleasantries, especially during the holidays."

"I know you're a grown woman but let me finish. It's the holidays and it's easy to feel warm and fuzzy now with all the talk of love and goodwill to men. I just don't want you to end up in another rebound relationship."

Mace smiled and placed a hand on Carly's thigh as warmth spread from her leg to her groin under his firm touch. She tingled with unexpected excitement, looking at his hand

and then back at his handsome face.

"Thank you, Nora, for warning Carly about the dangers of playing with my heart. I would hate to feel used by her."

Carly rolled her eyes at him.

"I see the two of you aren't going to take me seriously, so I'll leave it alone and let the two of you get back to catching up on old times."

"Bye, Aunt Nora. Love you."

"Love you more, Carly."

"Bye, Nora."

"Bye, Mace, and thanks for being there for my girl. Just remember, she doesn't need any more drama or hollow promises in her life."

"Consider me warned. I don't want your wrath over my head."

"Good." She laughed and ended the call.

Mace removed his hand and folded his arms, resting them over his lap.

"I didn't know you were here," they said at the same time and laughed at each other.

"I was in my office working on some things and I heard your voice. How was your workout?" He maintained contact with her, sitting hip to hip.

"My workout was good. I feel so energetic. How is your headache?"

"No pain at all." He rubbed the back of his head.

"I'll go with you to your doctor's appointment tomorrow." She placed a hand on his shoulder then drew it away, surprised a friendly gesture would reignite the warmth of passion in her.

"Don't worry about it. It should be a quick visit. I even thought of cancelling it since I feel better. I thought you had things to do tomorrow?"

"Nothing I couldn't do another time," she said. "Don't you think about cancelling your appointment. You took a nasty hit on the head."

He laid his head in her lap.

As if by reflex, she began tenderly massaging his temples and shoulders.

"Mmm. That feels good." He closed his eyes, placing his arms around her waist.

She looked down at his groin and noticed signs he found her actions pleasurable.

Opening his eyes, he looked down at himself before looking into her eyes. "I've been taking cold showers frequently. I guess I need another one now."

She licked her lips and took in a slow, deep breath. The sensual tension was growing between them. There was no hiding the outline of her hardened nipples signaling her heightened level of excitement. She turned his head and pulled on his lips before placing her tongue in his mouth, tasting his greedy tongue as it played with hers.

Smiling, he touched the side of her breast before taking the fullness of it in his hands and kneading it slowly, reverently. "I want you, Carly, and I'm not going to play coy. Nora is right. I don't want to do the cat-and-mouse game with you, so I'm asking you. Do you want me as much as I want you?"

She touched his pants and moved her hands along his thickened girth, which felt hard as steel. Rubbing it slowly, she grew wet with desire. Looking into his eyes, she lowered her head and rubbed her lips across his, kissing him possessively before answering, "Meet me in my bedroom and we'll both find out." Her voice was husky and demanding.

"I have a bigger bed. I'll meet you in *my* bedroom if you want me. I told you I wanted to be sure this is what you want."

She rose from the couch and extended her hand to meet his. "I'm sure. I want this and I want you."

"Let me turn out the lights and I'll be right there." He sat upright.

"All right, but don't take too long." She swayed her hips as she made her way toward his bedroom.

"Oh, baby. You don't know what you're doing to me." He watched as she walked away, heading toward the hallway.

"I think I do." She placed a finger in her mouth and sucked it before releasing it from between her lips.

Mason opened the drawer of the side table adjacent to the couch and peered inside, looking for a single foil package.

"There's *got* to be one in here." He hadn't had a woman in his apartment in two years. He'd thought he had at least one condom in the drawer.

"Damn." He pushed aside the contents, causing some of the papers to fall on the floor, but he couldn't find one. He got up and went to the small credenza near the door, stubbing his toe as he ran across the room.

"Ouch." He hopped for a few steps and placed his hand on the top of the piece of furniture, turning over a vase.

"Mace, what's taking you so long?"

"I'm coming, babe."

"Get in here. Now," she growled.

He jumped across the ottoman in front of the couch and made his way in a mad dash to her. "I'm coming," he yelled. "And soon." He ran into the bedroom where Carly was waiting and growing impatient. "I'll get condoms later."

Chapter

20

This has been a long day. Actually, too long." Mace took a sip of his drink and sat back in the chair in his office. He was glad for a little peace and quiet, even though he loved having Carly in the condo with him. Marlena was at the market doing some shopping. Alone to spend time with his thoughts, he pondered the conversation he'd had earlier that day with his doctor.

"My headaches were more frequent and worse for a few days after I got hit in the head – for the second time. They've gotten a little better, though."

"Have you noticed anything else?" Dr. Delano pulled a small flashlight out of his pocket.

Mace's skin warmed as he thought about what he was going to say. "I'm not sure why, but lately, I come harder, if you know what I mean." He sat up straight on the table as the doctor smiled at him while shining the bright light in his eyes.

"I'm glad your sex drive wasn't affected like it was when you took that first nasty hit." Dr. Delano pulled out the stool and sat in

front of Mace. "So, tell me, are you and your beautiful wife, Jamillah, back together and maybe thinking about starting a family?"

Mace frowned as he stared at Dr. Delano. "No and hell no. She's my ex-wife and will forever remain so. I'm not interested in starting a family at this point in my life."

"I see." He placed his hands in his lap. "Then the rumors I've heard must be true. The social circles here are small but filled with tongue-waggers. Are you and Carly finally going to get back together? I heard she was back in town."

"She's back, but we're taking it slow." Mason cleared his throat.

"All right, but we both know the term 'slow' is relative. How has your mood been?"

"Mood is fine, but there's one thing, Doc. My memory is becoming a problem. I'm preparing for a big company meeting and I'm having trouble remembering information. I'm getting so forgetful, and it concerns me that I'll make an ass of myself in front of my employees if my brain locks up on me."

"Mason, this is your second significant concussion." He straightened his glasses. "Can you give yourself more time to heal before you host a large company meeting? When is the meeting?"

"It's in two days, on New Year's Eve." Mason looked at the doctor frowning back at him.

"Are you telling me you make your employees work on New Year's Eve?" Dr. Delano took his glasses off and placed the tip of one arm in his mouth as if he needed to chew on the revelation.

"I make it fun, and it's always well attended."

"Okay, but maybe you could have some of the VPs you pay the big bucks to conduct parts of the meeting."

Mason's body language spoke louder than his response. He stood, shaking his head. "It's my company. It's important that I convey that I'm in charge." He tapped his feet as he leaned against the table.

Dr. Delano extended his hand and gave him a firm handshake before releasing him from the follow-up. "Call me if you have more questions, but I'm advising you, as your doctor and your friend, to take it easy. The nurse will come and give you your prescriptions. Goodbye, and see you next time. Oh, and tell Carly I said hello. I remember how long it took for you to get over her. Maybe it's wise to take it slow."

"Bye, Doc," *he told him as his friend exited the room.*

"I never got over her," Mason said out loud. Lost in his thoughts, he hadn't realized Marlena had returned with a club sandwich piled high with meats and cheeses. A sliced dill pickle was placed on the side of the small plate, just as he liked it.

"So you think about her even when she's not here?"

He jerked his head, looking upward, while she placed his lunch on the desk.

"What? What did you say?" Blinking, he tried to regain his focus.

"I said, you think of her even when she's not here, and don't even ask who *she* is."

The phone buzzed on the desk. He picked it up and looked at the screen.

"Thanks, Marlena. It's lunchtime already?"

"It's past noon." She frowned, looking at the trash can overflowing with wads of paper. "Maybe you should take it easy, Mason. It hasn't been that long since you took a blow to the head." She pulled the sides of the trash bag together and tied it in a knot before replacing the bag.

Mason's phone buzzed three times in rapid succession. Focused on the screen, he swiped through the messages while taking big bites of his sandwich.

"Things all right with the family?" She paused and looked

at him.

"Yeah, they're good. It's alerts on Carly sightings."

"What? You've got someone following Carly?" Her jaw dropped as she stared in disbelief.

"No. You know that's not my style. This is really a small town. Just like I remembered, people stay in each other's business." He hit the play button on one of the messages.

"Get your behind down here, Mason. Carly is back in town and she's fine. We all know you've still got a thing for her."

Marlena leaned over, gazing at the picture on the screen. "Is that Manny? It sounds like him."

Mason finished half of his sandwich and wiped his mouth with his napkin. "Yes, it's Manny stalking Carly, among others." The phone buzzed again with a text.

Jerry: Carly's at the battery taking pics. I think she's doing a promo for another book. Get down here man. I'll stay and be your wingman if you're scared. Haha.

Mason: I don't need a wingman. Thanks, but no thanks. C U later.

"People care about you, Mason. We know you and Carly were made for each other."

"Marlena, I need to take my time. You know I have the tendency to put my foot in my mouth. Not so much in business, but socially, things can get awkward real fast. I don't want to scare Carly away."

"Fine. I believe in you, and I know you'll do what's best for the two of you."

"You've always been there for me. You don't know how much I appreciate your loyalty."

Stunned by his sentiment, she was initially speechless. Lowering her head to avoid eye contact, she swallowed hard. "Stop it right now. Stop embarrassing me, boy, and finish eating your sandwich." She walked out of the room.

"Wow. Marlena didn't have a quick comeback for me, and no headaches. All of this in the same day. This has got to be my lucky day. Better get back to work so I can be finished by the time Carly gets home." He resumed work on the project on his computer.

"Carly's coming home. I like the sound of that."

His phone rang. He picked it up and looked at the screen. It was his mother. Taking the call, he placed it on speaker.

"Mason..." She paused. He heard the sound of her flipping through papers. "I just received a letter from your grandfather's lawyers on Broad Street. They sent it by courier to me." She sighed. "I called and told them that you were his personal representative. I thought you had already closed out his estate, but they said you would receive information about another trust he established before his death."

"I did, Mom." Mason looked up at Marlena coming into the room with a large brown envelope.

"This was just delivered." She placed it on the desk and turned to leave.

Looking at the envelope, he saw that it was addressed to him and had the name of the firm once used by his grandfather to handle his legal affairs in the top left corner.

"Are you still there?" Lucille's voice brought his attention back to the phone.

"Yes, I'm here." He picked up a letter opener and pried open the envelope. "I just got a delivery too. I'm sure it's nothing pressing. I did take care of everything years ago and closed his estate."

"Okay, I'll look at it and give you a chance to review it before we talk about it."

"Sounds good." He flipped through the pages.

A notification came up on his screen.

Alert. Important.

"Mom, I have to go." He clicked on the alert. "There's something at the office I need to address."

"Okay. Goodbye." She hung up while he frowned and responded to the alert.

Chapter

21

The sun was starting to set when Carly opened the door to Mace's home office.

"Hey, Mace." Carly came toward him with a sway to her hips before standing to the side of his chair. Leaning forward, she hugged him around the neck and kissed the top of his head.

"You've been gone all day." He turned his chair around and looked up at her. "I missed you."

"I missed you too, darling." This time she placed a kiss on his lips.

He pulled her down onto his lap.

"Darn it. Give me a minute. I forgot to take my pill. It's important that I take it at the same time every day. I'll be right back."

"Don't let me stop you." He rubbed her butt.

Why is he so happy? I'm going to take a pill. What's so exciting about that?

She looked over her shoulder at him for a moment before

exiting the office. She headed to the bedroom, remembering she had placed the pocketbook containing her bottle of pills on the nightstand. While popping one in her mouth, she saw something out of the corner of her eye. On a desk near the bed, there was a small gift box with a card attached.

"'I hope you like it. Love, Mace.'" She read the card out loud and tore open the colorful paper wrapped around the gift.

Gasping, she covered her mouth and screamed. Inside was something she could not imagine – a beautiful large pearl necklace with a sparkling diamond pendant hanging from it. There was also a matching diamond ring in a highly polished platinum setting.

She hurried back down the hall and found him in the dining room. "Mace, you shouldn't have."

He was standing there waiting for her as she flung herself into his arms. Planting kisses along the angle of his jaw, she tantalized him, sucking the tender skin down his neck. She looked up before kissing his mouth, open wide as if anticipating a sweet treat. He leaned in to kiss her as she eagerly received his tongue lavishing her mouth. Wrapping her legs around his waist, she leaned against his firm chest and felt the beat of his heart thumping in rhythm with her own. It reminded her of what she really hungered for. Him. His love.

God help me. I'm still in love with this man.

He placed his hands in her hair. She trembled as he pressed her hips against his erection, keeping her in a close embrace. She felt precious to him as he looked into her eyes. She moaned, enjoying the heat of passion between them.

"I'm going to assume you like it." He smiled and placed her back on her feet.

She caressed his face with the back of her hand before placing the box on the table. "I love it, but we agreed not to buy each other more Christmas gifts."

"It's not a Christmas gift. That was four days ago." He kept her close, tenderly running his fingers down her spine.

She melted in his arms as he continued to stare into her eyes. "I didn't think I needed to tell you not to get me a Kwanzaa gift either." She kissed him again. "Thanks. The jewelry is beautiful. It took my breath away."

"You're welcome, but the gift isn't to celebrate the holidays. I've had this set to give to you for years. No one can ever tell me I'm not a patient man. I've waited five years for this moment to give them to you and, baby, you didn't disappoint." He nibbled at her neck and inhaled her scent. "You smell so good."

"You're kidding me, Mace." She hit his chest in disbelief.

"No, I'm not. The set belonged to my grandmother. After I inherited it, I knew immediately they belonged to you, gracing your neck and finger."

"But, Mace..." She searched his eyes and found no answers for his desire to give such an extravagant gift to her, especially since with each passing year the chances of a reconciliation seemed more remote.

"Let's see how it looks on you." He took the necklace out of the box and placed it around her neck.

She touched the strand, silky smooth and cool to the touch, then placed her fingers on the diamond pendant. He observed her as she felt the necklace before he took the ring out of the box. Conscious of her actions, she balled up her left hand.

"I can't, Mace." She pulled her hands away from him as she dug her fingernails into her palms to slow her heart rate.

"Don't worry, babe. It's a right-hand ring. I'm not trying to play this to my advantage. Neither one of us is ready for an engagement. I accept it, for now." He took her right hand and placed the ring on her finger. "Perfect." He held up her hand, admiring the beauty of the ring.

"It is perfect." Her eyes glistened as she covered her mouth with her left hand.

"Let's go over to the mirror so you can see how lovely you look. These pearls were purchased originally for my grandmother, but now they belong to you. I knew it the first time I saw them."

She looked at her reflection. The pendant sparkled as the light from the candles Mace had lit while she was in the bedroom bounced off it. Brilliant flashes from the large stone danced around the room to the rhythm of her breath, giving it movement as she drew in air and released it.

"Please don't misunderstand me, but I don't want you to feel you need to purchase my affections." Her words were delivered delicately, but with a firm resolve. She looked at him in the mirror, standing behind her. Leaning against him, molding her body into his, she smiled as he brought his arms around her waist.

"Carly, I've purchased the goodwill of others in the past. Trust me, I'll never do that again." He nuzzled her neck and planted warm kisses below her jaw.

"My parents once told me to be cautious because what is purchased can be sold, but some things can't ever be bought." She placed her hand on top of his, still wrapped around her waist.

"Here's the only way I can put this. I'm a rich man, but I know I don't have enough money to purchase your love. I'll have to earn it and I'm willing to work hard to deserve it."

She turned around and guided his head to hers, kissing him until they were both panting and breathless.

Marlena opened the door, interrupting them, carrying a white gown wrapped in plastic. "I almost forgot about this. I got a courier to go to the dressmaker before they locked up for the day. They called and reminded me to come pick up the dress since they were closing early for the holidays. I would have remembered, but I got distracted."

"Thanks, Marlena. I meant to go get it, but I forgot too."

"That's all right. Carly, the dress will look wonderful on you at the New Year's Eve party."

Carly brushed Mace's arms away from around her waist and moved closer to Marlena. "Did I miss something?" She turned to face him. "I wasn't aware we were going to a formal affair. When did you get a dress for me?"

"I told you about it, Carly." His phone began ringing. He pulled it out and looked at the screen. "I have to take this. Excuse me." He left the room.

"Marlena, he never mentioned a party." Carly looked at her, blinking as she searched her mind for a recollection of that discussion.

"I know he probably told you not to go to his doctor's appointment with him, but he has been more forgetful since the attack." Marlena handed over the dress. "His company has a party every year in New York. I'm sure he's convinced he told you about it. Someone needs to go with him, Carly. I'm beginning to worry about him. He knows there is something wrong, because while you were gone, he was in his office the entire time working on his speech. It has never taken him that long to write one."

"He gives a speech at a New Year's Eve party?" She tilted her head, curious about the nature of the party.

"I understand that it's a tradition started by his grandfather. I don't think anyone can get him to end the tradition. He couldn't see that his grandfather was a lonely old man. After his wife died, he moved the company meeting to New Year's Eve in order to ensure he didn't spend that night alone. It was sad. The old man only had Mason, and before you came back into his life, Mason only had his business."

"That can't be true. He has a family who loves him." Carly refused to agree with Marlena's assessment.

"He loves them, but he doesn't allow too many adults to get very close to him. He's a good man, but he's busy. Maybe too busy. He beats himself up when he makes mistakes, as if anyone on God's earth is perfect. He needs you and he knows it." She pressed her fist to her mouth. "Maybe I've said too much, but I need to alert you that Jamillah will probably be at the party."

Carly's eyes widened and her jaw dropped. "What? You think Jamillah is coming to the party?"

"Yep. I think she comes every year."

"What the hell?" she sputtered, clutching her pearls. "So, I'm supposed to accept he hasn't gotten over his ex-wife?"

"I've known you since you were a little girl. You're smart. What I'm asking you is to help *her* get over *him*."

Carly flung her head back and looked at the ceiling.

Without further explanation, Marlena walked away.

"What have I gotten myself into?" Carly paced the floor. "Mace," she called out. "We need to talk, now." She walked out of the room to find him.

Chapter

22

Mace was sitting in the office. "What's the matter?" He rose from the seat behind his desk after Carly stormed in.

"There are a lot of things we need to talk about." She marched into the room. "Let's start with our visit to your mother's home. Man, was I in for a treat." She began pacing in front of him. "Your mother and Kate spilled the tea...all over me. I was trying to protect you by just filing it in my head for future reference, but it's beginning to mess with my mind." She threw her hands in the air then grasped the side of her head, massaging her temples. "I get to hear from everyone except you about a party and...Jamillah is going to be there."

Moving toward the desk, she leaned against it on the opposite side from him. She looked into his eyes. "This isn't working for me, Mason. There are just too many things you're keeping from me. I feel like I'm walking through a minefield, and something is going to blow up at any time."

He walked around the desk and took her into his arms. "I

know."

"You *don't* know, Mace." She pulled away from him. "There's something wrong that you refuse to face. There are big gaps in your memory. I told you that I'm concerned about it and you seem indifferent to it." She allowed him to take her hand and guide her toward the couch.

"Have a seat."

She took her time sitting down. As if needing to protect herself, she turned away, crossing her arms and legs.

"I see what's going on." He turned her head, causing her to maintain eye contact. "Carly, I've heard that word, indifferent, from my family for a long time now."

She tried to turn away, but he cupped her face with his hand, wiping away a tear with his thumb.

He sighed, looking up at the ceiling. "After I took that hit on the football field, I was seen in the emergency room and sent home to rest. One month later, I was still having headaches. My ears were ringing, and my memory had turned to mush."

She repositioned her body to face him as they joined hands. "I didn't know, Mace. Why didn't you tell me?"

"I was ashamed, Carly. I felt I was weak." He let out a deep breath. "I couldn't control my anger and after I started punching walls and throwing things, my parents arranged to have me placed in a rehab facility for a few months. It turned out to be a good decision. The staff taught me techniques to remain calm under the most stressful situations. It worked for me in business." He squeezed her hands. "I learned how to not crack under pressure, but as far as my personal affairs went, I came off as *indifferent*. Some people even thought I was an asshole. Sound familiar?"

She raised her eyebrows and ghosted a smile.

"After I got better, I tried to come to you to explain, but by that time, you had started seeing Tyson. I didn't want to stand in the way of your happiness."

"I started spending time with Tyson because he was trying to help me cope with our breakup."

"I realized that later. I'm telling you the truth now because I know we can make this work. I can't do this alone, Carly. I need your help. I've seen my doctor and so far, things look good. He thinks I should avoid too much pressure. I'm not in the same place I was ten years ago."

"What about the party slash business meeting in New York, or Jamillah?" She came closer.

"It's too late to cancel the party." He stroked the back of her hands with his thumbs. "If you don't want to go, I'll understand."

"Of course I'm going with you."

"Thank you." He kissed the palm of her hand. "Carly, I'm sorry we got our wires crossed." He rubbed his temple. "I thought I told you about the party, but the knock on my head may have rattled me more than I thought it did."

"How many hits did you take on the football field in addition to the hit you took a few days ago?" she wondered.

"The small ones on the football field are too many to count."

She looked at him with soft, caring eyes. "I'm concerned about you. I'd like to go to your next follow-up with your doctor to make sure you're telling him everything, if you don't mind."

"Don't worry about me. I'm feeling better."

"You're complaining less of headaches. I've also noticed you do better when you've gotten rest and aren't stressed."

"I agree, and I rest better when you're in bed next to me."

"Yes, and I've given myself the excuse that I need to be next to you at night to make sure you're all right." She kissed him on the cheek.

"You'll never need an excuse to be in our bed. I've been saving that space for you for a long time. I want you in my bed, not just to see that I'm still breathing or not having a nightmare, but because I love you. I want you to be the last person I see before I close my eyes and the first person I see when I'm blessed to wake up."

Carly rose from her seat and kissed him, touching him tenderly as if he was a precious jewel. "I'm concerned about all the hits you've taken. I feel strongly that we should go to a specialist."

"I'm not on the field anymore and other than the incident a few days ago, this hard head of mine hasn't taken a blow in years, but I'll think about it after the new year. I would stress less if I knew you were going to be here longer than a week. And as far as Jamillah is concerned, I'm not in love with her anymore. Our relationship is purely professional. She has a stake in a subsidiary we jointly own. I let her run it as she sees fit and it's profitable."

"Are you talking about the *Moore for You* lifestyle brand?"

"Yes, it was Jamillah's brainchild." He pursed his lips. "She was relentless when it came to pressuring me to finance the venture and she insisted that I remain a silent partner. I eventually provided the capital, but the products we sold… all Jamillah's idea."

"And the branding for the company?" She bit her lip, having seen the ads on social media and in magazines. "*Unforgettable. Enchanting. Love for a lifetime.*"

"Yeah, she green-lights all the ads." He raised an eyebrow. "You seem to know a lot about the company."

She shrugged. "Not a lot. I've just seen the ads."

"You ran across the ads while you were conducting historical research?" A sly smile appeared across his face.

"Okay." She rolled her eyes. "I googled Jamillah. The ads I saw for the company were interesting."

"Well, I won't be concerned about her business decisions much longer. I was planning to ask Evan to see if we can come up with a plan to buy her out or sell the company."

"Thanks for sharing that, but some members of your family think—"

"Oh yeah, that." He nodded. "They're probably concerned that I'll suffer a relapse and drive you away like I've driven others away."

"That's not going to happen." She placed her hand around his neck. "Not as long as we communicate with each other. No, I think they're concerned about our future together. That you're just interested in business, not in having a family." She bit her lip. "Mace, do you want children?"

"The idea of being a father hasn't crossed my mind recently, but sure, I'm open to discussing it in the future."

"What are you looking for in a mate?" She held her breath waiting for his answer.

"If you're asking who I want as my wife, it's you, Carly, but I don't want to pressure you."

"I don't want to be pressured either, but I want to be clear. If you want a woman to sit at home until you come back with gifts, I'm honestly not the one for you. I need a man who is present in my life. My father worked long hours running his business while my mother stayed at home faithfully supporting his dreams. I know you loved my mother, but I'm not her. I have my own dreams." The truth of it was in her eyes. She would not be deterred. "I've let one man turn my life into a nightmare. I'd rather go it alone than have that happen again."

"I get it, Carly. No designer bags, expensive outfits, or jewelry for you. You don't want a guilty, absent partner." He crossed his arms. "I won't be able to buy your affections."

"I'm serious, Mace. The clock is ticking for both of us. We either take advantage of the time we have to rediscover each other, or we lose the opportunity."

"I'll do anything to win you back."

"Even if it means giving up the ghosts of the past or surrendering something that was once dear to you?" Her heart skipped a beat. Would *she* have to give up her own closely held secrets?

"I swear to you, if that's what it takes, so be it. Love is about sacrifice." He took her into his arms, holding on to her tightly.

Chapter

23

What's in that red suitcase with my name on it? I didn't pack that bag." She looked behind her at the baggage handlers placing their things on the plane heading to New York.

"Marlena packed the gown I had made for you. The jewels and accessories to match are also in the suitcase."

"That was nice of you to have a dress custom-made for me, but it's white." She ascended the stairs to Mace's private jet. "I brought something else instead that I thought would be appropriate to wear. This is the holiday season. We're supposed to be festive and colorful. Did you want me to wear a white gown in December?"

"Trust me, white is perfect for the party." He gazed at her with a warm smile. "I'm sorry I didn't share all of the details with you, but my grandfather always had a beautiful white dress made for my grandmother when he was the CEO. She was the queen of the ball. He liked her in white. That was their tradition." He shrugged. "Besides, you know there's such a thing as a winter white gown."

She gave him a sharp, side-eyed glance, uncertain that he knew anything about female fashion. "If you believe it's perfect for the occasion, fine." She sat down in her seat. "It's your little soiree."

"I don't throw 'little soirees.' It's a big party and all of my employees working at the New York offices will be there." He grinned and took his seat beside her.

"Will we be staying at your home in New York?" She was curious about the place where he spent most of his time. His apartment in Charleston was very nice, but it wasn't the space he currently called home.

"Not this time. It's not close to where we're having the party. I usually stay at the hotel in Times Square because of the crowds gathered for New Year's Eve. My employees don't think I know it, but I see them slipping out of the party to join in with the crowd at midnight, see the ball drop, then come back inside." He chuckled.

Carly didn't think it was funny, but it obviously had become an inside joke. "Let me understand this. You have this New Year's Eve party every year and some of your guests leave at midnight? So, what's the point?"

"That's true." He shrugged. "It's hard to explain, but some of it is company culture. You'll see when you get there."

Carly wasn't sure he understood why his grandfather needed the *party*, but since he still hadn't said much more about Jamillah, she was at least going to know more about the event before they got there.

"Tell me, will there at least be food and dancing?"

"Of course there will be food, and plenty of it." He laughed good-naturedly, the one that rumbled in his chest before filling a room with good vibes when he found something genuinely funny.

Carly always smiled and laughed with him when she heard it. She couldn't help it. His laughter was one of the things she loved the most about him.

"What should I expect?" She turned to face him.

"You'll have fun." He patted her hand. "Don't look at it like it's only an obligation with a formal agenda. If it will make you feel more comfortable, here's all you need to know. First, we'll start out receiving guests, have a few cocktails, then sit down to a full-service meal before I talk." He raised his hand, bringing his index finger and thumb closer together. "Just a little business, then we'll close out the night with dancing. I'll keep it short, just for you. Doesn't that sound like a fun night?"

"Yes, but business at a party? Come on, Mace. It sounds like a camouflaged corporate meeting, not a party."

He raised his brow, then answered her question. "When I give out the year-end bonuses, believe me, my folks will have a reason to party for the entire year." He crossed his arms and jutted out his chin.

"Why not give the bonuses out before Christmas, then?" Their back-and-forth banter reminded her of the times he taught her to play chess. "Check." She cocked her head and smiled.

"Because I give them the bonuses New Year's Eve. Checkmate." He looked her in the eye and smirked.

"Well, of course, that makes more sense." She had no choice but to smile brightly at him after he filled the cabin with his disarming and beyond-charming laughter.

He was always better at making strategic moves. She had to concede – his company, his rules. She looked at him. That was her Mace, the man who knew how to take the lead and used it to his advantage.

She knit her brow as he placed his satchel on the chair in front of him and took out his notes.

* * *

They had arrived in New York with plenty of time for a power nap at the hotel before heading downstairs to the party.

Mace had awakened earlier than Carly and was in the front of the suite waiting for her. He checked the time and headed toward the bedroom. He was surprised she hadn't finished dressing and was sitting at the vanity dresser, applying the finishing touches to her makeup. He stopped at the doorway.

She looked up as Mace came closer. He was dressed in a white tuxedo jacket and white shirt, with a black bow tie and slacks that flattered his tall, muscular shape. It fit like he had been poured into it.

"Wow. Don't you look good? I could stare at you for hours and then take my time coaxing you out of that suit." She threw him an air kiss.

"Thank you, but I thought you would be dressed by now. As much as I would love to strip you out of your robe, baby, we've got to go, or we'll be late. It's tradition to start on time and end on time." He paced near the door, betraying his outwardly cool demeanor.

"I'm almost done." She turned back to the mirror and applied her mascara.

"Take your time, but I need to go downstairs and check on a few things. I'll meet you in the ballroom."

"What are you saying?" That was not a part of the plan. "Are you going to leave me to enter the ballroom by myself?"

She'd thought she would be going to the party on the arm of the host. She'd hoped it would help others know who she was and her connection to Mason.

"I figured we had more time before going downstairs." Carly's heart skipped a beat as she looked at her reflection. Her hair was still pinned up. She wanted a little more time to apply her makeup.

Too much chocolate on the cruise. She frowned as she looked at the little pimples that had appeared after daily consumption of a small treat for dessert.

Her dress was still hanging in the corner, neat and steam-pressed. "Don't you want to be the first one to see me in my dress?" She pushed her chest forward slightly and gave him a coy smile, the one that always caught his attention.

He smiled as he took slow steps toward her. He kissed the top of her head. After helping her onto her feet, he kissed her lips, and then lowered his head to caress the mounds of her breasts with his warm lips. "As much as I would love to have the honor of watching you model the dress for the first time for me and only me, I have to go. There will be staff on standby ready to escort you downstairs. There's a company phone in the outer room. Press eight and a special attendant will be dispatched to bring you, my queen, to me. Don't worry, we got this, right?"

"Right." She cast her gaze downward as he looked into the pocket of his jacket and pulled out a small card with his notes written on it.

Sure. We got this. She knew that would be the mantra for the night because she wasn't so sure if she could hold up her part of the bargain. She wasn't sure what role she was cast in and she hadn't met the ensemble of characters yet. Mason, so far, was short on answers.

She felt his hand nudging her shoulder and looked up at him.

"Did you hear me? You seemed a thousand miles away. I said I was going downstairs."

"Yes, I heard you." She leaned in to meet him halfway as he was about to give her another kiss.

"See you in a bit. Remember, you're my girl and you've always been my girl. Keep that in mind as you field all the questions I'm sure you're going to get."

"Mace—"

"No, Carly. We're doing it the way we planned. You'll be on my arm tonight. I'm the host and you're the hostess. You'll be great. See you soon. I love you."

"I love you too, Mace." She moved closer to him and placed her arms around his waist as he stood above her stroking the side of her face.

"No pressure, Carly. You're doing me a great favor. I gave you a complete rundown of what to expect already. Have you forgotten?" He tilted his head. "I just want you to have fun."

She looked at him, sensing there was no need to remind him that he hadn't given her the full story. That ship had already sailed. "I *plan* to have fun, and afterward, you'll return the favor by giving me your body. Sir, I'm taking what's mine." She pressed against him, feeling his boner rising.

"Stop it, Carly, before you make me a no-show. Bye." His laughter filled the room again as he backed away from her and waved before he left the room.

She waved goodbye, absently knowing she needed to go to his next doctor's appointment with him since he continued to remember things that hadn't happened, things he'd imagined he had discussed while continuing to forget things that were important, like what were her hostess duties? Who were the important players and what should she know about them? She placed her hands on the sides of her head, rubbing her temples. She knew the hit he'd taken to his head was serious. She sighed, uncertain of how to convince him of it.

"Oh well, at least for tonight, I'll try to enjoy myself." She turned back to the mirror and resumed applying her makeup.

If she needed to cover his memory lapses, she would do the best she could. His employees would understand she was new to the scene and that was why she was asking so many questions. That would be the cover she would use. Asking things about their roles in the company would be the deflection she would use to get through the night. She took a deep breath and smiled, comfortable with her look for the evening. All of those issues swirling around her gave her less time to obsess about possibly meeting Jamillah.

"Maybe she won't be there," she said out loud and frowned as she wondered how she had gotten herself into this situation. "Right. In my dreams."

She finished arranging her curls and rose to get the diamond jewelry set Mace had given her. Returning to her seat in front of the vanity, she put on the jewelry. As she fastened the necklace, she contemplated all that Kate had shared with her. Instead of letting her nerves get the best of her, she drew strength from the times she had sat before her mother's vanity, solving her most pressing problems while her mother helped style her hair. With recollections of overcoming past challenges, she took in a deep breath of renewed confidence.

"I got this," she repeated as she looked at her reflection. "There's nothing Mace and I can't handle together."

The cellphone buzzed, revealing the time.

"Oh shit. Where has the time gone?"

She got up and removed the dress from the satin-lined hanger and stepped into it. She had to admit Mace had good taste in clothing. He looked fantastic and the gown he had designed for her was a white, floor length, elegantly laced and beaded, sleeveless couture dress. Simply gorgeous.

It had been a long time, but she remembered how much he liked lace on a woman. It was just enough to make her look feminine yet alluringly sexy at the same time. The dress was formal, but cinched at her waist with flowing lines that accentuated her curves. After zipping it up, she looked at herself in the mirror.

"You clean up pretty good, girl, if I say so myself." She smoothed out a loose strand of hair before putting on her shoes and grabbing her bag. She picked up the black phone on the table and called for her escort.

"It's showtime." She smiled to steady her nerves and pressed the number eight.

"Someone will be right up, Ms. Rivers," the person on the other end told her before she could inform them of her request.

"I'll be waiting." She hung up.

Chapter

24

T here was a knock at the door. She heard an authoritative voice announcing the arrival of her escort. "Ms. Rivers, we're ready to escort you."

Opening the door, she saw a man dressed in a sharp black suit standing before her.

"I'm ready. Lead the way." Closing the door behind her, she followed the man down the long hall to the waiting elevator that transported them to the lower floors where the elegantly appointed ballrooms were located.

"Mr. Moore wanted me to direct you to the photographer waiting for you. He said you'll understand when you reach the space."

She walked along the gleaming black marble floor. "Sure, but I don't want to be late because I'm taking pictures." She tried to pick up the pace, but her escort continued to take slow, measured steps as he led her past the sparkling light fixtures and walls of mirrors reflecting the light.

"Don't worry about the time," he assured her. "He planned

for the delay."

Carly looked to the left after they passed the signs pointing to the Poinsettia Ballroom and smiled. In a small alcove was a Queen Anne style chair below a large picture of a scene in Charleston surrounded by a gathering of bright red poinsettia plants.

"This must be the space." She pointed over to the area decorated with a holiday vignette.

A woman with a camera strap around her neck and camera in her hand came forward to greet them. "Hello, Ms. Rivers. I'm Bev Allen. Do you mind if I take pictures of you? This won't take long."

"Of course. What would you like me to do?" Carly stopped and awaited Bev's instruction.

"First, let's get a few shots of you sitting down and then I'll take some shots of you standing in front of the chair."

Carly posed for the photos, including full-length shots.

Bev's assistant scurried around straightening out her gown and helping her strike the poses.

Bev completed the last series of shots. "There, we're done. Mr. Moore will love seeing these. You're very photogenic." She scrolled through the collection of photos she had taken on the camera's small screen.

"Thank you so much." Carly turned to the escort to continue on their path to the ballroom where Mace awaited her arrival. After a few more steps, he stopped in front of ornate double doors that were closed.

"Watch your step, ma'am." Two staff members dressed in tuxedoes stood on either side of the doors. "There's carpet in the ballroom and the flooring is a little elevated at this point. Be careful." They pointed to the floor then opened the doors.

She stood in front of the room with her hands held

together at her waist, awaiting the word to proceed.

No trumpets blew heralding her arrival, but everyone turned their heads in her direction and watched as she walked into the room. She looked up, locking her eyes on Mace as he stepped out of the crowd, handsome in his tuxedo. The lights were still bright and illuminated his gorgeous smile with its slight dimple in his cheek. She felt like she was in a dream, a fairytale, and the only thing missing was the pronouncement that the queen had arrived, ready to take her place beside the king.

Mace hurried toward her and planted a chaste kiss on her lips, covered in her favorite red lipstick.

"This is for you." He placed a small bouquet of white flowers surrounding small red tea roses tied in white satin ribbons around her wrist.

"Thank you, Mace. The corsage is beautiful." She beamed at him.

"Baby, you're hot... Like, *smoking* hot. Let me introduce you to some folks who I'm sure are salivating over you right now."

"But which ones bite?" she was quick to respond.

He leaned his head back and laughed, immediately calming the accelerating beats of her heart. Instead of using the center aisle, he led her to the side of the room, near a bar, and whispered in her ear, "You look lovelier than I could ever have imagined. You don't know how many times I've awakened from dreams of you walking toward me in a beautiful white dress while I'm standing before you, bursting with joy."

A small bead of sweat wet her brow. Her mouth became dry as she conjured up mental images of a wedding. She always enjoyed a fancy wedding, but the thought of marriage made her feel a bit faint.

"Are you all right?" He held her arm as she swooned.

"Yes, I'm fine." She covered the emotions warring inside with a smile.

He motioned to one of the waiters to bring her a glass of water.

She took it, drinking the cool liquid, which refreshed her resolve to make the best of the evening.

"Thank you for everything, Mace. The dress, the jewelry, and for this week. I can't tell you the last time I've had so much fun – all except the assault, of course."

"My pleasure, and I'll do more to keep you happy for the rest of our lives."

As if someone had made an announcement, his employees came forward and formed a line, greeting them.

"I guess it's time for the receiving line," she whispered.

As she shook the hand of one guest after another, she thought her skin would chafe from greeting those who held her hand too tightly and too long for comfort.

"I think we've greeted almost everyone here. Let's sit down before the fun begins." He led her to a table with multiple place settings.

She was curious. There were no name cards placed in front of the settings like the ones she saw on the other tables. The gathering, so far, had appeared very well organized, so she didn't think the absence of place cards was an oversight.

He pulled out a chair and held it before pushing it closer to the table. "Are you comfortable? This is our table. We'll be joined by the others shortly."

She felt a large weight fall to the bottom of her stomach. She ingested the word *others* with dread that it included Jamillah, who had yet to make an appearance.

He took a seat beside her and began looking at his watch. "I had a surprise for you, but I guess I'll give it to you later. We're running a bit behind."

"Don't worry about it. You have enough going on." She smiled. "I've had enough surprises to last awhile."

"I need to check on something." He looked around the room. "I hope there's nothing wrong. Will you excuse me?"

"Of course, I'll be right here waiting."

He kissed her and got up from the table.

Music was playing in the background and people were finding their tables and talking to their tablemates while she sat at the front table by herself.

"Excuse me, ma'am, I don't mean to disturb you, but Mr. Moore always waits until the program is about to start before he places name cards at his table. It's kind of a tradition," a woman dressed in a tuxedo told her as she laid the cards on the table.

Carly looked at the titles of the folks who would be seated there. Her and Mace, the CEO, then the CFO, the board chairman, the chairman emeritus, and their wives. She took in a breath to steady her nerves as she wondered what she would add to the small talk. Minutes were ticking away as the waitstaff scurried around with trays of appetizers and drinks.

"Where are my tablemates?" She pondered briefly what others would think of her scrolling through her messages, but she took her phone out of her purse and placed it just beneath the top of the table to flip through them. Some of the other guests were also doing it, so why not?

"It looks like you're bored, that's why not," she murmured to herself while looking over her shoulder at a man she had greeted earlier. Out of the corner of her eye, she watched as he lingered around in the shadows, trying to look as if he wasn't observing her. She wished she could remember his name to ask Mace about him, but she couldn't.

"Carly."

She turned her head in the direction of familiar voices. Her two best friends were waving as they came toward her table.

"OMG! What are you two doing here?" She kept looking back and forth between them, pinching herself, wondering if she was dreaming. She squealed with delight and did a little happy dance. "I can't believe this!" She greeted them with hugs and kisses.

They both laughed.

Carly just kept staring, waiting for an explanation.

"Sorry we're late, Carly," Yara, always the spokesperson for the three of them, told her as she stepped back from their embrace. "Mason asked if we could get here before you made it to the table. Oops, we didn't." She shrugged. "Anyway, surprise!"

"We didn't know your rich boyfriend was sending us an invitation to his fancy party *and* paying for our formal attire," Ariel added as they stood together in front of the table.

He did?

"Where can we get a drink?" Yara looked around the room.

Carly pointed and showed them the way to the bar, where the bartender prepared each of them a drink. Carly moved them to the more-secluded quiet area where the receiving line had formed earlier so they could talk.

"Look at you, Carly! You look amazing!" Both of her girls eyed her dress and jewelry in awe.

"You look like money, girl!" Yara said, looking at her from head to toe.

"Thank you." She tilted her head and smiled. "Wait a minute. Did you say Mace sent both of you formal attire?"

"He had one of his assistants coordinate with stylists in our hometown and sent each of us the most gorgeous crème and gold dresses with matching jewelry." They primped and turned slowly in front of Carly.

"We didn't know we were coming to such a swanky affair. Did you, by chance, tell Mace we didn't have anything fancy enough to wear?"

"I'm just as surprised to be here as the two of you. I found out about it a few days ago and I sure didn't tell Mace that—"

"Never mind." Yara waved away her comments, interrupting her again. "After I saw my dress, I at least wanted my nails done at one of the fancy salons around here." She extended her hand in front of Carly. "Hell, I barely had time to let them dry before the limo was outside waiting to pick us up."

Ariel nodded. "Then we got stuck in traffic. I hope Mace won't be angry. You've got to straighten this out for us, girlfriend."

"He didn't seem angry about anything. I guess you two were the surprise he promised me. I'm so happy you could come, girlfriends." She beamed with so much joy that others passing by gave her big smiles in return.

"So, what do you think about this? Instead of being besties, we could be sister-wives. You know, we could all marry Mason and share," Ariel suggested, laughing.

"No." Carly shook her head and sipped her drink before giggling.

"Well, at least you could let us borrow the jewelry. He told us we could keep everything purchased for us, but girlfriend, you look like a queen with that bling."

Yara covered her eyes as if blinded by the light bouncing off the large diamond pendant hanging from the pearl necklace.

"That's a hard no. These pieces belonged to Mace's grandmother, so they have sentimental value."

"Interesting," they said in unison and widened their eyes.

"I felt like a duchess in this dress, but Carly, you're definitely the queen." Ariel hugged her again.

Mason found them and came over to join them in the circle. "I'm glad the two of you finally made it. I was starting to get worried. Welcome to the party." He opened his arms wide enough to give Yara and Ariel hugs at the same time.

"Sorry we're late," they told him.

"You're not too late." He raised his eyebrows. "We have a few more minutes left before the dinner and program start."

"Great, so we can run back to make sure the bellmen placed our luggage in the right room?"

"I can have someone check on that for you, but sure, you have time if you'd like to freshen up, or you can use the private hospitality room adjacent to the ballroom. I'll give Carly the code and—"

One of his assistants came over and whispered in his ear.

"Paul, could you show these ladies where the hospitality room is located while I check on this situation? Also, can you make sure their bags are in their rooms?"

"Of course, Mr. Moore. Follow me." He took them to a side room, hidden from view, and punched in a code. He opened the door to a large suite of rooms with drinks and refreshments and a media center and bathrooms.

Yara peeped into several of the rooms, ensuring they were the only ones in the suite before continuing their candid conversation with one another.

"Let me guess, Carly, Mason picked out that dress for you. Am I right?" Ariel asked.

"It's gorgeous and it shows off your curves. It really shows off your ass nicely." Yara walked around her, smiling as Carly modelled the dress.

"Thanks, and yes, Mace did pick it out," she told them.

"Do you realize you look like a bride who hasn't put on her veil yet? I'm willing to bet he's going to propose to you tonight," Ariel told her.

"Did he tell you that?" She began wringing her hands and looked at the counter with folded cotton napkins placed on it. Grabbing one of them, she wiped away the moisture beading in the palms of her hands.

"Don't sweat it, Carly. He didn't say anything to us about it, but I've got a funny feeling, that's all. What man would ask their date to wear a long white gown to a New Year's Eve party where everyone else is in bright colors except me and Ariel?"

"It's a festive holiday affair, and besides, we're not ready for marriage." She placed her arms across her chest as if needing to cover and protect her heart.

"I hear you, but don't be surprised."

They all turned at the sound of footsteps and voices buzzing outside the door. The noise seeped into the room, demanding their attention.

"What's going on?" Carly was checking her lipstick as Ariel cracked open the door and inclined her ear to hear what was happening.

"People are whispering, 'Jamillah's here,'" Ariel said.

"What the hell kind of *Twilight Zone* mess is going on here? Didn't you tell us Jamilah was Mason's ex-wife? I'm going out to see who this Jamillah is. Come on, Carly." Yara began gathering her bag and walking to the door.

Carly took a deep breath and steeled her nerves. She resolved it was time to finally have her meeting with Jamillah. "You two go ahead and make yourselves comfortable at the table or refresh your drinks. I'll be right out."

"We can wait for you if you need to use the bathroom." Yara offered her support.

"No, I'm sure. I'll be right behind you. Dinner should be served soon." Carly took in another breath.

"All right. I want to get a look at this Jamillah." Yara walked out of the room with Ariel in tow.

Carly went to relieve herself and stopped in her tracks as she exited the bathroom. Standing near the door was a tall woman with an elegant swan-like neck and smooth, flawless skin wearing her hair in an updo of intricate twists. Her lashes were silken and long. Her makeup was the perfect complement to her outfit.

Jamillah. Clad in a bronze couture dress, she dramatized her appearance by caressing her perfectly round baby bump.

Carly's mouth opened and closed quickly. "She's pregnant." The words spilled out under her breath after the woman she knew had to be Jamillah turned and disarmed the keypad inside the door, locking it manually before she walked into the center of the room.

As she approached, she smiled, showing her dimples. There was no denying it. She looked divine. "Hello, I'm Jamillah. You must be Carly. I'm pleased to meet you." She extended her arm for a handshake.

Carly imagined Mason must have taken too many bumps to the head to let his gorgeous ex-wife go.

Chapter

25

I'm Carly Rivers." She held out her hand to greet Jamillah.

Jamillah's cocoa-brown hands, with their long, delicate fingers, smelled of an exotic fragrance as they encircled Carly's.

Carly's heart quickened as she kept her hand in Jamillah's grasp much longer than she felt was conventionally acceptable. It was quickly becoming awkward.

Here she was, in a locked room with Jamillah. She hadn't planned to be alone with her for their initial meeting, but she found something about Mace's ex-wife intriguing. With a resolve not to be the first to pull her hand away, her discomfort waned as she stared into the eyes of the stunning woman.

She knew Jamillah was sizing her up. She planned to measure up to any test, but… Kate was right. Jamillah's grace and beauty were disarming. Carly blinked as Jamillah slid her hand away then placed it along her graceful neck before she spoke.

"I'm assuming that was a gift from Mason?" She pointed to the pearl necklace.

Carly, stunned into silence, had to will her brain to speak. "Why, yes. So, you knew who I was before I introduced myself?" She looked at Jamillah, less out of awe than curiosity.

"Yes, I knew it was you. That's why I followed you to this room so we could speak in private. How could I not know who you are? Caroline Rivers, and you now go by the name Carly. Mason Moore's first true love." She laughed.

Carly felt she could taste the bitterness dripping from Jamillah.

"You didn't break up my marriage, but you were the ever-present ghost of the past. I just had to meet you, for my own sake, to have a few words with the woman who captured my husband's attention and affection, despite the fact that you left him a decade ago."

"I never—"

Jamillah cut her off with a wave of her hand before Carly could finish.

Carly closed her mouth. It was evident that Jamillah had played this scenario over and over in her head. As long as she could tolerate it, Carly decided to let her have her say.

Jamillah looked at her baby bump, then resumed staring at Carly. "Imagine living with your husband who kept his girlfriend's pictures. Mason put up all the pictures of you except the ones he kept locked away in the desk drawer in his office, but he was distracted one morning after a long night of working over reports and he left it open. I didn't have to look through his things because a picture of the two of you was on top. I asked him about it, but he blew it off, which made me angrier." She laughed again.

Carly shifted her weight from one foot to the other as Jamillah cast her eyes upward and looked away at a spot on the ceiling as if it was a portal that transported her back to painful memories from the past.

She shifted her gaze back to Carly. "That discovery began the pattern of arguments between us about you. To be honest, it often started over my jealousy of you, followed by some of the most intense, hot makeup sex." She sighed. "Forgive me. I digress, and truly, I have more important things to say…and ask of you. I also feel the need to warn you."

"Warn me? About what?" Carly smiled, trying to mask the heavy weight in her chest after hearing Mason indulged in hot, passionate sex with another woman.

She was his wife. She self-soothed by rubbing her chest below her collarbone to remind herself of that fact. Jamillah knew where to place the dagger.

"The necklace and ring are gorgeous on you," she remarked, looking down at Carly's hand.

"Thank you." Carly wasn't sure where the conversation was heading, but she hoped Jamillah would get to the point fast.

"Mason told me that jewelry set belonged to someone else. I was with him when it was delivered after the death of his grandfather." Her lips drew tight in a frown that distorted her beauty. "When I remarked how beautiful the set was, I assumed he would give it to me. When he didn't, I thought it was because it belonged to his mother. Figures he would give it to you." She wrinkled her nose as if she detected a foul smell.

"It could have been true that it was willed to his mother at the time you asked him." Carly rubbed her fingers along the silken pearls and turned away from Jamillah. Seeing her reflection in the mirror reminded her to keep her cool.

"Listen," Jamillah sighed. "Your timing couldn't have been worse."

"What are you talking about? My timing?" Carly cocked an eyebrow.

"Yes. I just closed on a very successful deal to continue the marketing campaign for my company. Are you familiar with luxury products made by *Moore for You*?"

"Oh, yes. Are you talking about the ads branded with actors who look like you and Mace?" Carly walked in a half-circle around Jamillah. "Your divorce is well-known in the media, but I noticed that you're selling beauty products that are supposed to make you memorable... unforgettable to any man. How does it go? 'Like a powerful goddess, you can cast a spell on him. Seize your moment.'"

Jamillah feigned a yawn. "I've made millions selling that illusion to women. So, since you seem to understand my marketing plan, I know you also understand why we can't have too many pictures of you and Mace on social media. The pictures of you and Mason in Charleston with hashtag MasonlovesCarly have to stop. I told my investors I would take care of anything that would hurt our bottom line."

"And take care of anyone?" Carly wrinkled her brow while a brief silence filled the room. "I don't control what folks in Charleston choose to post."

Jamillah rubbed her forehead. "What can I do to encourage discretion on your part, at least until we rethink our marketing options?" She took a step closer to Carly. "Can we speak later about compensation for your troubles? We can't have more events where it looks like you're the queen of the ball."

"I'm Mason's escort. Let's not assume that makes me his queen."

"Let me be clear, then. I can't afford it. If pictures of Mason with you in that dress are released, tongues are going to start wagging. I know he had it designed for you. I've done my homework too. I've seen those pictures of you, and none were in outfits like that." She gave Carly an appraising look.

"As you said, let me be clear. I won't be engaging in any *business* deals with you." Carly cast her attention to the door. "I'm sure Mace is wondering where I am. It was...interesting meeting you."

"Think about it." She rubbed her belly and smiled. "Think about your own self-interest, then. I don't want you to waste your time with someone who is a lying, cold-hearted monster." Her chest heaved as she made fists at her sides.

Uh, oh. Here we go. Carly stepped back as Jamillah's fake, syrupy smile morphed into unbridled hostility.

"Did Mason tell you he doesn't want children, or maybe, he can't father children? I wanted a child so badly and nothing happened."

Carly felt her heart sinking. She wasn't sure if she could hear this.

"I made lots of money as a supermodel, but I didn't care what effects pregnancy had on my body or my career. I just wanted us to be a family." She paused, placed her hands on her hips, and gazed at Carly with resolve. "My new husband and I had no problems creating life, so it wasn't me that caused us to be a childless couple. It was him. Carly, the man doesn't know how to give. He takes and takes until there's nothing left."

I've had enough of this witch. Carly let out a cleansing breath and focused on Jamilah's face, which just moments earlier she'd thought was enchanting. Now, she found her beauty contaminated and distorted by all the hostility and unresolved feelings about Mace. She remembered Marlena's challenge to intervene with Jamillah on behalf of Mason, but she knew better than to position herself between the two of them. *No way.*

"Jamillah, I don't think this conversation is necessary or appropriate. It was…nice to meet you, but I have guests waiting for me. Excuse me, please." Carly attempted to walk around her, but Jamillah stepped in her way, causing Carly to stop in her tracks to avoid bumping into the baby Jamillah was carrying.

"You'll want to hear this, Carly. Mason can be one of the most charming men you could ever meet, but underneath the façade is a demon, cold and calculating. That man married me knowing he was still in love with you." She choked on her words. "He broke my heart." Her voiced filled with emotion. "It took me years to heal from all the mess he put me through." She placed a fist to her mouth and closed her eyes to muffle a sob.

"Please, Jamillah, if you feel you have to do this, let's get it over with quickly. I came here to support Mace and to have a good time, not to dredge up the past. Besides, I had nothing to do with the relationship between you and him."

Jamillah laughed, the sound deep and threatening. "*Au contraire, ma chérie.* You had *everything* to do with what went wrong with our marriage. Don't get me wrong. I don't blame you. I lay all of it at Mason's feet. He pushed me into the arms of another man and when he found me in bed with him, do you know what he did?"

Carly backed away, shaking her head, and frowning as if a foul odor in the room was now assaulting her sensibilities. "This is TMI, Jamillah." She pivoted her feet. "I really don't need to hear this."

"Everyone I've talked to says you're a good person. Can't you see that what Mason did to me, he'll surely do to you? I'm just trying to warn you." Jamillah turned and looked toward the door. "I'll make it quick. What man catches another man in bed with his wife and does nothing but pause and tell them both to get out of his house? He gave me six minutes to grab my things and leave. He didn't defend his position as my husband. No, just an arctic-cold response. He has ice water running through his veins. I'll tell you what kind of man does that, an evil son of—"

She paused, letting out a big huff as her body shook while her eyes shot daggers at imagined people in the room. "And that family of his is like a bunch of locusts. They come over, eat all the food, and are around all the time."

"Stop it, Jamillah. Just stop it."

They both looked at the door, vibrating from someone pounding on it.

"I can see he hurt you and he hurt you badly. Your dreams of a life with him didn't come true." Carly looked at Jamillah's belly. "Move on with your life. Don't let your hard feelings be the reason you and your child are living in a nightmare."

A frantic voice coming from the other side interrupted them. "Carly? Are you in there?"

"Oh well, I guess we're done." Jamillah rolled her eyes.

"Open this door now. Carly Moore is in there." Carly recognized Yara's voice demanding that someone open the door. She heard the beeps of the code in the keypad, disarming the lock and opening the door.

"Are you all right?" Yara and Ariel came in and hugged her.

Yara turned to speak to the security person escorting

them. "Sir, thank you for your help, but we've got this."

"All right, I'll give you all some privacy." He hurried out of the room, leaving the women to sort out the situation by themselves.

"Yes, I'm fine. I was just leaving." Goosebumps began appearing on her arms. Carly rubbed her arm to warm her body from the chill in the air.

"You don't look fine. Do you need to leave while we have a few words with Jamillah? You know I'm famous for my Charleston charm." Ariel batted her lashes.

"No, please, no more talk of charm." Carly shook her head and reached out to encourage them to leave with her.

"Well then, you have a choice. Mason is looking for you as they are about to sit down for dinner and some kind of business announcement. He doesn't need to be concerned about you, so you either shake it off, or we let Miss Thing over there know she made a mistake upsetting you." Yara placed her hands on her hips, returning Jamillah's menacing look with one of her own.

"I'll shake it off. Let's go." Carly led the way to the door, intentionally not looking back at Jamillah. "'Carly Moore,' really?" She rolled her eyes and folded her arms for emphasis as she looked at Yara.

"It worked, didn't it? I told security that you were Mason's wife – you know, the man paying everyone's salary in this room – and what do you know, things started happening. One of the security guys said Mason told them we were his special guests, and they should take care of all of our requests. I love the power he wields. If you don't hurry and marry him, girlfriend, I will."

Carly pushed open the door and allowed them to exit. She didn't stop it from slamming behind them.

"Girl, you'd better watch your back with her." Yara gave voice to her feelings.

"I'm not worried about her now that I know her motives, but...I also know what it's like to be hurt by the man you love." Carly straightened her dress before heading back to the table with Mace.

* * *

Jamillah paced the floor, angry that she hadn't been able to manipulate Carly.

"I need to control this narrative." She was rubbing her belly when Fletcher opened the door and looked around before closing it behind him.

"Have you lost your mind, Jamillah? I told you I would handle it." He went to the bar and fixed himself a drink.

"How's that going, huh?" She narrowed her eyes, shooting fiery darts at him. "If you were handling things like I'm paying you to do, she wouldn't have been here."

"These things are delicate. They take time." He threw back his head and took a big swallow of his drink. "I tried discrediting her with pictures and information I sent to Mace, but...face it, girl, people like Carly Rivers."

Jamillah folded her hands across her chest. "Have you spoken to her ex-husband? Did he agree to sue Mace for alienation of affection?" She stared at him. "You reminded him that his legal fees will be paid by an anonymous donor, right?"

"He's not interested. The last time I spoke to him, he said he had other things to take care of. He wasn't interested in a lawsuit he probably wouldn't win. I've not been able to find any evidence that Mace was in contact with Carly during her marriage or during your marriage to him."

"Dammit, Fletch." She threw a box of tissue at him.

He ducked to avoid being hit in the head.

"That's not what I want to hear. I'm not going to let that bitch cost me hundreds of millions in profits. Get rid of her or else."

"Or else what?" He frowned.

"I would hate to see you not get your bonus check." She snarled and took her time heading out the door.

"*You're* not paying me enough to put up with this." He finished his drink and slammed the glass on the bar. "You heap trouble on my head, and I'll make sure it causes you pain too."

Chapter

26

A riel and Yara motioned for Carly to follow them as they left the table while Mason was still at the podium, having finished his speech, but talking to his chief financial officer with his hand over the microphone.

"We told Mason earlier we were leaving to join the crowd in Times Square after he explained what happens at his 'party.' Forgive us, but we're not spending New Year's Eve in the Big Apple listening to a CFO give a financial report when we can be out really partying. He said it was all right with him and besides, I think he was glad he would have you to himself," Ariel said.

"We're going upstairs to change into our party dresses so we can do some dancing. I don't want to bring in the new year listening to boring speeches... Blah, blah, blah," Yara added.

"I agree. Mason is a great guy, but he really needs some coaching on how to throw a fun party. Like, who plans a boring New Year's Eve party and invites other people to it? Carly, girl, that's not right." Ariel side-eyed her as Yara shook her head, feigning disgust.

"Stop it, you two." Carly burst out laughing and looked up at the clock on the wall in front of them. "You're both so wrong. The CFO's talk should last for about fifteen minutes and then the DJ will play while the band is on break. We can kick up our heels then."

"All right, let's go change our clothes. We can kick it with you for about a half an hour or so, then we're gone. I was speaking to the DJ while you were conferencing in the hospitality room with Jamillah. He has the playlist to liven up this party. Yes, I did it," Yara confessed.

"I declare we can't leave you alone for too long before things get interesting, but we can't stay here all night either. We're going to a real party. We're out," Ariel added.

"Got it, but I don't have another party dress to change into. I'm all right in my gown. It won't stop me from doing my thing on the dance floor. Are you sure asking the DJ to play a few songs is all right with Mason? Yara, we can't just hijack his party."

"He said he was cool with it since the band will be on break. Don't worry about a party dress. I brought the dress back that you lent me on the cruise. Remember, I wore it to the All-White Night Party? It's short and tight. I've always loved that dress on you. Besides, we're not going to bring in the new year looking like a trio of old women. Come on, girl."

They both took her by the hand and dragged her to the elevator.

* * *

Carly looked at the mirror, pleased with her reflection. Dressed in a short, white jersey dress designed to hug curves, her best assets were on display. She had changed shoes to silver-toned stilettos, setting off her outfit with just the right amount of sparkle to bring in the new year. She made sure to keep the white corsage with small red roses Mason had given her on her wrist.

Ariel had changed into a black dress with matching accessories and Yara was in a silver-toned party dress. They looked at each other and smiled, knowing that when the three of them got together, they commanded the attention in the room.

They returned to the ballroom and surveyed the action, which was almost on life support. The attendees were milling around the bar and along the sides of the room. The DJ spun tunes in the background at a subdued volume.

Ariel looked over at him behind the turntable, catching his attention, and gave him the thumbs-up.

"Let's get this party started," the DJ announced.

Ariel glanced at Carly, who was busy searching for Mason. The three of them walked to the center of the room.

Carly spotted him near the bar, smiling at her and raising his glass in a toast while the DJ cranked up the volume. That was the signal they needed. The three of them were going to run the town that night. They started dancing with each other with complete abandon just like they had in their suite when they were roommates in college.

Carly let out a deep breath of relief, feeling free and self-assured in the moment as the rhythms of the music coursed through her body. Swinging her hips, she moved sensually to the song's heavy percussive beat. She looked over her shoulder as she felt the heat of Mason gazing at her. Smiling, her attention was locked on him.

Blowing her a kiss, he encouraged her to continue the

dance with her besties.

They moved to the music as the DJ let loose his playlist. The crowd became more excited, joining them on the dance floor. Two of Mace's junior executives, Chance Baker and James Maxwell, came into the circle, coupling with Ariel and Yara, while a third man came forward to dance with Carly. She laughed as she saw Mason making huge strides to get to her on the floor.

"This lady is mine, Todd. Find your own."

Carly threw her head back and laughed as Todd backed away.

Mason stood before her, his hands folded across his chest.

"Are you just going to stand there like a tall tree or should I call Todd back to dance with me?" she asked before he grabbed her hands to sway with her.

"Mace, this is a fast number, if you haven't noticed. I'm not going to swing dance." She leaned back and looked into his eyes.

Drawing her closer, he spoke into her ear. "You know I don't dance." He kissed the top of her ear.

"You can dance. I know it because I taught you how to dance. Just look at me and do what I taught you." She pulled away from him and turned around to back it up. Her back was close to him, but their bodies didn't touch.

He placed a hand on her shoulder and surprised her as she looked back at him dancing lightly on his feet and smiling with her. Another song came on and he kept dancing, his level of comfort growing as he added more steps to his repertoire.

"You deserve the grand prize, Mace. You're a great dancer, babe." She moved over to give him a kiss.

He took her into his arms then looked over at the DJ, motioning for him to slow it down.

"I had a great teacher." He looked at his guests applauding them while they partied on the dance floor.

The DJ spoke to the crowd. "This is dedicated to our host and hostess. As we begin saying goodbye and reconciling with all the mistakes and mishaps of an old year, we look forward to a new year full of new beginnings, new hopes, and new joys." The DJ spun a medley of slow songs, including the song "Perfect."

The mirror ball reflected the light while the smoke machine added an ethereal feel to the room. As the white vapor lightly filled the air, other partygoers joined them on the floor. Carly and Mace both swallowed the lumps in their throats and gazed into each other's eyes, feeling the pain of their separation, and asking each other for forgiveness without words, but with the beat of their hearts drumming a synchronous rhythm while they pressed hard against each other.

As the song ended, Carly felt an emotional weight lift as she took a deep breath, sensing that for the two of them, all was forgiven.

"I love you, Carly." Mace lowered his head and kissed her, his lips lingering on hers for a long time.

"I love you too, Mace. I'm grateful my prayers have been answered. We've been given a new beginning and now we can move forward." She placed her hands on his head and guided his lips back to hers.

"Yes, I want to move forward with you as a part of my life forever. I'm sorry, and I'll never hurt you again. I'm a different man now. Will you mar—"

She pressed her finger to his lips, preventing him from finishing his question.

"I don't want to rush things, Mace. Do you understand

why I don't?" She searched his eyes as his chest heaved.

"Yes, but a man can hope." He sighed.

The DJ interrupted him with an announcement. "All right, Ariel and Yara, that was a bit heavy and maybe we should speed things up."

"No," came a slight roar from the crowd.

"One more slow song. You know which one to play." Mace surprised Carly with his request to keep the DJ playing, even though the band had returned and was ready to take their place back on the stage. He frowned as he pressed her close, then smiled as she smoothed out his brow's frown lines while they danced to the slow song he'd requested.

"You won't have to wait long, I promise." She gazed into his eyes.

The corners of his lips rose with the return of a lighter mood.

They waved back at Ariel and Yara, who were busy gathering their things and preparing to leave.

"Whew." Carly blew out a breath. They had been on the floor for a while. She looked up at Mason. "Do you mind if I freshen up a bit?"

"Sure, go ahead." His eyes didn't hide his disappointment.

"Is there somewhere I can go that's private?" she asked him as he escorted her off the dance floor. *Don't think I'm going back to the hospitality suite. Had enough of being ambushed.*

"Sure, I have a corporate suite with a private restroom attached on the floor above this one. I heard about what happened in the hospitality suite. I'm sorry that happened to you. Here's the card with the code embedded to open the door. Take your time. I'll be here waiting for my best girl."

"Thanks, but no need to apologize. It wasn't your fault.

I'll be right back." They embraced before she left the room.

Chapter

27

arly looked up at the signs directing her to the central grand stairway leading up to Mace's private suite one level above. She could see her path within view, but she bumped into a man coming around the corner. Their proximity was so close, she smelled the champagne on his breath.

"Pardon me." A nervous smile spread across her face. She attempted to go around him as they engaged in a you-move, I-move maneuver that still had him blocking her way.

"Okay, I'll stop and let you go on." She smiled again and stood still, waiting for him to pass her.

"You're Caroline Rivers, right? I'm Fletcher Daniels." He extended his hand.

She tried not to frown as she reached out her hand to meet his. After a quick appraisal, she recalled he was the same man who'd been standing in the shadows earlier.

"Yes, but I need to get going. I'm expected back in the ballroom." She tried not to show her irritation. *Why can't a girl just go to the bathroom without drama*? She shifted her weight and tried to pivot around him and be on her way.

"I'm on an ancillary team with Moore Investments. Do you need an escort? I'm free and available."

"No, I know where the private suite is. So, if you'll excuse me…" She moved away and he came closer.

"You're a beautiful woman," he whispered. "Maybe you don't know as much about Mason as you think you do. Stick with me and hopefully you won't get hurt the way Jamillah was. I did her bidding, and I can work for you."

She backed away and held her hands up. "I'm not Jamillah, and you don't have to worry about me. Now. If. You'll. Excuse me." She narrowed her eyes and tightened her lips.

"Mason has a pattern of kicking women to the curb." He ran his eyes down from her head to the floor. "I'll give it to him, he has great taste." Surveying her body once more, he came closer, extending his hand toward her.

She waited for him to lessen the space between them before raising her knee and slamming it into his groin.

"Ahhhh!" he yelled and doubled over, dropping to the floor and gathering his legs up in a fetal position.

As he groaned in agony, Carly stood over him like a champion boxer scoring a knockout. Her fists were balled. "I said excuse me!" She raised her shoulders and growled over him, unaware of the staff members coming around her with dark suits and gold security badges with the words "Hotel Security" etched on them.

"Can we help you, ma'am?" one of them asked her as another man came forward displaying credentials that identified him as Christopher Saunders, Chief Security Officer with Moore Investment Group.

"Carly, I can escort you to the suite which is right up these stairs for a little privacy. I'll contact Mr. Moore while you guys take care of Fletch, you piece of sh— Sorry, ma'am." The chief looked at him on the floor while talking to his security team at the same time.

Carly canvassed the area, wide-eyed and trying to catch her shallow breath, which quickened as a crowd gathered around.

"No, I need to get out of here." She ran around the corner and spotted the elevators, leaping in as the door was closing. She pressed the number on the panel. She needed to get to her room as fast as she could.

Chapter

28

Hastening her steps, Carly turned in the direction opposite her suite, heading toward Ariel and Yara's room. She inclined her ear and heard the elevator door open.

She mumbled, "Maybe they came back early to escape the cold." Her pulse quickened as she heard unknown male voices communicating the urgency of their situation with someone over their handheld radios, buzzing louder as they closed in on her position. She hurried down the hall and disappeared into a small linen closet.

"We'll find her, sir. Don't worry about it."

Carly's heart threatened to beat out of her chest and beads of sweat gathered on her brow. She remained hidden as security continued their search down the long hallway. After they turned in the direction leading away from her, she tip-toed back toward her besties' room. She needed to get away from the mess downstairs.

"Yara. Ariel." She kept her voice low while knocking at

the door. "It's me. Open the door, please." There was no answer.

Hearing the sound of footsteps approaching, she slipped into another small room where the ice machine was stored. With her back pressed against the wall, she remained still until the sound of footsteps faded.

"Jamillah. That Fletcher person. Dammit. I need some time to think." Gritting her teeth, she placed her fists to the sides of her face. "It wasn't supposed to turn out like this. I wasn't supposed to screw things up for Mace on his big night, especially in front of the board and his employees."

She made sure she hadn't been discovered before heading to her room. Looking around one last time, she quickly made her way to the suite and closed the door behind her before letting out a deep, heart-wrenching sob.

"Get it together, girl. You've gotten through worse times." She closed her eyes and wiped away the tears. She drew from a strength deep inside her – she wasn't going to allow herself to crumble. She pulled out her phone. Ariel's smiling face and contact information came up. She bit her lip. Pausing the impulse to call her friends, who she knew would be there for her, she decided against involving them. *Not now.*

Walking toward the window overlooking Times Square, she looked at the throng of partygoers huddled together in a mass of excited bliss, less than one hour before the ball dropped. She sat on the ledge of the window, contemplating her next move as she scrolled through social media posts. She'd almost forgotten her church back home was broadcasting their New Year's Eve service online. Clicking on the link, she caught the live broadcast of Pastor Jacks speaking to the flock with a message that seemed just for her.

"There will be times when you don't know which

direction to turn. In some ways, it will feel like the scary place you've been in before. You're anxious, afraid of making the same mistakes over and over again." The pastor stared into the camera, making her feel he was baring her soul.

"But even if you feel you can't trust your own instincts, or your heart, the thing you felt led you astray in the past, then, my beloved, trust the One who created you, looked over you, and protected you, even when you didn't know you were in need of protection. Trust the heart of God. He has already given you the keys to unlock and move past the pains of the past. You have the keys of perseverance, truth, faith, forward thinking, and courage. You don't have to be a prisoner of your past. Stop looking for a sign when the truth is standing in front of you, looking at you," he told the congregation.

Carly looked up from her phone at the doorknob turning. Her fingers tingled, hovering over the screen. Maybe it was time to call Yara and Ariel. She wasn't leaving with security and facing the possibility of running into Fletcher again. Her heart calmed.

It was Mace standing at the door.

The truth was clear to her. She would walk through the fires of hell with him if she had to. She already had.

"Can I come in?" He stood in the doorway, awaiting her answer.

"Sure."

He came inside and stretched his arms out wide.

She got up and ran to him.

"Baby. I'm here. Tell me what happened." He placed his forehead to hers and his hands on her shoulders.

"He told me his name was Fletcher," she spilled to him. Her eyes were wide with near panic. "He wouldn't let me pass. He had the gall to put his hands on me. I guess I feared he would assault me, and I hit him in the groin. I wasn't going to be traumatized by him – or any man, for that matter – not ever again." She placed her fists, trembling with anger, on her sides.

"My security folks told me there was some bruising of the jewels." He squeezed his eyes and lips closed, imagining Fletcher's pain. Opening his eyes, softened with concern, he placed his hands on the sides of her face. "I'm sorry this happened to you. Fletcher isn't a primary member of my team. He has worked with me in the past on recommendation from Jamillah. I need to deal with this situation personally. Will you be okay? I promise it won't take me long." He leaned her head against his chest. "I can have a trusted member of security outside of this room to make sure you're not disturbed."

"You have nothing to apologize for, Mace. It's not your fault these people keep trying to intrude on our happiness. Please don't leave. I don't want what is already a bad situation to get worse." She held on to him while his phone buzzed in his pocket.

"It's probably Chris, my head of security." He took the phone out of his pocket and put it on a table on speaker. After freeing his hand, he continued caressing Carly. "Hey, Chris."

"Hello. We got info on Fletch. After Carly took care of him, he tried to run away, but he had a groin injury, if you know what I mean."

Mace looked down at Carly and winked. "So you had a chance to deliver my message to him?" He continued to comfort her, rubbing her back.

"Oh yeah, boss. We let him know he was fired. You were right. The bastard had the nerve to be angry with you."

Surprised by what she was hearing, Carly flinched. She

moved closer to the bed with Mace as he sat down and gently lowered her onto his lap.

"He knows that only my employees and contract staff on January first qualify for the year-end bonus," Mace responded. "Since he was fired on December thirty-first, his bonus check is void. Hold him downstairs until I get there, I have a few more *words* for him."

Shaking her head, Carly held tight to Mason, grabbing his shirt to stop him from leaving.

"That's the other thing I have to tell you. Fletch sought out Jamillah and things got heated between them. Her husband, Nick, intervened. We tried to break them up, but Fletch got away after Nick landed him on his butt again. The man has nine lives."

Mason leaned back against the headboard. "All right. Try to find out where he's headed. We need to find him before he climbs under a rock to hide out. Goodbye, Chris."

"Bye, Mason. I'll handle it."

"What are you planning to do to him?" Carly asked.

"It's best you don't know. He's not going to frighten you and get away with it." Mace grabbed her tight and placed a kiss on her temple. "I'm not going to hurt him, but we need to press charges against him."

"I don't want to press charges, but...but Jamillah said something that made me wonder. She said you didn't fire Nick when you found the two of them together. You didn't say anything to him when you discovered him coming out of your bedroom partially naked. Is that true?"

"Yes, it's true. I heard them before they saw me. Also, Jamillah didn't sound like she was being assaulted, trust me." He looked away from her.

"It had to hurt. I know you had some kind of feelings."

She placed a hand over his heart, thumping in his chest.

"Yeah, it hurt." He continued to look away.

His skin was heating beneath her hand, but she felt she needed to understand his response to Jamillah's infidelity. "So why are you acting differently tonight?" She tilted her head in the direction of his gaze, hoping he would resume eye contact with her.

He did. "I was hot as hell for a brief second." His chest heaved, causing her hand to move off of it. "When I went inside myself to gain control like I had learned in therapy, the anger drained away. For the first time in a long time, I had mental clarity. I saw a picture of you in my mind. I had to admit I'd always wanted to be with you."

He hugged her tight. "I wanted to get back to you. Marrying Jamillah was a mistake. For the first time in years, I allowed myself to hope we'd be together again. I didn't know how, but I knew I was getting a no-contest divorce and I could move on. I felt free."

A smile appeared across his face. "I also checked in with my therapist, who stopped me from kicking Nick's ass and catching a case. Besides, tonight is totally different. Nick loves Jamillah in a way I never could. He defended her honor. Likewise, I love you with every fiber of my being. I'll never let anyone disrespect you. For whatever reason, Fletch's problem with you is his problem with me. I plan to solve it."

"Chris said he would handle it." She grabbed his chin and kissed him, hoping it cooled his anger.

"I heard him." He turned his body to face her. "Why did you and Jamillah have that conversation? I don't get it."

"She felt I needed to know. She wanted to *warn* me. While I was alone in the hospitality suite, she came in and spoke to me."

He shook his head. "Welcome to the craziness called my life. I heard she had you locked in the suite with her, but I didn't know what she said to you. I'm going to tell you something, and I hope our conversations about Jamillah don't extend past tonight."

She sat back to listen.

"You're aware I got my fortune, including this company, from my grandfather?"

She nodded. "Yes, I heard you inherited the lion's share of his fortune."

"Well, Jamillah met him before he got sick. We were already married at the time. I told her of his plans to leave the bulk of his holdings to me. After he died and before I could shed a tear that my grandfather was gone, she looked at me and said she wanted a copy of the accounting of his assets since half of it belonged to her." He gritted his teeth. "That woman told me that shit while I was still in pain. My grandfather wasn't even cold in his grave." His eyes darkened like a storm threatening to erupt.

Mason looked down at her and rubbed the goosebumps popping up on her arm. "She insisted on being kept in the loop, mainly about the finances. It shouldn't have surprised me, because I met Jamillah through one of my clients, a professional ball player. We'd set up a portfolio for him. He introduced me to his baller friends and the women who hung around them."

"Jamillah was one of them?" Carly stroked his chest. His heart rate had slowed, but his skin remained hot to the touch.

"Yes. She showed me her cold heart before we were married, but I ignored the red flags because she was fun. She was one of a few people who made me forget the pain of losing you."

"I see. I think we've both made the same mistake – trying to soothe the pain of a broken heart with other people."

"So, do you understand why nothing she did after that could hurt me? Not even her infidelity after her callousness when I lost my grandfather."

"I understand, but it's strange to keep the man in your employ who you discovered sleeping with your wife. Can you understand how that makes Jamillah and you look?"

He looked at the ceiling. He continued to hold her close.

"He wasn't my employee when I discovered them together. He worked for another firm. I contracted their services. When his firm found out, they fired and blackballed him for bringing shame to their company. I think the owners thought I was going to try to ruin them, but Nick is brilliant and good at what he does. He was broken by the mistake he made and started drinking. He has been sober and a loyal employee ever since I hired him." He lowered his chin on the top of her head.

"The truth is, I helped push Jamillah into his arms and…Nick didn't take anything I wasn't prepared to lose. Jamillah and I had stopped having sex a year before that. I could put my ego aside when I realized the value Nick would bring to the company. The man can create algorithms in his sleep. God doesn't create brains like his and send them to Earth very often. He's a genius, but a geek and socially awkward. He once told me he was a four and Jamillah's a ten."

Carly raised an eyebrow while he paused and laughed.

"Never in his wildest dreams did he ever think he could get the attention of a woman he thought was out of his league. Jamillah was in a loveless marriage and blindly ambitious. That's what initially led to the attraction between them. Nick had no other place to go and worked hard to redeem himself."

He looked up at the ceiling. "My grandfather and my mentor, Alexander Okafor, always said both international business and politics make for strange bedfellows. Literally."

"You've really processed this." She rubbed his hand. "But you still punished Jamillah by giving her nothing in the divorce, and forgave Nick?"

"Yes, I guess. I never thought about it like that," he reflected, looking into her eyes. "Back then, it was important for me to serve it to her cold."

"Now that you've had time to think about what's really important to you, could you reconsider your settlement with Jamillah? She was the glamorous face of the company for a few years, wasn't she?"

"She did help build our brand and connected us with the pretty people." He rolled his eyes.

"It may help her let go of the thread of a relationship with you."

"We don't have a relationship." He frowned at her.

"Um, excuse me... Let's call it a connection. You have an ex-wife that comes to your New Year's Eve party every year."

"Carly, you don't understand. It's tradition. While my grandfather was grooming me to take over, I accompanied him to New York. He thought it was important the employees had some idea of his succession plans. We would have the party, then fly back to Charleston, where Marlena had our New Year's Day meal hot and waiting for us when we came home."

"So three lonely people spent New Year's Day together?" She widened her eyes, surprised at her own clarity.

"For years, it was three lonely *and* angry people. My grandfather never got over the loss of my grandmother. Marlena was grieving the sudden loss of her husband – and later her son, who died a hero in Afghanistan – and I was trying to get over losing you."

They sat quietly in each other's arms.

"It does sound pitiful, doesn't it?" He focused his attention on her with sad eyes as she stroked the side of his face.

"I'm more impressed that you all were there for each other. I know the pain of loss."

"Since we're being transparent, I have to ask. If you know how much we love each other, why won't you marry me?" He nestled her hands in his.

She swallowed the lump in her throat and tried to make saliva to relieve the dryness in her mouth.

"I don't feel we need to rush things. We've been back together for a week, Mace. I don't feel you need to put a ring on it to prove anything." She held up her left hand, letting her fingers dance in front of him. "I feel we're in a committed relationship, with or without a ring."

He nodded, letting her words sink in. "As in, committed to each other, good times or bad times?"

"Yes, fully committed to each other, as in soul mates. That, for me, is more important than any protections the law could give me as your wife."

"As in, working toward a lifetime of commitment?" He came closer and brushed his lips against hers.

"I would say that. My heart has been ruthless. It constantly reminded me that the decision I made to not fight for us was a mistake. It wouldn't let me feel anything with Tyson that was close to the joy I felt when we were together. Sometimes, I had to make myself respond with something close to warmth when he touched me." She placed a hand above her heart. "It didn't miss a chance to let me know it was beating to regain a connection with the only man I could ever truly love. My heart belongs to you, Mason Moore."

"And I love that wild, warm, and committed heart of yours." He kissed her again, his tongue playing with hers as he ravaged her mouth with passion. He laid her on the bed, covering her body with his as he planted kisses along her neck. He pulled at the hem of her dress, exposing her hips. Panting, he pulled away, distracted by the sound of the alarm on his phone beeping.

She spoke with haste, trying to get his attention before losing the courage needed for self-disclosure. "I need to tell *you* something. It's time. I want us to go into the new year with it behind us."

He looked at the phone. "Can it wait until later? We only have fifteen minutes until the new year comes in." He began moving them toward the side of the bed. "We need to catch the elevator and get back to the ballroom in time."

"All right." Sighing, she pulled away, preparing to get off the bed.

"Do you know how many years I was in that same ballroom wishing you were with me, in my arms and looking into my eyes when the new year rolled in?"

"Not only do I understand, but I've wanted the same thing. Let's go. We can talk later." She smiled, sensing his excitement.

He grabbed his phone and took her hand to begin their race downstairs.

"Oh, wait. I have to use the bathroom." She ran to the other room to relieve herself.

"Make it quick, babe. I want to start the year off right."

Chapter

29

W e weren't sure you were coming back," Chris greeted them as they entered the ballroom. "Everyone knows your party ends at 12:10 sharp, so I guess they weren't hanging around this year if you weren't going to be here."

Mason and Carly looked around the nearly empty room, still decorated for a grand party, but most of the guests had left. The few who remained were seated at their tables or gathered around the bar getting their last drinks before it closed.

"Well, we're here." Mason kept his fingers intertwined with Carly's.

The illumination of a clock shined the numbers 11:50 on the wall. "The new year is almost here." He looked at Carly, side-eyeing the scene of what was left of his party.

"This is perfect," he noted as he led Carly to the dance floor. With the spotlight shining on them, he took her into his arms and swayed to the sound of the smooth jazz the band was playing in the background.

"In five minutes, I want you to turn it up," he yelled to the band.

They nodded and prepared to play upbeat party tunes while more people gravitated to the dance floor.

"I'm sorry I ruined your party, Mace." She leaned her head against his chest.

"What are you talking about? I'm having a great time." Rolling his hips, he began showing her his dance moves while the band ramped up the volume, playing a medley of fast songs.

Carly matched his hip action with her own rump shaking to the music. Caught up in his infectious joy, she abandoned all inhibitions. She looked around and saw Yara and Ariel dancing their way to them. The ballroom floor was getting crowded with revelers, while waiters scurried around with trays full of champagne.

"Five... four... three... two... one!" the crowd yelled as the new year came in.

Silver, gold, and white balloons fastened to the ceiling dropped on the partygoers toasting each other. The waiters remained close to the action on the floor as those dancing placed their glasses on trays to kiss the ones they loved or at least the ones nearby.

"Happy New Year, Caroline." Mace intentionally chose her given name, the one she'd used to introduce herself to him so many years ago. The same name that caused his heart to jump whenever he heard it.

"Happy New Year, Mace," she answered, closing the space between them.

Lights were pulsing around them. Their eyes caught. Her pupils darkened as he gazed into her eyes. The intensity of the moment became more palpable. He placed his arms around her waist, drawing her closer. Hoping to cement the bond and connection severed by years of misunderstanding and heartache, he lowered his head, moving closer to her lips, but unwavering in his wanton look into her eyes. He wanted to recover the way it used to be with them. Passion. Heat. Flames.

"I love you and I'll never let you go again," he declared.

Yielding to his desire, she opened her mouth as he crashed his full lips hungrily against hers. Caressing her flesh with his tongue, he enjoyed the warmth of her smooth touch. Blood coursed hot through his veins, burning with desire, and his heart threatened to thump out of his chest.

The lights were lowered to near darkness. The band brought down the action with a slow-tempo tune, changing the vibe. Mace saw the others on the floor swaying to the beat, but he was lost in his own world. One in which he imagined that he and Carly would share more moments like this, filled with new memories, new adventures.

Lowering his hands and rubbing her buttocks in a slow, sensual motion, he pressed his rod, flesh hardened like steel, against her belly. His nerves popped like rows of fireworks exploding within. He could no longer deny the scorching passion between them. It didn't matter who was looking. He didn't see himself just as the CEO of a *Fortune* 500 company. He was a man fortunate enough to know love and he couldn't care less if the world knew it. Carly was the one he planned to share his heart, his fortune, and his future with – if she would have him.

"Promise me, Carly. Promise we'll never let go of each other again." He searched her eyes as "Auld Lang Syne" played over the noise of people whooping and yelling.

She placed a hand behind her ear. They were having problems hearing each other, so they read each other's lips, delivering messages from their hearts.

"I promise," she mouthed to him as she laid his hand over her heart. "I'm committed to you." She pointed at him before he kissed her.

He pointed to her and said, "And I to you."

They gazed at each other, mouths parted and hearts filled with words yet unspoken, until Yara and Ariel came alongside them and tugged at their arms. They didn't resist being pulled off the floor to a quieter area.

"Now this... *this* is a New Year's Eve party. It was way too cold outside, and we came back, surprised to see you had gotten your party swag on." Ariel looked around at the party that somehow had more life breathed into it than before they left.

Yara and Carly laughed and danced with her while Mason spoke to a member of his staff, who whispered something in his ear. Mason whispered back before he scurried over to the area where the band and DJ were waiting for instructions.

Seamlessly, the band faded out as the DJ took over the party, urging everyone to come to the dance floor.

"Let's do this. We're gonna party till we're broke," the DJ told them. "After those large bonuses I hear y'all got, it's going to take a long time." He rapped over the mic while playing popular songs that had almost everyone on the dance floor. With the party in full swing, he spoke directly to the host. "Mr. Moore, thanks for the extra paper to start off my new year. I plan to earn every dollar of it."

They lifted their glasses in a toast and Mason turned to dance with Carly, Yara, and Ariel. Chance and James, who had been looking at the women all night, came over, requesting another dance. After they left him with Carly, Mason grabbed two more glasses of bubbly off a tray.

"You know I don't drink a lot. Trust me, you don't want to see me drunk." She laughed as she took a few sips from her glass.

"I remember you don't know how to hold your liquor, but our room is upstairs, and I'll have my eyes on you the rest of the night. Go have some fun."

"Well, Yara, Ariel, and I have a tradition too. When we were lucky enough to bring in the new year together, we always did our girls' dance in the middle of the floor, even when I was married."

"So, don't let me stop you. They're calling you on the dance floor."

"Thanks, babe. After our dance, I'm all yours." She threw back her drink and joined her besties on the floor, dancing and laughing. He kept his promise and watched her as she had fun with her friends.

* * *

Minutes later, Carly led the way as Yara and Ariel weaved and wobbled on unsteady feet back to Mason, sitting at the bar.

"Okay, ladies, I think I've had enough for one night. No, it's morning." She giggled as she leaned into Mason's embrace while Ariel and Yara looked on.

"That's some damn good champagne you have flowing." She placed her glass on the bar.

"Nothing but the best for my girls." He held on to Carly while Ariel came close and placed a small kiss on his cheek.

His phone began buzzing in his pocket.

He heard his ringtone. Mason pulled his phone out to look at the screen, which had Ian's smiling face on it. He had given his nephew a phone for Christmas, with his direct line. There was a text displayed above the voice call.

I need you Uncle Mason. I need you Uncle Mason.

"Excuse me. I have to take this."

"Uncle Mason, Mommy is hurt in the bathroom and the door is locked. She's screaming and, and…" Ian, who was four years old, tried to explain. His voice was high pitched as his words frantically spilled out. "Help me, Uncle Mason. Help me." The boy began crying.

"Calm down, Ian. I'm here for you. Who's there with you other than your mother?"

"Nobody else is home," Ian sobbed.

"Ian, I need you to stay on the line and listen to me." Mason spotted Carly coming toward him. "Let me have your phone," he told her.

She looked into her handbag, pulled out her phone, and gave it to him.

"Daddy's not answering his phone. I need to help Mommy. She's on the floor. She's hurt."

"Okay. We got this, buddy. You're still my guy, right?" Mason dialed 911 with Carly's phone. "Stay on the phone with me, Ian. I'm getting you some help." The boy's breath was audible over the phone. "Hold on."

"911, what's your emergency?"

Mason moved to the corner of the room and began speaking to the dispatcher, who he hoped would connect him to emergency services in Charleston while he held Ian on the other line.

Luckily, she was able to manage it. "We have an

ambulance on the way."

"Don't hang up, Ian. Help is on the way," he told the boy, who was now whimpering instead of crying.

Motioning frantically to Bernie, he got his attention and ran to meet him outside of the ballroom. "Ian, Carly will talk to you while I get ready to come to you, okay?"

"Okay." Ian let out a deep breath.

Carly took the phones while Mace ran to speak to Bernie.

"I've got to leave." He was out of breath when he got to him. "There's an emergency in Charleston."

"No, no, Mace, you can't leave. We have fires to put out here." He began wringing his hands. "What about the meeting with our international investors this week? Can't a family member down there handle the emergency for a few days until you finish with business here?"

"I need *you* to handle business here." Mason pointed his finger with force, then ran his hand through his hair. "Arrange a teleconference. Listen, I don't have time to discuss this." He backed away and headed back to Carly, who was talking to Yara and Ariel.

It was a new year and an infant's life was hanging in the wind. He had to be there for his family.

Chapter

30

Buckle in," Mace told Carly as the plane taxied down the runway, about to take flight.

"We should be back in Charleston in three hours." He checked his seat buckle again, even though he knew it was securely fastened. Staring at Carly, who was peering out the small window, lost in her own world, he wondered what thoughts were going through her mind.

"Don't worry about Kate and Ian. She's at the hospital. Evan is flying into town with the boys. I was able to get in touch with my mother. She has Ian."

"I'm relieved everything is working out." She kept looking outside.

The roar of the engine drowned out his thoughts as he grew more anxious that there was something else bothering her.

"Carly." He broke the silence after the plane had climbed to twenty-five thousand feet.

"Mace..." She called his name at the same time, after

turning to face him.

"You go first," he told her and braced against his seat, prepared for whatever was to come.

She reached across the aisle and grabbed his hand as they sat in the plush chairs of his private jet. "I could have stayed with Yara and Ariel while you took care of things in Charleston." She covered her mouth with her hand. "I'm sure you could tell they were a little tipsy. I'm feeling guilty that I abandoned them. They've always been there for me. Since you came back into my life, I've been disappearing on them." She looked down at her lap. "That's not how a woman should treat her friends. That's not how a woman should treat her family."

"I agree," he answered, nodding. "Don't worry. I have staff members who'll make sure that their every need will be taken care of, including taking them to the airport. I know you didn't have time to fully explain what was happening, so while you were gathering your things, I went to their room to tell them we had to take care of our family matters."

"*Our* family matters?" She tightened her grip on his hand.

"Yes, our family matters," he repeated, then looked her directly in the eyes. "While not by blood, we've been bound together by love for a long time. We're family." He paused. "So, while we're discussing family matters in Charleston, we should discuss other things as well. We haven't talked about our living arrangements going forward." He took a glass of water from the tray beside his seat. "I want you to tell me what *you* want to do. I've waited for the past week, and you've said nothing about your plans."

"Your business takes you all over the world. I thought you would be leaving Charleston soon," she replied, fidgeting in her seat.

"Carly, I thought I made it clear that I could conduct business from any place in the world." His tone was deliberate. He didn't want to come off like he was negotiating another transaction when matters of his heart had become important to him. "I want you to stay with me in *our* place, but what do you want to do?"

She blinked, doing a double take.

He waited for her response.

"After a week together, you want me to make the decision to move in with you, long-term?"

"No, please understand me." He placed two fingers between his brows. "I'm asking you to move in with me permanently after almost a decade apart. This isn't an impulsive decision, at least not on my part. If I had my way, it would have happened a lot sooner."

"Well, I have good news. I did accept the offer to work at the college for the next year, so the answer is yes. I'll move in with you." She flinched as he leaped out of his seat and unbuckled her belt before helping her to her feet.

"I thought you told me to buckle in my seat?" She playfully recalled his directions.

He took her into his arms and placed kisses along her neck until he reached her plump lips, waiting to be claimed. "We'll go to the hospital first. I'm sure when we get home, Marlena will have a delicious and traditional meal waiting for us, but before then, I have some plans for you in the bedroom."

"So you want to *talk* some more?" she asked him, moving backward as he walked her to the compartment in the rear of the plane.

She stopped him. "Let me be clear about something." She placed her hands on her hips. "I won't be calm if I ever come home and find you in bed with another woman. I'm going on record to let you know there will be some ass kicking and may the best warrior come away, bloodied and bruised, but alive."

He laughed and raised her fist to kiss the back of her hand. "I have no doubt that the successful warrior will be you, the woman who knows how to fight to win. Consider me warned, but you have nothing to worry about. After the lovin' you put on me this week... Gosh, I can't even think about it without getting excited." He untucked his shirt to hide the boner tenting his trousers. "Don't think I'll be calm like I was when I discovered Jamillah's infidelity. My response will not be pretty."

"You have nothing to worry about." She stroked his cheek. "We've waited too long to find our way back to each other. You're the only man for me."

"And..." He looked at her while a warmth crept across his cheeks. His voice tone was low. "I was your first. I took your precious virginity and I plan to be your last." He rubbed her knuckles with his thumb.

"Yes, it was precious to me, but you didn't take anything I didn't willingly give to you. Even with the benefit of hindsight, I would give it to you again. I loved you then and I love you now."

He looked down, reflecting on the power of her words then raised his head to meet her eyes. "Thank you, babe." Struggling with his emotions, he swallowed the hard lump in his throat. "That means a lot to me."

"I'm finished talking." She laughed to lighten the mood while he continued to walk her backward toward the bedroom.

"Oh yes, we're going to do many things that won't involve talking." He turned the knob and kicked the door open as he led her to the bed.

Chapter

31

Baby Emerson is beautiful. Congratulations, Uncle Mace. I guess four times is the charm. Kate and Evan finally got that baby girl." Carly took a bite of her bagel from the tray. They were enjoying a break in the hospital cafeteria after Kate's night in labor.

"We can go back upstairs and say goodbye before we leave. I'm tired of hospital coffee." He yawned.

Her phone vibrated, drawing their attention away from the conversation. She reached for it, clenching her jaw while looking at the name on the screen.

"If it's not a call you want to take, let it go to voicemail. It's early and we haven't finished breakfast." He frowned at the phone.

"I need to get this over with. I don't want this hanging over me all day. It's Tyson."

"Why is he calling you?" He looked over at the screen and saw the name on caller ID. "Place it on speaker, please."

She hesitated but granted his request. "Yes, Tyson. How

can I help you?" Her tone was direct and formal, denoting there was no love lost.

"Good morning, Carly. I'm sorry if I'm catching you at a bad time, but I needed to talk to you. I'm at the hospital in Charleston with Mom. I thought I saw you last night. Are you still in Charleston too?"

She looked up at Mace, who remained silent, with his arms across his chest.

"Yes. I'm listening." She rolled her eyes.

Mace pushed back from the table and crossed his legs.

"You know how much my mother loved you. It devastated her when we got divorced." Tyson spoke in sad tones.

Carly looked at Mace. His chest heaved and his breaths were audible as he breathed in irritation and breathed out hostility at Tyson's voice, as if it was assaulting his ears.

"My mother's health is failing. I think she's giving up. She asked about you this morning. When I saw you, I thought it was divine intervention. Carly, she needs to see you. It would be good for her."

Carly leaned in. Her voice softened. "What's going on?" She hovered her finger over the speaker icon, but Mace blocked her hand before she grabbed the phone.

I want to hear this, he mouthed to her.

She accepted his request and listened intently.

"Are you still there, Carly?"

"Yes, I'm braced for what you're about to tell me. You know how much I care for your mother."

"Her kidneys have stopped working. She told the doctors she'd rather die than depend on dialysis for the rest of her life. We can't find a donor for her."

"What are you asking me, Tyson?" She leaned forward.

"No, no, I'm not asking you to see if you can be a donor. I'm just wondering if you could come visit her, in case we can't find a donor and she doesn't change her mind about the dialysis."

"I have a lot going on right now. Are you asking me to come now?" Her fists tightened as she awaited his answer.

"Yes, can you come now? If things don't change soon, I don't think she has much time left."

Mace shook his head and placed a fist to his mouth, muzzling himself.

Carly scratched the back of her head, contemplating her response.

"Fine. Tell your mother I'll see her shortly, but I don't expect to see you. Please don't think about staging a *chance* encounter. You and I have settled everything between us."

"Sure, Carly. Anything you say. My mother will be so happy to know you're coming. She's on the ninth floor."

"Goodbye, Tyson."

"Goodbye, Carly."

She ended the call and waited for Mason to say something, but he remained silent as he looked at her squirming under his scrutiny.

"Don't sit there judging me. You don't know the full situation. Edna Matherson is a good woman. She had nothing to do with what happened between me and Tyson."

"That may be true, but you don't believe Tyson is going to let you come see his mother and not attempt to see you, do you?"

"I can only take him at his word. The last time we saw one another was in court when I was granted the divorce. We didn't end on a good note, but I'm all right with it. I have no need to seek closure with him. The divorce gave me all the closure I needed."

"Listen, I don't trust Tyson, but I trust you to do what you feel is the right thing to do. So, here's what I propose." He grabbed her hand. "I'll go upstairs, see Kate and the baby again, then I'll meet you on the ninth floor."

"I accept your proposal." She raised his hand and touched it with her lips.

"Good. Now, can I enjoy my breakfast with my girl before we get interrupted again?" He pulled his chair closer to hers.

She leaned over and placed her head on his shoulder. "It's going to be okay, Mace."

* * *

Mace: I'll be down there shortly.
Carly: Ok. She's in room 925.

Carly placed her phone back in the bag. She had gone to the hospital store to get flowers prior to heading to the ninth floor and was in the elevator on her way to Edna's room. The doors opened and she looked up. There he was, appearing tired, but that didn't hide his devilish good looks.

Tyson Matherson stood with his large hands held in a defensive posture, blocking her exit. "Carly, I was just leaving." He smiled, backing up as she moved to the side to allow him to get on the elevator.

"Don't let me stop you." She headed for the chairs in the sitting area outside of the ward to await Mace's arrival.

"Honestly, I didn't plan this." He followed her. "I was telling Mom you were coming to visit. The doctors came in while I was there to let me know about her progress – well, really, *lack* of progress. She's becoming more confused."

She stood and tightened her grip on the potted plant while maintaining eye contact. "Why were you expecting progress if she's terminally ill? That's the impression you gave me on the phone."

"The Carly I used to know never gave up hope of something good happening in any situation." He tilted his head, not breaking eye contact.

She turned away from him and sighed. "I believe the terms of our agreement were we would spare each other another unpleasant face-to-face meeting. I want us to stick to it. I don't want to upset your mother with bad vibes between us. She's already dealing with a lot."

"The nurses were giving her a bath and they should be finished soon. Let's sit for a few minutes until they leave her room. Look, you can see room 925 from here." He pointed to the room down the hall.

"As I said, please don't let me keep you. I'll be fine waiting here by myself." She tightened her lips in a show of defiance. "No, better yet, I must insist you leave, or I'll have to leave."

Her body stiffened as he came closer and placed his hands on her arms.

"What about us? Let's not lose this opportunity to correct mistakes we both made." He loosened his grip after she flinched. A brief scowl crossed his face, quickly replaced by a camouflaging smile once she freed herself from his grasp.

The heat of anger coursed through her body. She had seen that smile before. "What *about* us? There is no 'us.'" She managed to speak through gritted teeth.

He came closer, further fueling her temper despite her attempts to control it.

"Carly, please."

She moved away quickly, but not before he grabbed her hand.

"We said some awful things to each other, but despite it, I still love you. If you had allowed me to come on the cruise with you, I would have had the chance to show you. I know in time you'll love me again. I'm sorry, Carly." He choked and tears fell down his cheeks.

"Let. The lady. Go." They both turned to the voice, tinged with hostility, growling behind them.

Carly backed away. Tyson looked over his shoulder as Mason approached them, closing the space with long strides. He walked past them, toward the chairs that provided a barrier between him and Tyson before he looked down the hall at the nurses' station.

"This is about as low as it gets, Matherson. You used your sick mother to lure Carly back here. Carly, can I speak to you?" He beckoned her to come to him as he took a few steps toward the corridor leading to the patients' rooms.

"What are you doing here, Moore?" Tyson hissed at him.

"I could ask you the same thing, but I already know the answer." Mason snickered.

"When are you going to learn, Carly, that Mason Moore is no good for you, or any woman?" Tyson turned to face her. "I tried to protect you from him by blocking his number from your phone after he kept calling you all those years ago." The admission of his past clandestine activities spilled out.

Carly looked at him, pausing, eyes wide, jaw dropped. He'd finally told the truth, an unforced error on his part. It shouldn't have surprised her. She had learned that he was a master manipulator. She decided to remain quiet and let him keep talking.

"I even had my friends intercept letters he wrote to you

after he left school, but I'll be damned if I'm going to save you again. You've been an ungrateful bitch." He pointed his long finger at her. "The two of you deserve each other."

Carly thought about slapping him across the face, but out of the corner of her eye she saw Mace about to charge him. She moved forward and stood between the two men coming face to face. Mason's nostrils flared. He looked into her eyes, softening under her gaze. She touched his arm, supporting his efforts to control his temper as he breathed through his pursed lips.

"Mace, I don't want to create a scene. Tyson was *just leaving*. Can you wait for me until I finish my visit with Edna?"

Mason came close to her and brushed his lips against hers before turning to whisper in her ear.

Carly turned her head, startled by the noise of Tyson slapping his hand against one of the decorative columns defining the seating area.

"Can you do me a favor and keep walking toward the room and not look back?" Mason spoke so that only she could hear. "You know every time I focus my attention on you instead of the matter at hand, it doesn't work out for me. Can you do that for me? No one will get hurt."

"Yes, if you promise. Please don't do anything rash."

"I promise. Babe, nothing rash will happen. I've thought about my actions for a long time."

She kissed him and looked up as the nurses came out of the room.

"See, there's security here. We'll be fine." He waved at the security guard walking by on his rounds.

She lifted her chin and kept her gaze forward as she walked, undaunted by fears of what may happen between the two men. *Just keep walking Carly*. She took long strides to the room.

Thump. Thump. The sounds of flesh colliding against flesh.

She looked out of the corner of her eye. Mace was still standing, and Tyson was sprawled out on the floor.

Arriving at the door, she knocked to announce her arrival. "Edna, can I come in? It's Carly."

Chapter

32

The new year had started on a different note. Partying in New York, followed by spending hours in a hospital awaiting the birth of a baby. Carly couldn't have imagined the new course her life had taken. After seeing Baby Emerson and visiting with Edna, Carly and Mace went home and slept the rest of the day away. Determined to get the new week on track, Carly had insisted Mace accompany her to the grocery store. They decided to purchase items to prepare their first meal together at home in the new year.

"I gotta pee." She wiggled at the door. After pushing it open, she stood there, startled by the unexpected guests who made her forget nature was calling.

"Surprise! Happy New Year, I guess," Mace's mother Lucille and his brother, Evan, yelled at Carly, pausing her bodily functions.

She gasped, her breath caught in her throat.

"Breathe. I'm sure you weren't expecting us, but please don't pass out." Lucille came forward.

Despite the surprise, Carly's initial intent to get to the bathroom came back. She placed her bags on the table near the door. "Happy New Year." She darted down the hallway, slamming the door behind her.

After taking care of her needs, images of what had just happened crossed her mind. What had happened to the plans to spend quiet time with Mace? The warm water, mixed with the fragrant, bubbly soap, flowed… cleaning her hands, and soothing her nerves.

"Ready or not." She opened the door, turning the knob slowly enough to muffle the sound. *Not. What's next?*

Thinking she needed time before facing the family, she eased into Mace's bedroom and plopped on the bed. Directly in front of her, on both sides of his rectangular mirror, framed in silver, were the pictures she had taken around the city as her holiday present to him. On his dresser was a folded white card with her name in fancy print on the front. Curious of what was written on the inside, she got up to read it.

Carly, The love of my life. You're the last image I want to see when I close my eyes at night and the first when I open them.

Her body warmed with feelings of gratitude. She had a man who cherished her. She felt his love, deep and satisfying, down to the marrow. Reflecting on the New Year's Eve message her pastor had given his flock, she wondered, *What are you waiting for*?

The sound of laughter broke her musings. She looked into the mirror at her own image. She could use a little freshening up, but if she continued to avoid the inevitable, Mace would come looking for her. Straightening her top, she walked into the hall and overheard the conversation he was having with his family as he placed a little black box in the drawer near the couch.

"All right, let's stop dilly-dallying. We need to talk about the new addition to the family. I thought I would be celebrating this day welcoming Carly, my third daughter, into the family." His mother seemed to be venting to Mace. "Instead, we need to discuss how to handle this mess."

"You have Emerson. She's the third girl," Mace responded.

"This isn't a joke, son," she came right back at him. "Wait a minute. You've haven't reviewed the packet your grandfather's lawyers sent, have you?" She sighed. "I tried calling you several times, but my calls went to voicemail."

"No, Mom, I haven't yet."

Carly heard footsteps across the floor followed by a plop on the sofa.

Carly stepped back into the doorframe to avoid being seen as she continued listening. She could see portions of their reflections in the large mirror as she peeped down the hall.

"Why are you so concerned about the packet? I told you I'd get to it."

"While you were in New York, I received a visit from a young man." Lucille placed her hand to her face. "Anyway, he said his mother and her family worked for my father many years ago, before she moved to Maryland."

"What's going on?" Mace furrowed his brow.

Evan was closer to the hallway and spoke for her in hushed tones. "Mom requested that the packet and all of Granddad's personal papers be sent to me to review."

Carly leaned in to hear what he was saying.

"She's not talking about Emerson, Mace. She's talking about—"

Carly's phone pinged, alerting them that she was nearby.

Evan stopped talking abruptly.

"Oh boy." She reached for the phone in her pocket while walking down the hallway.

"I was starting to worry about you."

She saw Mace give Evan a knowing look before he patted the sofa cushion, signaling he desired for her to sit next to him. She obliged his request by snuggling in his arms and kicking off her shoes before drawing her feet up under her. She placed her phone on the table. Looking at the mantel, she saw the portrait of her taken at the party as she entered the ballroom. A smile spread across her lips.

"Do you like it?" His eyes twinkled, reminding her of his boyish charm. A beautiful smile accenting his chiseled good looks spread across his face.

"I love it."

"I had Marlena let my interior designer in. She had it hung after we left."

Carly placed her hands on the sides of his face before pressing her lips to his in a full-frontal kiss. She rewarded him with a caress as if no one else was in the room with them.

He pressed his forehead to hers. "Glad you like it." Nervous laughter escaped him. "I had to negotiate with a lot of people to get it completed so quickly."

Carly knew his family had never seen them openly display affection since most of the time they'd spent together in their late teens and early twenties was with her family and not his.

"Are you sure you're all right?" he asked again. His cheeks turned a rosy red while he rubbed her back and looked into her eyes.

In her peripheral vision, she saw his brother looking concerned about something. She rubbed the sides of his face, staring intently into his eyes.

"I'm fine. I felt a little lightheaded, but the feeling passed."

"All right." He leaned in to kiss her cheek.

Her phone rang this time. She grabbed it from the table. Seeing the picture of Yara, she pressed the accept call icon.

"Excuse me. I've got to take this." She got up and went to the bedroom, closing the door behind her.

* * *

Mace looked at Evan peering down the hallway, this time ensuring their privacy before he resumed speaking while their mother paced the floor.

"Mace, we wouldn't have come if it wasn't important, but time isn't on our side."

"Yes, the chickens have finally come home to roost." Lucille looked over her shoulder at her sons.

"It's a 'sins of the father being visited on the sons' scenario." Evan poured himself a drink.

"What?" Mace leaned forward, looking between his family members. "What are you two talking about? Spill it and don't hand me another old saying."

"You know the history of your father's... unfaithfulness." Lucille cupped her neck. "I can't say I'm surprised by the news. This young man claimed that he was your father's son."

Mace remained silent, tightening his lips.

"He said after his mother's health had taken a turn for the worse, he started looking through her papers. He discovered monthly checks from Cameron for years before your father died. He also said there was a mention of a trust your grandfather had set up for him."

"Okaaay..." Mace tried to remain calm and respectful of

his mother's feelings. "Why are we talking about this now? So he comes with claims – not a birth certificate, not a paternity test, but *claims* – that he's related to us. Where's the proof?"

"Mace." Evan turned to face his brother. "You're the personal representative for Granddad Mason's estate. The packet that was sent to you has information that he knew about this son and colluded with the mother to keep it a secret."

"What? So you're both telling me Granddad knew there was a secret baby, and he hid it from his own daughter?" Mace jumped up. "I think I need a drink."

Evan took a swallow of his drink then placed it on the bar. "According to the story he told, Dad and his mother went to Granddad to ask for his help. His mother's family, the Grants, once worked for him. Granddad provided immediate funds for the young woman to relocate to live with family members in Maryland. Dad couldn't move that kind of money without Mom knowing about it."

Lucille rubbed her arms while listening to Evan.

"After Dad died, Granddad kept the monthly checks going to the mother of the child. Did I get it right, Mom?"

Lucille looked at Evan and nodded.

Mason, pacing the room, looked back at his mother and then went to her, taking her into his arms. "I'm sorry I wasn't there to handle this for you. No way this man should have dropped this load on you." He clenched his jaw. "I promise, I'll handle this." He gave her a tight hug around the shoulders.

She leaned back and patted his arm. "You're here now. Go on, Evan."

"Well, we know it's true that Granddad set up a trust fund to educate him, under the condition that he never knows the secret of his paternity. His mother agreed to the terms. It seemed like a done deal when the woman married, and her husband legally adopted her son."

"So, why was this not a part of his estate papers? I promise you," he paused, "I went over every single sheet before the estate was closed." Mace placed his hand on his forehead. "I'm sure I did."

"It's not your fault, son," Lucille said. "This was intentionally left out. It was to be sent to you five years after Granddad's death."

"Mom, he didn't say anything to you about it?" Mace turned to face his mother.

"No." She looked at him with sad eyes. "Your grandfather knew me and your father well. He also knew that your father's best friend, Edmund Hollison, was a philanderer and a bad influence on him. Cameron and Edmund were thick as thieves. They went to college together and served in the army together. At the time this child was conceived, Cameron and I were going through a tough time. The frequent deployments were taking a toll on us as a couple. We had Deuce, and you, Evan, but I was thinking about leaving your father. Before I made up my mind to leave, Edmund was killed in battle. Because of his grief, your father started drinking heavily and staying out all night. I told him he needed to seek help, or I was leaving. He realized I was serious and swore to me he would stop drinking and become a better man." A tear fell down her cheek. "My father knew he was cheating on me. Women were calling the house asking for your dad, and my father overheard me cursing one of them out."

Frowning, she placed her hands on her hips. "I was a spitfire back then and, at that point, if things didn't get better, someone was going to get hurt. I know it's hard hearing this." She turned away from them.

"No harder for us to hear than it was for you to do," Mace reassured her. "So, the old man took this secret to the grave with him, but he made sure the secret would be revealed in the future?" He spoke aloud, trying to digest yet another family dilemma.

"It sure looks like it, but I also think he didn't say anything because a year later a miracle happened, Mace." She gazed at him. "We thought our family was complete, but then we had you and you brought the light with you. We grew stronger as a family. I had troubles with your father, but I can't deny he gave me three precious gifts. You boys mean the world to me. I forgave your dad before he died. I'm not going to hold bitterness in my heart for flawed dead men." She pulled her arms tightly around her. "He confessed he had an affair. We're all flawed, but never so much that we can't receive forgiveness and grace."

"I'm glad you see it that way, Mom." Mason wiped his brow. "This is the first time I'm hearing about this and I'm not there yet." He rubbed his chest, attempting to relieve his stress.

"I know how much you both respected your father and grandfather. This is hard to swallow." Lucille tried to comfort them.

Mace lowered his head, heavy with the thoughts of everything he was hearing. Moments later, he raised it again with steely resolve.

"Y'all aren't telling me the whole story." He prayed he could bear the weight of the full truth. "You haven't once told me this man's name."

"Brace yourself, brother," Evan forewarned. "As the PR, Granddad left it to you to decide if and when this son gets the remainder of his trust fund now that he's at least thirty years old. The fund is now close to three-fourths of a million dollars."

"And...?" Mace remained silent. His heart was beating hard in his chest and sweat moistened his brow.

"The woman is also a widow," his mother answered, just above a whisper. "Her name is Edna Matherson and her son, Tyson Matherson, is claiming to be your half-brother."

Mason's jaw dropped. It felt like the air had been sucked out of the room.

He took a deep breath before saying, "He's Carly's ex-husband."

"Oh." Lucille slumped into a chair and grabbed her stomach. "This is worse than I thought." She closed her eyes and turned her body away from Mace. She was speechless.

Mason stumbled backward. Tightening the grip on his drink, he avoided shattering the glass on the floor.

Although his life was breaking apart, he didn't need Carly to come out of the room, wondering what was happening. He couldn't let her get caught up in this madness. Not this shitstorm.

Chapter

33

I 'm so glad you're back in town." Carly hugged Aunt Nora.

"It's good to be back home." She smiled. "I enjoyed being with Daniel and his family, but I was glad to leave Chicago and the cold. I'm sorry I couldn't make it for dinner." Aunt Nora finished her wine, sitting with Carly in front of the picturesque window overlooking the twinkling lights around the harbor. The two of them were enjoying each other's company. Everyone else had left.

"So, you thought things were interesting around here?" Aunt Nora asked.

"I guess you could call it interesting." Carly swung her legs as she spoke and finished her wine. "First of all, when we got back from grocery shopping, Lucille and Evan were here. Mace seemed just as surprised as I was when we opened the door and there they were."

"What did they want?" Aunt Nora raised an eyebrow.

"I'm not sure." Carly shrugged. "I can tell you that there was a clear shift in the atmosphere when I came out of the bedroom. I was in there for several minutes on a call with Yara before we connected with Ariel. The three of us were busy laughing about our time in New York."

"Sounds like you had a good time." Aunt Nora reached out and patted Carly's leg.

"We all had a great time, including Mace." She sighed. "Something has definitely soured his mood, though." She stared out the window at the Ravenel Bridge, lit up against the dark sky.

"What else happened?"

Carly turned her head toward Aunt Nora and refocused her attention. "Well, then Marlena came over with boxes full of food." She rolled her eyes and shook her head. "I was planning to cook our meal. While she and I were taking the food out, I asked if Mace looked sad to her and she told me, 'I can't say he looks sad to me, but he'll be mad as a hornet when he realizes he's not having *my* Hoppin' John, collard greens, and pork roast.' Really?" Carly sighed. "He went to the store with *me*." She pointed to herself. "He knew the assignment. He agreed to tell Marlena we were cooking our first meal of the new year together. She said she didn't get the call telling her she didn't need to come over, but that's not all. She asked if I knew what Hoppin' John is!" She crossed one leg over the other.

"I held my peace, Aunt Nora." Carly placed her hands on her hips. "I know what Hoppin' John is as sure as I know I'm a native daughter of Charleston. Mom always prepared black-eyed peas and rice for good luck, collard greens for money and good fortune, and pork as a symbol of looking forward to things to come in the new year. She served it with rolls, cornbread, and her famous bread pudding for dessert. I know the tradition is to eat it on the first day of the year and I was excited about marking our first full day in our home together. Deuce and his wife, Kim, came over after we laid out the food, and stayed a little while. Evan took Lucille home a couple hours later. He needed to check on Kate and the kids."

"Something must have caused Lucille to come over unannounced." Aunt Nora frowned. "She really wants the two of you back together."

"I know." Carly widened her eyes. "Sometimes I wonder if all of this is what I want, but… I know *who* I want. It's Mace." She paused again. "Something is bothering him, but I don't know what it is. He picked at his food and wasn't present much after we ate. His phone kept ringing and now he's holed up somewhere answering another phone call."

Aunt Nora whispered, "Today has been quite unusual."

"Definitely different. It's been just the two of us most of the time, with Marlena coming and going during the day. We've been home together almost every night except when he accompanied me to see Tyson's mother, Edna, and of course when we went to the party."

"How is Edna?" Nora asked and placed her empty glass on the table in front of her.

"She's not doing well, but we got some good news." Carly clasped her hands. "They found a donor and her team was optimistic the transplant will be successful."

"Did Mace have anything to do with her chances for a transplant improving?" Aunt Nora raised an eyebrow.

"He made some calls, but the decision will be a clinical one. I didn't ask Mace to pull any strings on her behalf."

"I see." Aunt Nora laced her fingers together. "I'm happy about the news, but what I'm really concerned about is your happiness. Are you happy, sweetheart?"

"Yes, I can honestly say I am." Carly smiled with her

whole face and giggled as she once had when their love was new and caused every fiber of her being to fire with excitement.

"Okay, I won't press you on it. Let me help you clean up." Aunt Nora sat up and grabbed her glass.

"Please leave it. I'll get it later. You need to get home. Let me see if Mace is off the phone. He can come and tell you goodbye. I'll be right back."

"Okay, while you're doing that, I'll call for a ride."

"No, don't worry about that. We have a service we've been using since Mace got hit on the head. I don't want him driving at night or when he gets his headaches."

"All right, I'll gather my things while you get him."

Carly walked down the hall and entered Mace's study. "Aunt Nora is leaving and wants to say goodbye to you."

Mason turned in his chair to face her and clicked off the phone. "I'm sorry about today, but things aren't going as planned with my investments in Africa."

"Can we talk about that later?" She extended her hand to him. "Come say goodbye to Aunt Nora."

He got up and placed his arms around her waist as they returned to the front of the condo where Nora was waiting at the door.

"Nora, I'm sorry I wasn't more hospitable, but business has occupied much of my time today. I hope you enjoyed your visit with Carly." He came forward, kissing her on the cheek.

"Of course I did. Any time I get to spend with my niece is a good time. I had hoped to spend more time with you too, but maybe another time. Please give your family my regards."

They all focused their attention on the sound of someone fumbling with keys at the door. The doorknob turned and Marlena came in. Their jaws dropped as they stared at her.

"You all didn't think I was planning to meet this mess in the morning, did you?" Marlena took off her jacket.

"But—" Carly closed her mouth after Marlena held her hand in the air, silencing her.

"But nothing. Nora, I'll talk to you later this week at church. Goodbye for now."

"Goodbye, Marlena." She shook her head and laughed.

"The driver is out front," Marlena advised her.

Carly grabbed her jacket and let out a sigh when Mace's phone went off again.

"Carly, I'm sorry, but I may have to leave in the morning." Mason pressed the accept call button. "It's business."

"So soon?" Blood pulsated through her veins, leaving her feeling heated. "Where are you going? What's happening?" She closed her eyes, centering herself in silence. "Don't worry about it. Let me walk Aunt Nora downstairs while you answer the phone."

"Yeah, Bernie, I'm listening."

She heard him answering the call before she closed the door behind her. "Ready, Aunt Nora?" She guided her toward the elevator as her aunt looked at her with sad eyes and closed lips.

"Don't worry." Carly patted her hand. "Mace and I will talk this out."

* * *

Carly came back inside the condo. Marlena was busy at work tidying up the place.

"Marlena, we don't expect you to be here at our every beck and call. You've been working all day. I wasn't expecting you to return."

"Don't worry about me. After tomorrow, things will slow down tremendously. I enjoy having days like this when I have something to do. You and Mace will be gone sometime this week. I'll be here alone counting the time until you return. I've packed his bags already. You're the one who should get some rest after you pack."

"What do you mean?" Carly asked as she folded a small throw blanket. "*We're* not going anywhere. At least, I can't leave now."

"Mace always leaves on business somewhere during the first week of the new year. Judging from the amount of calls he has gotten today, I'll wager he'll be gone early in the morning. I know when you two dated while you were in school, he probably complained about the responsibilities his grandfather placed on him, but now, Carly, it has all fallen on him. This is the world he has chosen. He likes international business and, from what I've read, he's good at it. I beg of you to please enter this relationship with your eyes wide open. I care about both of you and I want the two of you to be happy. You're like your mother. She was an independent thinker and so are you."

Marlena's words warmed Carly inside like sunshine. She always liked being compared to her hero, her mother.

Mace walked toward them, interrupting their conversation. "Carly, can I talk to you for a moment?" His shirt was unbuttoned, revealing his muscular chest.

Marlena said, "I'm glad you're starting to fill out a little more. You were getting too thin, Mace."

"I'll remember while I'm eating that you think I'm starting to chub up."

She shrugged and moved the conversation along with other issues of concern. "So, you're preparing for your business trip tomorrow?" She picked up another glass before making her way to the kitchen.

He ran his hand through his hair and turned away from Marlena without answering her question.

"Mister," she spoke with an air of sarcasm, "I've already got you packed." Marlena disappeared into the kitchen.

"Let's go to the bedroom. We need to talk in private." He took Carly's hand and led her down the hall, closing the door behind them.

"Mace, I can't go with you on this short notice. I'll be starting at the college soon. I don't want to start this new position asking for time off." She plopped on the bed.

"I understand." He paced. "My time this week will be fluid and could change at a moment's notice. I know I'll be connecting with my team in New York. It's not a sure thing, but I won't be surprised if I need to fly to Africa sometime this week to intervene in negotiations. I hope to wrap up everything in a week." He took off his shirt and stepped out of his pants. Walking around the room in his boxers, he started gathering his personal items.

She salivated as he stood near the bed. She had to admit his six-pack was more well-defined and no, he wasn't *chubbing* up, but beefing up. She shook her head. Closing her eyes, she hoped to clear her mind of the desire to rip his shorts off instead of talking about his departure.

"So you want me to deal with the fact that you'll be gone for a week, depriving me of your body as you parade around here almost naked?" She lay back on her elbows and watched the muscles ripple along his back, down to his tight rear end, and then to his thighs, flexing as he placed his things in a carry-on bag.

He turned around, smiling as Carly ogled his naked chest

while spreading her legs across the bed in response to his maleness, thickening with excitement.

"Carly, be good. I've got to get some sleep before I step into the hornets' nest tomorrow."

"Okay, I'll be good… if you tell me what was happening with you today. Why were you sad?" She crossed her legs again and he drew nearer and stood before her.

"You're very observant." He rubbed his cheek and sat beside her.

Carly sensed he was contemplating what to say. She hoped it would shed some light on what had happened between him and his family.

"I was sad because…" He looked away, avoiding eye contact as he spoke. "I couldn't get the thoughts out of my mind that my grandfather was gone, and here I was happy for the first time in a long time. I got my wish. You're back in my life, as I always had hoped for." His chest expanded slowly then deflated before he turned back to face her. "My grandfather, on the other hand, had to suffer for years after my grandmother died. Marlena also got caught in the depths of grief and had little chance for happiness. The loves of their lives were gone forever."

"Mace, Marlena doesn't seem unhappy." She placed a hand on his shoulder. "You don't believe that your grandfather didn't want you to be happy, do you?"

"No, I guess I don't think he had a problem with me being happy, nor that he didn't desire my success. Hell, the man built an empire and left it to me to manage." He got up and took fresh underwear out of his drawer. "I'm just a little conflicted."

"All of you had the choice to move on with your lives. Living a life without love wasn't your fate, but your choice.

I'm glad you chose to fight for love."

"I only fought for love with *you*." He came back toward the bed. "Marlena actually was the first one to decide for the better, out of love. She chose to go to therapy to get better for her family. She also insisted I go to therapy to move past my depression and anger. My parents and grandfather came to some of my sessions. I know it was because they loved me. And now here I am, back with you. You may think I'm being superstitious, but the year I ate an extra helping of Marlena's Hoppin' John, I discovered Jamillah in bed with another man."

She raised a brow and cleared her throat. "And that was a good thing? You aren't one of those guys who gets excited watching their wives have sex with another man, are you?"

"No, I'm not." He gave her a side-eyed glance. "I've explained that to you already, and we're focusing on food, not sex." He cleared his throat. "As I was saying, I ate another large dose last year and then I reunited with you." A smile spread across his face.

"Okay, so how much did you eat this year?" She narrowed her eyes and crossed her arms.

"A lot, and who knows what's going to happen." He came forward and scooped her off the bed, drawing her close and rubbing her buttocks.

"I thought you were busy preparing for tomorrow?" She laughed as he cradled her in his arms.

"I need to take care of *you* tonight." He pressed his lips to hers and nibbled at them. "I'll let tomorrow take care of itself."

She looked down at his hard-on peeking out of his shorts. "Take me, I'm yours." She placed her arms around his neck and her legs around his waist, giggling as he carried her to shower with him.

Chapter

34

Carly was asleep when Evan came over for a late-night talk with Mason.

"I know you'll be gone by tomorrow, so I came over for our usual nightcap before you leave on your business trip for the next few months." Evan stretched his long arms and rubbed the stubble on his face. "You know, I had to stay with Ian because he wouldn't stop crying about you. I told him you'd be back soon, but the poor fella cried himself to sleep. I also needed to get out of the house after Kate and I shared a few choice words." He frowned and narrowed his eyes. "I told her she overstepped her boundaries with Carly when she told her about Jamillah. She told me that was my opinion and hers differed. I didn't want things to get too hot between us, so I told her I was coming here for our visit before the two of you left."

"Carly's not going with me. Besides, I won't be gone long, maybe a week." Mason interlaced his fingers and massaged his knuckles.

"You don't believe that, do you, Mason? You're never gone for just a week. The timing couldn't be worse for you and Carly. The two of you need more time together before you're off in a different part of the world. I'm also sorry Kate may have told Carly you don't want children. I've regretted that I shared that with her for years. Pillow talk can get a man in trouble."

"You got it wrong, bro. What I shared with you, to set the record straight, is that I don't want children with a woman I don't love and respect. I couldn't have children with Jamillah for that reason alone."

"Enough of the small talk. Are you sure Carly is sound asleep?" Evan looked over his shoulder down the hall. "I don't want her to overhear the update I'm about to share."

"She's out." Mason smiled. "I did my job satisfying my woman."

"Yeah, right." Evan snickered. "If she's listening, it's on you. I would hate to be the one to tell her that Tyson," he whispered his name, "may be Dad's son."

"Did you put a gag on him until we have a chance to sort this out?" Mace sat on the couch opposite Evan. "There is a new group of clerks at the law office and the firm is now being run by the son of Granddad's lawyer. They're double-checking to make sure the packet of information is complete. I'm never going to believe the words of a liar."

"If you mean did I give Tyson three hundred grand for his cooperation for now, yes, I did." Evan tightened his lips. "He said he also needed time to *process* the news, but he agreed to your request to stay silent. So you don't have to worry about him blurting it out to Carly."

"And he agreed to meet with me in New York for a face-to-face discussion?" Mace placed his hands behind his head as he leaned back against the couch.

"Well, that was a sticking point, because he didn't understand why he couldn't meet with you here in Charleston, but he needs the money, so I'm almost positive he'll show up at my office in New York tomorrow."

"Listen, there's no give on that." He pointed his finger. "I need to get him out of town, away from Carly, before I leave the country. He doesn't show and it will be a long time before he sees the rest of the money. You can use the excuse that he has to meet with my lawyers in New York to go over the terms while I'm gone. I have to buy myself some time. There's a lot to do in the big city. I'm sure he won't have trouble keeping himself entertained."

"Mace, don't get into a pissing contest with this guy." Evan shook his head. "As your brother and your lawyer, I advise against that. Things could get out of hand. Let's just settle this as fast as we can and move on. I don't think he wants a personal relationship with the family and neither do we. Deuce had to go out of town, but he's on board with the plans to close the trust as soon as possible. I'll go over the entire packet, including Granddad's additional personal papers, which may shed some light on why he established the trust." Evan got up and grabbed two glasses. "Let's share a drink. Scotch?"

"Sure." Mace leaned his head back, looking at the ceiling. "This is some shit. Just when I get Carly back in my life, this gets dropped in my lap."

"How did you handle her questions after we left?" Evan poured the brown liquid into the crystal glasses and handed one to Mace.

"She sensed something was wrong, but I told her I was sad that Granddad wasn't here to share in my success, or to see that we were back together." He took a sip of his drink.

"She bought it?" Evan returned to his seat.

"I think she just didn't want to pry, especially after I told her I had to leave on business. She's never been one that likes ending the day with a fight. We've done that already." He let out a deep sigh, filled with sadness. "I know I have to tell her about Tyson, but I'd prefer to wait until I get back from handling business. I may have to go to Africa."

"So that's your story and you're sticking with it?" Evan cocked an eyebrow. "You're only going to be gone for a week, and during that time you believe Tyson – or anyone else, for that matter – won't spill it to Carly?"

"Yeah, that's about right." Mason placed his glass on the table.

"You're a gambling man, bro." Evan crossed his arms in front of his chest. "I hope Lady Luck is with you. I'd better get going. We have an early flight to catch in the morning."

* * *

The next morning, Mace waited in Evan's New York law office while his brother was on a conference call. While maintaining a cool exterior, he was struggling on the inside to harness his fighting warrior spirit, the same thing he used to close his most important business deals. He couldn't risk letting his emotions get the best of him. There was too much at stake.

Mace looked around at the office, which more modern, practical, and subdued than his own. Mace's designer intended his space to speak to the fact that he was successful and used to winning at business. Was it meant to be intimidating, with its high-end luxury décor? Yes.

In contrast, this interior space, with high ceilings, timber-framed beams, and built-in cabinets, was filled wall-to-wall with leather-bound books. Large windows flooded it with natural light and the décor left visitors with the impression that its owner was competent and knew how to get the job done. The cool grays and accents of warm beige in the paint and carpet softened the space. Definitely calming.

Mason looked at the time on his Rolex watch. "He's late," he said out loud as he drummed his fingers on the wood desk. He wasn't about to tolerate tardiness from anyone. His body heated with irritation coursing through it.

Intimidate Tyson? No.

At that point, he wanted to *annihilate* him.

"I can't wait to see his face when we tell him the truth." His smile was syrupy sweet, but he couldn't hide the bitterness dripping from his broad, upturned lips. Evan had pulled an all-nighter and come across some interesting details, including a personal letter he'd shared with Mace on their plane ride to New York.

"Listen, Mace." Evan rushed back into the office. "Tyson called and just threw us a curveball. While I was in my meeting, he left me a voice message. I'll play it for you."

Mason and Evan leaned over Evan's phone to listen.

"*I'll make this brief. I won't need to meet with you two. I have my own legal team that will be representing me. I thought about this thing and it occurred to me that you wanted to conduct business out of town and put a gag on me so that dear Dad and Granddad's reputations aren't dragged through the mud.*" Tyson raised the volume of his voice. "*You want to pay me off and deny me my birthright. I'm a Moore too!*"

Evan pressed stop. "Mace, he just starts to ramble at this point."

"No, let it play!" Mace gave him a sharp look, narrowing his eyes.

Evan resumed playing the message.

"See, I'm a self-made man. I didn't grow up having everything given to me. I had to make my own way in the world, you bastards." He grunted.

"Oh, that's rich." Mace snickered.

"I'm going to have some fun with my money in Vegas, and when I get back, I'm going to win back my Carly. We'll have the money for the family she wants." He paused. *"I regret that I didn't agree to the fertility treatments she wanted...but I'm going to do right by her now. See you in court, suckers... I mean, brothers. Bye-bye."*

Mace rose from his chair and pounded the desk. "Who in the hell does he think he is?" His chest was tight. He balled his fists and placed them to his temples, pressing hard to stop his head from exploding.

"Get him on the phone, Evan," he demanded, and began pacing the room. "Never mind. I swear I'm going to find him and then strangle him with my bare hands." He moved toward the door.

Evan pivoted to block him from leaving. "Wait a minute. I'll call him, but don't you see he's baiting you?" He spoke in calm, even tones. "He threw in that part about Carly to push you over the edge, hoping you'd do something stupid."

Mace's heart stopped thumping hard in his chest. He thought about what Evan had said. He took in a deep breath, letting rational thoughts fill his mind, and then slowly let loose some of his anger. "Thanks. I see that." Turning to look out the window, he stood still, contemplating his next move. "Don't call him. He still has to come to me."

"What else do you want me to do?" Evan focused his

attention on Mace.

"I know he will call, so take the call. Tell him you can't do anything until I get back from Africa on business. I was going to send a team overseas and stay here to handle the matter, but my office notified me that my business associate, Alex Okafor, will be leading his team in the negotiations. He's not only been good at helping us expand our holdings in Africa, he's my friend." Focusing on Alex made him smile. "He's also going to have a high honor bestowed upon him by his government next week. He asked if I could come to the ceremony. I'm thinking I should go, but for the first time in a long time, I'm not sure what I should do." He rubbed his forehead. "Can you handle Tyson's foolishness until I get back?"

"Go support your friend. You know I've got you. It will give me time to review the entire packet in detail." He extended his hand for a fist bump. "I'll look out for Carly too."

"I already have that handled. I assigned a security team to provide coverage for her safety. You know I take care of what's mine." Mace placed his hands on his hips.

"You might need to tell the frat brothers to stand down," Evan advised him. "One of them works at the hospital and was told about the *encounter* you had with Tyson. I don't like Tyson, but no one needs to get hurt."

"I don't control them." Mason smiled. "I would *hate* for Tyson to discover that if you mess with one of us, you mess with all of us. They are brothers of my soul for life." Mace looked at their fraternity's gold and purple paraphernalia on the shelf behind Evan's desk. "I've got to go."

"Okay." Evan walked Mace to the door. "Don't worry about anything."

"I'm not the one who should be worried." Mace walked

out of the office, confident that this was a battle he would not lose.

Chapter

35

I know you don't want to hear this, but I'm almost finished with business here. I promise I'll be home soon." Mason's smiling face, with a little bit of stubble on his cheeks, looked back at her on the small cellphone screen.

"No, I *don't* want to hear it, because my heart sinks a little lower every time you call and delay returning home." Carly picked up her pen to distract herself and began doodling, surprised by her candor.

"I know, babe." He closed his eyes and sighed. "I know it's not fair to continue to ask for your patience, but many things have been outside of my control. I told you Alexander got sick. His blood pressure rose to dangerous levels, and that slowed down the negotiations."

"I hope he's all right now?" She looked into the camera.

"He's better, but it was a scare for all of us." Mace rolled his eyes upward, as if looking toward heaven. "I won't even let myself think what it would have been like if we lost him.

He's a giant in the business world."

He paused then looked into the camera and smiled. "I took your advice and signed the agreement amending the divorce settlement with Jamillah. Nick said she has been feeling better since she received the new settlement giving her a fairer amount of money. Maybe it's just a coincidence, but she was having contractions and was on bedrest since her encounter with Fletcher at the party. Over the last week, the contractions have stopped." He paused again. "In light of the complications with Jamillah, tell me you understand why I couldn't ask the man to leave his wife alone?"

"Yes, of course I understand, but you didn't think there was anyone else in the organization up to the challenge of negotiating with your associates in Nigeria?" She asked the question but, she already knew the answer.

"No, not this level of negotiations. Alex confided in me that he was glad that I chose to lead the delegation for my company. After he became ill, he invited me to stay at his home so we could speak privately. He said he had something to show me. He hasn't told me what it is, so while I'm waiting, I've been spending time with him and his family. Hold on. I'm going to place the phone on the stand while I talk to you. It may make my image seem farther away."

She watched as his bathroom in the background came into view.

"Listen, I don't want to see you take care of your bodily functions." She smiled as he snickered at her. "I want intimacy, but some things should forever remain a mystery."

"Agreed. I have another meeting and I need to shave."

Observing him as he took the warmed shaving cream with steam coming from the container, she watched in silence, thinking the white lather might be too hot for his face.

He spilled it on his nightshirt. "Damn. That's hot." He took off his shirt, exposing his broad chest.

"So you're torturing me now?" She breathed in and let out an audible huff of air in exasperation at how familiar their routine over the phone had become.

"What are you talking about?" He wrinkled his brow.

"Never mind. You've got a full day today. We'd better hang up. Love you."

"Don't hang up, Carly. I look forward to our conversations. It's worse when I go a day without hearing from you. Listen, I know this is difficult. It's hard for me too."

She looked away from the screen at the clock on the wall. It was very early in the morning his time.

"Are you happy, Mace? I mean with working constantly and the constant travelling?"

He came closer to the phone and his face appeared larger on the screen, as if he needed to make their personal connection as close as possible, eyeball to eyeball. "Well, I do like the thrill of negotiations and the gratification of having a hand in things that can change the lives of many for the better."

"So your business is a source of deep, personal satisfaction for you?"

"That, among other things. My relationship with you has and always will be important to me. I'm not sure where we're going with this. What are you really asking me?"

He grabbed the shaving cream after it had cooled and lathered his face before he began shaving.

"I don't want to be another acquisition, like another business agreement, a merger. Hell... I didn't want to go there with you, but it's how I feel." Carly pressed her lips together and then continued, "Like I said, I know you're busy and so am I."

She stiffened her back, sat upright in her chair, and put a brave smile on her face. They would get through this. When he returned, she would discuss how they could have more of a work-life balance.

"There's not much to do in the condo, so I told Marlena she didn't need to come in. I thought she would use the time to rest, but she's been away taking care of family members. That woman thrives on caring for others." She shook her head. "We spoke before she left and agreed the kitchen and laundry were her domain, but our bedroom and my office belonged to me."

"I'm glad the two of you worked things out. I want you to feel comfortable in our home. How have you been spending your time?"

"Work. My job is going well, and I've used the extra time to continue the joint research with my colleague in Barbados. I may have to go there for a meeting."

"Sorry, hold on. I have to accept this request." His hand came forward while he continued shaving. He placed his razor on the counter and wiped his face with a towel.

Without any warning, their screen time was taken over by an image of stock prices scrolling on a display of international market indicators.

She clicked off the video, not wanting to say anything she would later regret. Her jaw tightened.

"Calm down." She spoke softly and placed a finger on the pulse in her neck to slow her heartbeat. Biting her lip, she tried to stem the tide of emotions. It didn't help. Nothing averted the hot tears flowing down her face.

"Are you still there?" She sensed the concern in his voice. "I can't see you anymore."

"That makes two of us. I have to go. Have a great day."

She pressed the end call button, grabbed her bag, and headed out. "I can't stay in this condo alone again tonight." The door slammed behind her. Covered by the veil of darkness on the moonless night, her tears were unseen by the people she passed as she walked toward one of Mace's cars.

Chapter

36

Two weeks later...

The holiday glow had dimmed. Carly was settling into a routine in Mason's condo, a space that still felt like it belonged only to him, despite her attempts to add her own personal touches. She had only moved in the things she needed. The rest of her things she kept in storage.

Looking out at the harbor, she enjoyed the sight of the sun setting over the calm water as she sat in her office in the back of Mason's condo – a place he hadn't inhabited in weeks. The top of her desk was filled with papers she had reviewed throughout the day. In Mace's absence, she had spent most of her time at the Avery Institute, conducting research for her latest project.

Deep in thought, she wasn't sure if she heard her phone ring. She located the phone under her legal pad filled with notes and looked over at the screen. The number was from an unknown caller.

"Maybe one of the couriers who delivers contracts for Mace to sign is calling." His office had her number to call since Marlena was on vacation. She grew excited, thinking it meant he might be coming home soon. She answered the phone, trying not to get her hopes up only to be disappointed again.

"Hello, this is Carly."

"Sweet Caroline, you're my girl." A familiar male voice began singing her name to the tune of the famous song.

She rolled her eyes. She wasn't amused. "What do you want, Tyson?" She placed the phone on speaker.

"Now, is that your attempt at Southern hospitality?" He laughed. "You really need to work on it, girl."

She looked around the room as his voice filled the office, giving her chills. "Like I said, what do you want? Answer the question or I'm hanging up."

"Hold on," he quickly responded. His voice was way too jovial for her liking.

She frowned, waiting for him to drop the hammer. It wasn't going to be good and she knew it.

"I'm allowing you to be the first to congratulate me."

Carly grabbed the cup of chamomile tea she had prepared and took a sip.

"I just rented a condo in Laurens Place. Well, actually, I'm subleasing it until one becomes available. You're not the only one with friends in high places. I'm your new neighbor."

"You're *what*?" She grabbed her throat after choking on the news. "How? Why?"

"My unit is near Mace's, and guess what?"

She shook her head in disbelief. "What?"

"Since I live in the same gated community as you do, I have the same privileges to come and go with my security card. I was thinking maybe you could come see the space and help me decorate."

"You're delusional, Tyson. Do not come here and no, I will not be visiting you." Her voice was breaking with anger. "I don't believe this."

"Believe it, baby." She could hear the anger in his voice. "I came into an unexpected inheritance and Lady Luck shined on me. I went to Vegas and turned over a quarter of a million into almost one million dollars. Since you like rich guys, I thought it would improve my chances of winning you back. What do you think?"

She took deep breaths, knowing it wasn't in her best interests to engage him in a tit-for-tat. "Go to hell, Tyson, that's what I think."

"Did I hit a nerve, sweetheart? Well, it's time to own up to the truth. I think lover boy needs to know the whole truth too. Don't you?"

"I'm going to hang up."

"Listen, girl, if I can't have you—"

"Goodbye." She hung up the phone and seconds later it began ringing again.

"I've got to get out of here." She ran to the bedroom and opened the safe where Mace kept his loaded gun before gathering a few things in an overnight bag.

* * *

Carly pressed the button to start the metallic gray Lexus parked in the garage in Mace's designated space. Looking in the rearview mirror before she pulled out, she made sure she wasn't being followed.

"I'll call Aunt Nora after I find a room somewhere. I can't go to her house just yet. She'll know something is wrong." Her heart was racing as she stopped at a red light. She wiped away the tears forming in her eyes that were obscuring her vision.

"Calm down." She placed a finger on the pulse below the angle of her jaw and let out a cleansing breath. The light turned green, and she was almost in the intersection when a car came out of nowhere, racing down East Bay Street. Startled, she slammed on the brakes to avoid a collision. Turning her head, she quickly looked on both sides before driving through the intersection.

Her phone rang. She placed a hand above her heart when the name Evan Moore came up on the console. Pressing the button on the steering wheel, she accepted the call through the car's Bluetooth speakers.

"Hey, Carly." His friendly voice was calming. "I got a notification on the tracking system that the car had been moved and was racing down the street. I'm calling to see if everything is okay."

"Hey, Evan." She attempted to camouflage her fears with a cheerful voice. "Mace told me I could use the car. Is there a problem? I didn't know you would be notified."

"No problem that you're using the car. It's just that you've been using the ride-share contract Mace had set up for the both of you until yesterday," he explained.

She looked in her rearview mirror and noticed that she was being followed by a black SUV. For a few minutes and after a series of turns, the vehicle continued to follow her.

"Are you there?" Carly noted the urgency in Evan's voice.

"Yes." Her voice trembled. "I can't believe this is happening to me." She reached over to ensure that she could get to her pocketbook in the passenger seat. "I'm being stalked, Evan."

"Is it a black SUV?"

"Yes, it's still following me." She looked in the rearview mirror again.

"That's an employee of Alpha and Omega Security. They provide security for Mace any time he needs it. The owner is one of Mace's frat brothers. Are you heading to your aunt's house?"

"No, that's the first place he…" She stopped, realizing that she would have to divulge that Tyson had contacted her. She took his threats seriously, but she hadn't come back into Mace's life to place him or his family in danger. She would handle Tyson. He was her problem.

"It's been harder than I thought staying in that large condo without Mace." She searched her mind to come up with a reason for her sudden departure from his home. "I'm just used to writing and going through my research materials in small, cozy spaces. I thought if I stayed in a hotel – you know, one set up for business and pleasure – my mojo would come back."

"I understand." His voice resonated with empathy.

She drove around, calmly taking in the sights of the beautiful city while talking to Evan. It had been a long time since the two of them had a conversation.

"When I'm preparing for a big case, I may stay for days in a hotel just so I can hone in on my thoughts, talk to myself, and present my arguments to my imaginary jurors."

They both laughed. She was grateful for the comic relief.

"Carly, why don't you head to the Hotel Bennett on King Street?"

"The luxury one by Marion Square?" She shook her head. "Oh, no."

"We have…" He cleared his throat. "…No, Mace has a corporate account with them. I'm texting them as we speak."

He was silent for a few moments. "There, it's done. They will be expecting you."

She turned, heading down King Street to the hotel. "Thank you, Evan." She felt the anxiety leaving her body.

"No need for the thanks. For better or worse, you're family."

She felt his warm sentiment coming through.

"That's what we Moores do. We show up for each other and sometimes even when you don't need us, we still show up."

"I know, but can you do me a favor? Please don't bother Mace with this?" She bit her lip, waiting for his response.

"Bother him? Is there something *else* going on?"

"No, Evan, of course not. Say hello to Kate and those beautiful kids of yours."

"Sure thing. Goodbye, Carly."

"Goodbye." She slowed and came to a stop in front of the lavish hotel.

"We were expecting you, ma'am," a man dressed in uniform greeted her.

She grabbed her purse, carrying her new favorite thing at the moment – a Smith and Wesson.

Chapter

37

Ms. *Rivers, you're pregnant.*" The words kept sounding in her ears.

Carly had attended a doctor's appointment earlier that day. The results had thrown her for a loop, but if she was being honest, she had suspected it. She wasn't sure how to handle it, but she'd decided she would wait and have a face-to-face conversation with Mace. She needed to tell him first. Not Aunt Nora or her friends.

She had busied herself the past few days spending hours on research some days and on others alternating between keeping up with Aunt Nora and Edna. That day had been hectic as she had run errands, then finished packing for her trip to Barbados. Her position at the college in Charleston included research time at the facility it shared with the college on the island. She had accepted the offer for a temporary assignment.

"I'm tired." She was back at the condo, and stretched out on the bed for some needed rest. Grabbing for the television remote, she knocked over her bag, spilling the contents on the floor, including her phone, which was vibrating.

"Hey, Auntie. Yes, I'm home." She felt more secure returning to the condo knowing she was protected by Mace's security detail.

"Good. How are you?" Aunt Nora asked. "You looked a little tired the last time you were here."

"I've gotten a little more rest – Auntie's orders." She smiled. "How are you? Have you taken your blood pressure pills today?"

"I'm all out of my medicine, but I can wait until you bring them tomorrow when you come to visit. Do you mind picking them up for me?"

Carly leaned her head against the headboard. She was tired, but there was little she wouldn't do for her aunt. "Nonsense. You need your medication. I'm on my way." While she was there, she would tell Aunt Nora that she was going to leave the next day, a little earlier than she'd planned, for Barbados.

She gathered her things and headed for the car. Once inside, she started the car and passed the guard shack, waving at the guard standing at the front of the building. The phone rang. She looked at the console. She hadn't heard from Tyson in over a week, but she wasn't going to take the chance of accepting one of his calls. It was from Yara. She pressed the accept button.

"Hey, girl, what's up?" she answered while keeping her eyes on the road. There was light traffic.

"I had a dream," Yara replied. "Stop rolling your eyes. I know that's what you're doing."

"Okay, so is this the part when I ask, what was it about, dream queen?" She smiled and made several turns, heading to Calhoun Street to the drugstore near the hospital.

"Before you dismiss my powers, let me tell you that it was definitely about you and not me or Ariel. I spoke to her yesterday. It started with visions of a bee, and we know you're the queen bee, and it ended with visions of a fish."

Carly groaned as she listened to Yara.

"You know what our mothers used to say about dreams about fish..." Yara waited for Carly to answer. When she didn't, she said it herself, "Someone is pregnant."

She waited again for Carly to speak. Finally, she said, "I just know it's you. Remember when our periods always synced up when we lived together? Well, this is like a linking of our psyches. I can feel when something is up with you, so spill it."

"It's me. I'm pregnant." Carly put the car in park while listening to Yara squeal with delight.

"I'm going to be an auntie! Ariel and I are going to spoil that kid for life. I'm so happy for you. How is Mace taking it?" She peppered her with questions. "Is he happy about it? Say something."

"Slow your roll." Carly looked out the window. "I haven't told him, yet."

"What? Uh-oh."

Carly heard a little regret in Yara's voice. "'Uh-oh'? What does that mean?" Carly raised an eyebrow. "Time for *you* to spill it."

"You remember Chance Baker, one of Mace's executives? We met at the party in New York, remember?" When Yara added unnecessary details, something was up.

Carly gripped the steering wheel.

"He and I have been seeing each other since then. I wasn't going to share it with you or Ariel until I was sure it was more than a thing…a one-night stand. Anyway, call it pillow talk, but I shared my dream with him before he left for New York yesterday. He was about to freak after he mistakenly thought it was a confession that I wanted to have his baby, but to calm him down…I told him it was you. I just knew it was you."

Silence.

Music thumping from a car nearby finally broke the silence. A horn blared.

"Carl, are you still there?"

"Yes." She leaned her head against the steering wheel. "How many times have I said you talk too much?"

"Counting since our teens, about a million." Yara quickly added, "But you love me anyway."

"I do love you." Carly leaned back and placed her hands on the sides of her head. "Let me think a minute. I'm not going to overreact. Mace is still in Africa, so he won't run into him."

"Sorry, Carl. I was just so excited for you and Mace."

"No harm, no foul, Yara. Listen, I've got to go. I have to run an errand for Aunt Nora and then make sure she's okay before I fly out to Barbados tomorrow."

"Okay, love you, girl." Yara smacked her lips.

"Bye, big mouth," Carly laughed.

She looked down and gave her belly a gentle press. "We're going to be all right, sweetie. You have a village of aunties who love you already. Let's go get Aunt Nora's medicine."

She opened the door and hurried to the store.

Chapter

38

As usual, the morning came, and it was another day Carly wouldn't be seeing Mace. What was unusual was the time he was calling her.

He was yelling frantically, "Carly, you can't do this to me, not to us. Aren't you the one who talks about fairness? How is this being fair to me?"

She lowered the volume on the phone's speaker.

"Why don't you activate the video so we can at least look at each other?" His breath was shallow and audible as he volleyed one question after another at her. "What's really going on? When were you going to tell me that you were in Barbados? Why do I have to hear what's going on in my life from my security guys and from Chance? And why are movers calling, confirming the order to move things out of my house?"

She rubbed her eyes. "Whoa. Wait a minute. First of all, you're going to stop yelling at me or I'm going to end this call. I've been busy since I got here. I planned to call to tell you everything tonight." She tried to remain calm despite the slight tremor in her hands.

"I don't want to look at you on video, Mason. You've been stringing me along for almost a month. All the while, you knew it was highly likely you wouldn't be able to return home in less than two weeks. Now you're angry that I'm out of town on business? I have a job too. I didn't return to Charleston with the hopes of being the woman waiting for her man to find his way back home. Thanks, but no thanks."

"Carly, I don't want to have that discussion with you over the phone. Despite my absence, you can't possibly think I'd be all right with you taking my child away from me. I want to be a part of its life. I'm in the air and will be landing in London soon. I planned to surprise you by coming home early. Where are you staying in Barbados?"

"What?" Her eyelids fluttered and her jaw dropped. She couldn't believe what she was hearing. "What…what are you talking about, Mason?" she sputtered. Her tongue grew dry and stuck to the roof of her mouth, making it hard to speak. "What child am I trying to keep from you?"

"You know what I'm talking about." He huffed. "Chance is a part of the team that will be coming to Africa. Before we hung up the phone, he told me 'Congratulations.' He said we would have to smoke a cigar to celebrate that you're pregnant with our first child." His voice went up an octave. "Then I hear you're gone and in Barbados. I know I haven't committed to the idea of being a parent, but please, let's discuss this before you decide on anything. Don't shut me out."

Her heart was breaking for him into a thousand pieces. She sensed he was holding back a sob. He was choking as he pleaded to be in the life of the child, the child he'd had to hear about from someone in his company.

"Mace, I promise you, I'll be at the condo waiting for you. I was leaving Barbados today, as I was only scheduled to be here for a week, but I finished my work early. Let's talk in person. This is too important to discuss over the phone."

"All right." His voice calmed. She sensed the crisis he was imagining had been averted with her decision to meet as soon as possible.

"It's going to take at least nine hours to get there. I'll come directly to the condo."

"I'll be on the evening flight and there waiting for you. Have a safe trip. Goodbye."

"Goodbye. And Carly..." There was silence on the phone. "I love you. I always have and I always will."

"I love you too, Mace. You know that. See you soon." She tightened her lips, uncertain their love was enough to keep them together.

* * *

Marlena was standing in the center of the room when Carly entered after returning from Barbados. She'd missed her initial flight and arrived early the next day. Luckily, she had returned before Mason, who had experienced a weather delay.

"Hi, Marlena," she greeted her. "How was your time off?"

"It was good seeing my family members in Florida, but I'm glad to be home."

Mason opened the door and rushed in. Sweeping Carly into his arms, he kissed her and waved at Marlena before he bolted out of the room. "Gotta go. Give me a few minutes." He ran down the hall and slammed the door to the bathroom. Minutes later, he came back to join them with his tie undone.

He looked tired in his rumpled business suit. "I got here as fast as humanly possible."

"My pocketbook is in the kitchen. Let me go get it and then I'll leave you two to talk." Marlena disappeared into the kitchen.

"Carly, can you give me a few more minutes to shower?" He placed his hands on her shoulders. "I'm grungy and I feel like shit. A quick shower to relax should help. I want to be calm and really listen to you."

"I just got back too. I could use some time to decompress while you shower. I've been up for hours also. Afterward, we can both decide if it's right to have this talk now."

"All right. I'll be right back." He disappeared behind the bedroom's closed door.

Seconds later, she heard the water flowing in the shower. Sinking onto the couch, she placed her feet up.

The doorbell rang.

"I'll get it." Marlena had her coat on and her pocketbook on her shoulder, heading for the door. "Excuse me, but why are you here?" Carly heard her asking.

"Ms. Rivers scheduled a pick-up of some of her things?"

Carly saw the man had a clipboard in his hand and was clad in a shirt with his company's logo. Slapping her forehead, she realized she had forgotten to cancel the moving arrangements to transfer her things to Aunt Nora's house. "I can take care of this, Marlena. Please don't let me hold you up."

Marlena stood there, refusing to leave, as Carly escorted the man to her room to get the boxes she'd packed before she left for Barbados. "Mason, come out here, now," she yelled, so loudly her voice was probably heard in the next unit.

Mason came out dressed only in exercise shorts. His

exposed chest appeared broader and more sculpted than ever as droplets of water beaded on his beautiful pecs. His thick leg muscles were flexing, and his feet were bare as he came running out.

"What's going on?" Looking around the room, he waited for an answer.

Carly and Marlena were speechless as they looked at him, a handsome hunk of masculinity.

Chapter

39

No answers were forthcoming while Mason quickly assessed the situation. "Did you forget something?" Carly nodded after he directed the question to her.

He looked at the man dressed in a uniform identifying himself as a mover pushing a metal dolly filled with boxes labelled in Carly's handwriting.

Marlena was standing at the door, blocking his egress, while Carly stood beside the two of them, mouth open wide, staring at him.

"Sir, there's been a bit of a misunderstanding here. The order should have been cancelled. Please, let me pay you for your time and inconvenience. I'll be right back. I need to get my wallet." He felt eyes focused like lasers on his bare back as he retreated to his room and came back with some cash, placing a wad of it in the man's hand.

"I'll need Ms. Rivers to sign this document agreeing that she didn't require my services before I can accept your money as a cancellation fee."

"Carly, can you help this man? Please sign his forms agreeing that he presented for services contracted and you declined them." He took the clipboard and pen from the man and gave them to her for her signature.

She remained silent and signed it without protest.

"Thank you, man." Mace escorted him to the door and closed it, turning to face the women. The three of them stood there at a silent impasse. Carly was licking her lips with what he hoped was appreciation at the sight of him.

"You're ogling him, Marlena." She turned to the older woman, who was speechless.

"Have mercy." She placed a hand to her chest. "You're ogling him more than I am, Carly. I need to get out of here and get some air. I'm not comfortable with my thoughts. Get thee behind me, Satan." She raised a hand in the air and proceeded to the door, leaving without saying goodbye.

* * *

"Have you been working out every day?" Carly asked, keeping her distance in order to avoid losing her composure. The thoughts running through her mind were already jumbled in a haze of longing and lust. She missed him and wanted nothing more than to taste and feel him. The heated charge drawing her to him, tingling down to her core, was taking control. Flowing like electricity firing up and down her spine, she feared her excitement was going to short-circuit her brain.

"Did you hear me, Carly?"

She shook her head. "What did you say?"

"I said I worked out, sometimes twice a day, to take the edge off my horniness. This has been the longest three-and-a-half weeks of my life. It was getting old taking cold showers. Thanks for giving me a moment to take a nice hot shower. Can I ask you to join me on the couch?"

She stood there as he extended his hand to her.

"Are you all right? I know you're disappointed in me, but let's talk this out." He cocked his head. "I asked if you'd join me on the couch."

Her brain registered the words *me, join,* and *couch,* but she just stood there, still looking at the man, a hunk she was preparing herself for the possibility she might have to leave. A hard lump of regret settled in her throat as she ruminated over the thought that they would not stay together. If he wasn't going to be present in her life and the life of their child, she knew she only had one choice to make.

"Can you put on a shirt?" She placed her hands in front of her as he attempted to approach her. "Please. I don't want my lust to prevent me from saying what I know needs to be said."

"Of course, I'll get a shirt and then can you join me on the couch? I won't do anything that makes you uncomfortable. I promise."

She summoned her strength to make it through the discussion that was long overdue. She had questions that needed answers. He was always better on his feet than she was. Starting with small talk would make it easier to maintain her nerve.

He came back clad in long pants and a shirt. As an invitation to join him, he extended his hand to her again. The electricity between them shocked her, just as strong as it had been the first day they'd professed their love for each other.

"May I kiss you, first? I missed you so much."

She answered by placing her hands on the sides of his face and guiding his lips to hers, deepening the connection between them. At first, they tenderly touched before devouring each other. Lips pressed together and her heart wildly throbbing, she savored the feel of his tongue rubbing along the inside of her cheeks.

She opened her eyes and watched as he pulled away and tilted his head, looking at her from the crown of her head down to her toes. She moved closer and, like tasting candy, she sucked his lips, pulling on them sweetly. She breathed in his manly scent and opened her mouth wide, allowing him access to deep, gratifying pleasure. They broke contact at the same time, taking in deep breaths to calm the storms of desire.

"We need to talk." She panted and allowed him to guide her to the couch.

"I'm listening, Caroline." He sat and repositioned his body in order to maintain eye contact.

"Please don't call me that. I changed my name to Carly after we broke up because any time someone who sounded like you called me Caroline, I thought I was going to fall apart. It's hard explaining to people that I'm crying because they sounded like my ex-boyfriend. It got easier when I started going by Carly since you never knew me by that name." She lowered her head to avoid seeing the pain in his eyes.

"I never meant to hurt you." He closed his eyes then opened them with resolve. "I'm willing to hear whatever you feel you need to tell me, no matter how uncomfortable it gets."

"I don't want to hurt you either, but I feel you need to hear the truth from me."

He grabbed her hand.

She buried her lip between her teeth, looking at him as he knitted his brow, seemingly struggling with the idea that there was another *truth* that hadn't already been shared.

"Is there a greater truth than we love each other? Tell me,

I need to know." He rubbed the top of her hand with his thumb. "Is that why you didn't tell me about the baby? I feared that you were planning on leaving and taking my baby from me." He touched her belly.

She looked down and placed her hand on top of his. "There is the truth that sometimes love isn't enough to keep two people together if one of them thinks they were betrayed."

"All right, I see where you're going with this, so talk to me. Did something happen while I was gone?"

She felt the sweat from his hands moisten her palms. "Not in the way you think." She sighed. "Tyson called and threatened to tell you the whole truth, something that happened to me years ago. I think he planned to tell you I was pregnant before I married him."

"Oh. Something from your past." Mace leaned his head back and blew out a breath through pursed lips. "I thought it was something else."

"You knew? How?" She placed her hands on top of his.

"Yes, I already knew you were pregnant before marriage and had lost the baby. My grandfather did a background search on you when I wouldn't stop wanting to be with you. I guess he thought if I realized you had moved on, it would help me to do the same thing."

"Your grandfather did a background search on me? Why was my business any of his business?" She pulled her hands away.

"*I* was my grandfather's business. He didn't do it to hurt you. His intentions were good. He was trying to help me."

"What makes you so sure he wasn't trying to hurt me?"

"He didn't spread your secret and he only mentioned it one time because he realized it didn't change how I felt about you."

"There's more, Mason. Tyson knew the baby wasn't his, but he insisted it was and he was going to raise it as his own. No paternity test and no questions asked. I was about to tell him my ultrasound showed I was almost four months pregnant when I miscarried in January."

Mason sat back and listened. Carly sensed his mind was performing quick math, placing the information on a timeline.

"I left the university in November, before the end of football season, and —" He looked up at her and placed his hands on her shoulders before asking the question.

"Are you telling me the baby was mine? We created a baby and you didn't tell me?"

She sat up and decided she needed to face him as a woman who had lived with the burden of her secrets for over a decade.

"Yes, Mason, you and I created a baby, a girl." She lowered her head and gathered her strength before raising it again. Feeling the courage to get through it, even if it meant saying goodbye to the only man she had ever truly loved, she knew she needed to be honest.

"I betrayed you by initially going along with Tyson's plan to raise the baby as his own, but how could I tell you I was carrying your child when I hadn't gotten over the pain of losing you? At the same time, I felt you had turned your back on me. You ghosted me." She turned away from him and wiped away a tear. "I wasn't going to let my child live with the reality that her father didn't want her or her mother." She pulled away and rubbed her arms to soothe herself while allowing herself the freedom to sob.

He took her into his arms.

Gathering her strength, she pulled away and continued. "I was a mess after you left. To deal with the pain, I partied too much. For a moment, I lost my moral compass, until I discovered I was pregnant. Our baby gave me a reason to move past the pain. I planned to be a good mother to her. I began taking care of myself, eating the right foods, and getting rest. Yes, I slept with Tyson on the rebound, but there was no way he could have been the father of my child. The math didn't add up. I've come to the realization, after all these years, that he thought you took something from him. I loved him, but I was never *in* love with him. Do you get that?"

He nodded and grabbed her hands, stroking them.

"He was envious of you and that motivated him to take something from you... Your child."

Slowly, Mason got up and began pacing in front of her. "This is heavy." His breath was audible as he fumed. "I'm trying to process that you didn't trust me enough to tell me you were carrying *my* child." He held up one finger, then another. "You were willing to go along with Tyson and let him claim the baby – *my* child. And now that you're pregnant again, you were planning on leaving me and taking *my* child?" He resumed pacing.

She placed her hands on the sides of her face, rubbing her temples. "Don't you understand, I thought you had left me. I loved you for your strengths, but I wasn't blind to the fact that you could be arrogant and self-centered back then." She turned away and looked down at her hands.

"This time, after it took so long for you to come back, I can't deny that it made me wonder if you were able to commit to a life with me...and a baby. I've also had my doubts if you ever wanted to be a father. You never said that you saw it in your future." Her tears flowed as she struggled to speak. "But I've been through a lot, and I've learned so much. Even though I'll always love you, I have no doubt me and my child will make it, with or without you."

She stood, her back straight and tall, stopping him in his tracks. She didn't flinch as she gazed up at him.

"Carly, I don't hold it against you for making what you thought was the best decision. We were different people back then." He tightened his hand into a fist and pressed it to his lips. "I only regret I wasn't there to share your pain and grieve the loss of…our child."

Carly placed a hand on her belly.

He reached out and placed his hand over hers. Sweat began beading on his brow. "Let me be clear. I want you and I want our child. I'm not going to *let you* walk out of my life." His voice was louder than usual and rumbled in his chest. He rubbed the back of his neck.

"Sorry, that came out a little angrier than I intended." He looked around the room. "It's getting hot in here. Do you want some water?" He went to the bar and grabbed a bottle.

"No, thank you." She watched him as he returned and motioned for her to resume her seat on the couch.

He threw his head back and took a big gulp of water. "Can we at least admit that this wasn't planned?" He looked at her, searching her eyes. "I would have been more careful and continued to use a condom, but I thought you were on the pill, and we were covered against an unwanted pregnancy. I recalled you telling me that you had to go take your pill."

She laughed. "My thyroid hormone replacement pills. My doctor thought it may have contributed to my years of infertility."

"Oh…" He raised his brows.

"I can see how we got our wires crossed. But, Mace, before you found out I was pregnant, I got the impression that having children wasn't something *you* wanted." She pressed him, searching his eyes. "I know you haven't had time to get used to the idea of my pregnancy, but are you being truthful? Do you want this? There's no pressure to do something you don't want to do."

"Carly, I'm not the same man." He frowned. "You want to hear the truth?" He looked deep into her eyes, baring his soul. "While I was obsessed with building my business, I believed having children would have been a hindrance to my success. I was also sad I didn't have you in my life anymore, so I decided that if I couldn't have children with you, I would have no children at all. I've been very focused and, yes, very selfish. Does that answer your question?" He leaned away and sucked in his cheeks while narrowing his eyes.

"I didn't mean to put you on the defensive, Mace." She settled in his arms. "I needed to feel you out. So, tell me, why the change of heart?"

He raised her chin and kissed her forehead. "Before I do, I need to know one thing. Do you feel this baby is a blessing or an inconvenience?"

She answered right away with tears glistening in her eyes. "This child is a blessing to me, even if I have to raise him or her alone."

He pulled away, frowning and frustrated by her response. "I have to tell you, Carly, you're beginning to irritate me. Why do you think I'd let any child of mine be raised without me in its life, or are you just trying to push my buttons?"

She turned to face him, grabbing his shoulders. "I'm sorry. I didn't intend to irritate you. Can you own that you spent the last four weeks, plus ten years of your life, pursuing your passion without me? Face it, you love running your empire. There's little place in it for me or a baby."

He shook his head. "No, you're wrong. I spent the last four weeks, throughout most days and late into the night, divesting myself of the majority of my international holdings so I could be with you. I'm beyond happy we're having a child." He kissed her on the forehead. "I love the sound of that."

Laughing, he made the gesture of his head exploding. "I can't tell you how happy it would make me to be a father. I was in the process of closing a deal worth millions where I would purchase the stock in a company I've been in negotiations with for months. We slowed down the negotiations for several days after Alex became ill, then the stock tumbled as irregularities in the management of the company were discovered. Me signing with them would have been a fiasco, at least in the short term."

He rubbed the back of his neck. "While I was staying at Alex's home, I saw how devoted he was to his family and them to him. We spoke about business no more than a few hours a day, then we enjoyed each other's company, either sharing memories of old times or relaxing in his media room."

He smiled. "He said what he wanted to show me, by his example, was that my family was my greatest asset and not a hindrance to my success. He also said I should remember what I learned in business and apply it to my personal life."

"What's that?" She yawned and blinked her eyes.

"He reminded me that there are no permanent friends or permanent enemies. I only have permanent interests. My biggest interest, without a doubt, is you. I'll do whatever it takes for us to stay together. I don't want to lose you, Carly. Not now, not ever. I'm over the moon about the news." He placed his hand on her belly then cupped her breast as he looked at her body.

"Babe, I hope you're ready for the changes your body is going to go through, because I think you're up a cup size already." He caressed one breast and then the other as he placed a kiss on the tops of her breasts, peeking above her V-neck shirt.

"Are you a breast guru now? Because you're right. I have grown almost a cup size."

"You know I'm a man who loves to look at your boobs."

She got up and extended her hand to him. "Let's go to bed. We can finish this talk in the morning."

"Okay, but your body is looking pretty good. You're hot in those jeans. I don't know if I can keep my promise to be good." He picked her up and cradled her as he took her to their bedroom. "It's great to be home. I plan to make up for lost time."

"It's great having you home, Mace. I've missed you so much."

"We'll never be separated for that amount of time ever again, I promise."

She placed her head against his chest and envisioned a night of sweet lovemaking.

Chapter

40

Carly yawned, covering her mouth with her hand. Looking out over the picturesque Charleston harbor, she knew she couldn't have imagined how much her life had changed in a month.

"Why didn't you come back to bed?" Mace came into the room dressed in lounge pants and bare-chested. "Gosh, I'm tired." He rubbed his eyes. "All that traveling is catching up with me."

Carly walked across the room to the couch. Dressed in a navy-blue crop top and loose-fitting yoga pants to match, she grabbed her cup of decaf coffee. "I couldn't sleep. I had too much on my mind."

"Give me a chance to put your mind at ease." He motioned for her. "Come back to bed, babe."

"If you had gone to sleep last night instead of ravaging my body..." She wiggled her eyebrows. "You would be more rested. I sense that you're still feeling frisky."

"Can you blame me?" He licked his lips. "You're walking

around with your belly exposed." He ran his hand down his six-pack. "That top hugging your breasts is a real turn-on."

"Come sit with me, Mace." She pointed to the couch.

He hesitated, then, trudging across the floor to sit next to her, he frowned.

She poured a cup of hot coffee from the pot on the table and gave it to him. "Thank you for your cooperation." She patted his leg.

He grabbed the cup and blew over the top of the hot black liquid.

"I have to ask you about Tyson. Why—?"

"Yes. Let's talk about Tyson. Why didn't you tell me he was stalking you?" He frowned. "I know Tyson moved into the complex and...you didn't tell me that." He cocked his brow. "Don't worry. That has been taken care of. He's out of here. For the record, he'll be eating humiliation gumbo when my lawyers are done with him, and I plan to serve it cold."

"So Evan told you?" She mirrored his frown by tightening her lips and furrowing her brows. "I asked him not to bother you. I wasn't going to run to you like a frightened girl, and besides...I saw you had big guys following me at all times. Evan shared that you had a security detail here in Charleston." Her eyes softened. "Thanks."

"You're welcome." He leaned over to kiss her. "In the future, please don't ask Evan to keep secrets from me."

"Understood." She placed a hand on his leg. "So, as I was saying, since we're coming clean with each other, why didn't you tell me that Tyson thought he was your brother?"

He coughed, sputtering drops of the coffee onto his pants. "Ouch. What?" He turned to her. "How did you find out about that?" He gathered the damp material covering his crotch in the palm of his hand, squeezing it. "Are you trying to scorch the family jewels?"

"Okay, I see you're buying some time, but I'm waiting." She turned and placed her cup on the table, then repositioned her body to face him.

"Carly, you can't expect me to talk about that fool on an empty stomach. I'm hungry." He rubbed his bare belly with his hand in slow, sensual circles.

She looked at him, salivating as she viewed his muscular chest. "I know what you're doing." She turned away and gathered her thoughts, squeezing her legs together to resist his efforts. "Don't tantalize me. It's distracting."

"Clearly my intent." He smiled. "I was expecting to have you under me by now, put it on you, girl, then eat." He leaned his head back against the couch. "I wasn't prepared for another heart-to-heart talk."

"I've seen you conduct business for hours without eating. Breakfast can wait," she insisted. "If I feed you, you'll complain that I'm asking you to talk with your mouth filled with food."

He smiled. "Let's do this, then."

She ran her hands through her hair. "Good. We need to have this discussion."

His stomach let out a loud growl. Pressing firmly on his abdomen, he tried to suppress the sounds coming from him.

Carly smiled and gave him a side-eyed look.

"I told you I was hungry."

"Come on," she finally relented. "Let's go to the dining room. I've ordered breakfast. There's also fresh coffee."

"Why didn't you say that in the first place?" He grabbed her by the hand, dragging her along to the other room. He slowed his approach to the table, clad in a starched white tablecloth and topped with fine porcelain plates and crystal glasses for mimosas for him and plain orange juice for her.

"This is nice." He looked around. "Have a seat. I'll remove the covers from the servers and fix us a plate."

Carly waited while he pulled out her chair. He took his time uncovering the foods she had placed in the small servers.

He inhaled the aromas as the steam and scents escaped into the air. "Yum." He placed pieces of French toast, crepes, and assorted meats on their plates.

Carly removed the cloth covering the breads. Slices of fruits in bowls were already on the table. As they prepared to consume their meal, the sun shone through the window, providing natural light and warmth in the room.

He sat down and quickly picked up his fork, eating with pleasure. "Baby, this is good."

After swallowing a few bites, Carly brought it up again. "Why did Tyson think he was your brother? *You* still haven't told me." She frowned. "Edna was confused and out of her mind in the hospital when Tyson confronted your mother. Her health improved last week and then she was able to undergo transplant surgery. She was appalled after she recovered, and he told her that he had visited Lucille and told her things that weren't true. I didn't press her on the details since she's still weak from the surgery."

Mason held his fork midair, contemplating his answer. Taking his time, he placed the fork on his plate and reached for his napkin to wipe his lips. "I'll tell you why, and unlike Tyson, I'll lead with the truth."

"I encourage that." She tilted her head and crossed her hands in front of her chest.

"Tyson isn't my father's son." He wiped imaginary sweat from his brow. "His biological father was my father's best friend, Edmund Hollison. He and my father made a pact while they were in the army that they would care for each other's kids if either one of them was killed on active duty. My father kept the promise by providing funds for Edna and Tyson, even after she married Gerald Matherson. My grandfather established the trust to honor my father's promise after he died. The trust was only active until Tyson was over thirty years old. My grandfather could support a child, but he believed a man should stand on his own two feet."

"Wow…" Carly paused. "Edna told me he found out that Gerald Matherson wasn't his biological father after he went through her private papers. He was also misled with information provided by someone else. I cringe just thinking that he was happy thinking you shared the same father." She closed her eyes and scrunched up her face. "Married to two brothers." She grunted. "We could have been messy reality-show stars." She covered her mouth with her hands.

"Stop thinking about it." He placed a hand on top of hers. "It was never true." With his index finger, he lifted her chin and looked into her sad eyes. "Hold on. I'll be right back."

He got up and went to the side table in the front room, taking a small black box out of the drawer and placing it in the pocket of his pants.

"You don't have to worry about the two brothers thing anymore." He raised his hand and batted the thought away. "But I like the other word you used."

"What?" she wondered.

Standing in front of her, he drew the box out of his pocket, but kept his hands behind his back. "I like this, Carly, just the two of us."

"Well." She smiled and rubbed her belly. "I believe in including everyone, so it's the *three* of us."

"There's something about this situation that's missing. You said the word and I'm ready to make it a reality." He lowered his body and, on one knee, opened the box in front of her.

"Carly Rivers, will you *marry* me?"

She looked at the box, containing a platinum wedding band and matching engagement ring with a sparkling diamond, while he held his breath awaiting her answer.

"Yes, I'll marry you."

He slid the ring onto her finger then rose to his feet, taking her in his arms. Placing his hands on the sides of her face, he gazed into her eyes, grateful she had fulfilled his soul's desire.

She tilted her head as her lips parted and yielded to his kisses.

He felt her body heating up as he wrapped her in his arms. "This feels so good." He delighted in the delicious warmth of her body as he kept her close. "I wanted our engagement to be a grand gesture, but at the end of the day, I realize that it boils down to two people who love each other and are committed to spending their lives together."

"This is perfect, Mace." She hugged him.

Unable to contain his excitement, he shouted, "You've made me one happy man!" He swung her around in the air before placing her gently on her feet. "This past month has been stressful for both of us."

She stood, her arms wrapped around him, and remained silent.

Mace placed his chin on top of her head, holding on to her as his heart rate calmed.

He took a breath before speaking and looked down at her. "Did you find Barbados relaxing?"

"It was relaxing in Barbados, but not as relaxing as

spending time *together* anywhere with you," she answered.

"Here's my suggestion." He took her in his arms and began swaying as if music was playing in the background. "Why don't we go down to Barbados, get married on the beach, and spend a couple of weeks there on our honeymoon?"

"Without family and friends?" she asked, the uncertainty evident in her voice.

"There's a glimmer in your eyes." He tilted his head. "I can tell you're finding my suggestion enticing. When we get back, we can celebrate with them and throw the biggest party this town has ever seen."

"Yes, I'm enticed." She flashed a big smile, brightening her face. "We don't need to have the biggest party ever, but I want to share our happiness with them. I do, however, have another concern."

"What is it?" He peered into her eyes.

"If we're going to get away, I hope you intend to get away from business too."

"That won't be a problem." He tightened his arms around her waist. "I was talking to Evan the entire time I was away. I plan to downsize. I found out that Fletch, along with others, were trying to sabotage our relationship to save the profits from *Moore for You*."

"Others like Jamillah?"

"Yes, Jamillah. Nick was made aware of it too. He was so furious, he threatened to leave her and sue for custody of their child if she didn't change her ways...but she's his wife, his problem." He grunted. "Several of the subsidiaries have already been sold off. So, babe, I'm all yours. I finally have a good executive team in place. I feel it's a good time to get away...with my wife."

"But I'm pregnant." Her lips parted slightly. "At my age, I need to make sure I stay close to my doctors."

He cocked his head and uttered an incredulous gasp. "They have doctors in Barbados, but if you need to be seen here, I have a plane. I can get you to your appointment. We've got this."

He picked her up and cradled her. "Can we finish eating now? You're eating for two."

He led her back to the table, then grabbed fresh plates, filling them with warm food.

He waited for her to pick up her fork. "Eat," he insisted. "You'll need your strength."

"What do you have planned?"

"You'll see when I get you back in bed." He wagged his eyebrows.

Chapter

41

I 'm going to make more time for exercising this year. Charleston is a beautiful town to get out, walk, run, or join a fitness group." Carly spoke to Mace as they packed for their trip to Barbados. "With the baby coming, I'll need to focus more on my health."

"We both need to focus on health issues. Thanks for coming to my last appointment with me. You asked questions I wouldn't have normally asked." He hugged her around the waist while she finished placing her clothes in the suitcase.

"I'm happy you've had a complete recovery from your concussion. Getting rest this past week and taking care of yourself have made it easier for your memory to improve. Don't you see the difference now that you're more relaxed?" She leaned back into his embrace. He kept one hand on her waist and with the other he caressed her breasts and belly as she felt his girth ramping up the growing tension between her legs.

"We need to finish packing." She removed his hand from

her breast.

"Okay." He kissed the side of her face before returning to his side of the bed and closing his suitcase. "I'm not as anxious as I have been the last four weeks."

"You, anxious?" She looked up and widened her eyes.

"Yes, and if you recall, it was my anxiety that landed me in your bed before the big game." He joined her as she sat on the side of the bed to listen to him.

"Remember that I called you in a panic two days before the big game against our rivals? You told me to come over to talk to you and I ran over to your dorm room. You sat there and listened to me for hours. By the time we finished talking, it was early in the morning. I was going to get into trouble if I went back to the athletes' dorm after curfew." He took a seat and leaned against the headboard. "So you said, 'Just stay here. You can say you're coming back after an early morning run.'"

She nodded. "I remember being worried about you. Back then, you were the man who always played to win. People put so much pressure on you... The team, the fans, and the alumni, but never more pressure than you placed on yourself. I wanted us to win, but not at your expense."

"You have always been in my corner, Carly. I didn't intend for us to make love for the first time, but that bed of yours was so small and my body so big compared to yours. No matter how much I tried to stay on the edge, you kept rolling into my arms while you slept. I couldn't help myself. You were like an angel to me. I just held you, thinking I was the luckiest man alive."

"I woke up and there you were, staring at me." She moved next to him. "You looked so tired."

"How could I sleep with the most beautiful woman on

campus in my arms?" He looked into her eyes. "I wanted you so badly, but not until you were ready to have me."

"You awakened something in me that I had never experienced before. My heart was racing. My body was tingling all over. If you had asked me my name that morning, I wouldn't have been able to remember it if my life depended on it." She moaned as he nibbled at the flesh down her jaw. "I was so excited, I felt I was going to explode, but I remember how good it felt being in your arms, especially after you began nuzzling my neck with your nose. Then you started using that wicked tongue of yours."

"My wicked tongue loves that mouth of yours."

She placed her hands on the sides of his face. "Then, those beautiful brown eyes of yours piercing mine did it. I was ready to take off all of my clothes. I knew who I shared my body with for the first time was important to me. I valued my virginity, but I was ready... My heart, mind and soul wanted to share the experience with you." Her chest heaved with passion.

He kissed her softly on the lips and looked into her eyes. "I was so nervous. I wanted to be a tender lover to you. I cherished the touch of your soft skin, and damn, when I saw your breasts...oh my gosh. I got so hard. I felt every nerve in my body fire off like rockets. When we came together as one... I still don't have words to describe what it was like penetrating and being inside you for the first time."

She bit her lip and closed her eyes, savoring the memories.

"Feeling your warmth and tenderness made me feel invincible, loved for the man I was, and so alive. I would dream about us being together like we were the first time for years, even after we separated. The dreams evolved from us making love to dreams of you coming down an aisle to me in a beautiful white dress." He took her lip into his mouth and sucked it before filling her mouth with his greedy tongue.

"Is that why you had the dress designed for me?" She cupped the side of his face and tenderly rubbed his cheeks.

"Yes, I had a designer create the dress from the images in my dreams. You've always been the woman of my dreams. I'm looking forward to spending the rest of my life with you."

"I'm looking forward to our life together also. I'm surprised how supportive everyone has been of us getting away. Your mother whispered to me that she hopes we come back married. Now that I have a home health nurse to come in and check on Aunt Nora, I can relax knowing someone will be there to keep an eye on her or call me if something should come up."

She frowned. "My girls are going to kill me that I didn't tell them about our plans to elope."

He patted her hand. "Blame it on me. Maybe I can pay for my mistake by giving them both gifts." He laughed. "We've taken care of things in Charleston. I guess we're ready for the flight tonight."

"Agreed." She patted his chest.

Epilogue

Carly and Mason married on the beach in Barbados in a ceremony at sunset with a witness and a minister presiding as the sun painted ribbons of pink, yellow, and orange across a clear, cloudless sky. The trees blew in the soft winds, waving and saluting them on a beautiful warm February day. The fourteenth would not just be Valentine's Day, but their special day, when they'd honored the strength and endurance of their love.

Mason smiled as the minister stated her formal name.

"Do you, Caroline Angelica Rivers, take Mason Jefferson Edmund Moore as your lawfully wedded husband?"

"I do," she replied, gazing at Mason, dressed in a short-sleeved white shirt that displayed his tattoo of the initials CAM enveloped in a heart on his left bicep. He was a handsome sight in his fine linen khaki pants.

"You have always been my angel on earth." He looked up at the sky. "I take you as my wife – and our daughter, Taryn Avery, whom I'm looking forward to meeting – to love and cherish you both forever."

She had relented in humoring him. He was convinced she was having a girl.

"Mace loves Carly." He read the white banner flapping in

the wind attached to the small jet he had rented for the day. He knew she didn't need grand gestures because nothing for the two of them was grander than to be committed, loving spouses to each other.

"Mace loves Carly, and Carly will forever love Mace." She looked into his eyes, anxiously waiting for the minister to finish the ceremony and give his direction.

"And now you may kiss your bride."

Mason pulled back the white, shoulder-length tulle veil trimmed with lace that she had designed to match the dress he had made for her to wear on New Year's Eve. She'd had a little more lace added to the dress, as she knew he loved lace. She'd wanted to wear it one last time to make his dreams come true. With his profession of love, he had made *her* wildest dream come true.

She kissed him for the first time as the newly declared Mrs. Caroline Angelica Moore, his much-loved and cherished wife, now and forever.

About the Author

Michele Sims is the "author-ego" of Deanna McNeil, MD and creator of the Moore Family Saga. She loves writing hot love stories and women's fiction with multigenerational characters. She is the recipient of the 2019 RSJ Debut Author Award, the 2018 RSJ Aspiring Author Award, and first runner up in the Introvert Press Poetry Contest for February 2018. She is a member of LRWA, in Charleston, SC.

She lives in South Carolina with her husband who has been her soulmate and greatest cheerleader. She is the proud mother of two sons and the auntie to many loved ones. When she's not writing, she's trying to remember the importance of exercise, travelling, listening to different genres of music, and observing the wonders of life on this marvelous planet. She has worked on several collaboration projects and plans to work with other authors in the future.

Email: michelesims2122@gmail.com

Visit her website at:
authormichelesims.com

Made in the USA
Columbia, SC
16 June 2023

18172665R00163